HOMECOMINGS

With love and gratitude
for our discussion in
Lamalou.

Enjoy the second reading,
08-09 2009
Yvette

HOME
COMINGS

Yvette
Rocheron

Matador
9 Priory Business Park,
Wistow Road, Kibworth Beauchamp,
Leicestershire, LE8 0RX
Tel: 0116 279 2299
Email: books@troubador.co.uk
Web: www.troubador.co.uk/matador
Twitter: @matadorbooks

ISBN 978 1789017 939

British Library Cataloguing in Publication Data.
A catalogue record for this book is available from the British Library.

Printed and bound in Great Britain by 4edge Limited
Typeset in 11pt Sabon by Troubador Publishing Ltd, Leicester, UK

Matador is an imprint of Troubador Publishing Ltd

To Mustapha and his son
In memory of peace

Contents

1.	Damasacus *October 2008*	1
2.	The Clinic	14
3.	Leaford	26
4.	Damascus	43
5.	Tugs of Love	55
6.	Troubled	64
7.	Damascus	71
8.	Waiting	82
9.	Fish in a Bowl	95
10.	Damascus	101
11.	Old Flirts	110
12.	Damascus	119
13.	Self-healing	128
14.	Meeting the Al-Sayeds	139
15.	Touring Syria	155
16.	By Themselves	165
17.	Aleppo's Citadel	174
18.	Opening Gambits	184
19.	The Deal	195
20.	On The Road	205
21.	Flights	214
Epilogue: For Those Who Like Tidy Ends		227

– 1 –

Damascus

October 2008

KHALID AL-SAYED PUTS THE PHONE DOWN ON HIS DESK and, irritated, walks into the inner courtyard, feet bare, indifferent to the cold floor inlaid with extravagant strips of marble to match the best of Levantine rugs. In the last few days, whenever he rings his father, the line to Hama is full of interference or echoes of their own voices. Ironically, the antiquated technology is reassuring as he remembers a sarcasm which clung to the 12-year-old boy, then a refugee from the massacre which destroyed their Hama home: the British and Hafez Al-Assad's men couldn't have been fairer, his father joked – they shared the job equally, watching and criminalising us Sunnis. This is why, maybe, his father felt the move to Leaford as a safe homecoming.

Khalid smiles ruefully: his family is no longer subject to state-of-the-art bugging but he is still trying hard to forget the two years spent in that Lebanese camp infested with rats and spies.

And now, coming back to Syria more than 20 years later, it is taking him longer than he expected to adapt to the hustle and bustle of his birthplace. How many times had the Al-Sayeds built a home only to leave it, nomads again? Father, twice. Himself, twice. May Zaida be spared such a destiny!

1

Since the divorce, he's had little opportunity for fatherhood – a few weekends in Britain acting the funfair dad, buying tickets for dodgems and Aladdin shows; keeping on the good side of Virginia for Zaida's sake. Until now there has been nothing to replace the normal family life which providence, or his ex, denied him.

Yesterday Zaida went to stay with her grandfather in Hama. Already he is missing her.

A gust of cold air. The servants should have switched off the rattling air conditioner high up on the wall. Khalid sucks in his cheeks, chilled, unsettled. He is through with being at the Franklins' beck and call. After the separation, Walter and Gwen opened their home to mother and child, forgiving Virginia's double ineptitude: first falling pregnant so young and then marrying him, a student at Leaford University.

It is their turn to miss the child for a while. There will be little room to manoeuvre, and there will be a terrible fuss, but both families can shield Zaida from the fallout. She is so excited, so avid for anything Syrian – food, stories, clothes, family history, you name it. As she grows into her mixed heritage the choice will be hers. His duty now is to give her the resources of her Syrian self.

The budgies again! He can't get used to them fussing above the door leading down to the servants' basement. Zaida enjoyed looking after them to the delight of their owner, his housekeeper. Mariyam Ajemian, an ageing Armenian woman from Aleppo, hangs the cage together with a rusting Byzantine cross the size of a fist but fortunately without the tortured body. Such knick-knacks undermine Khalid's décor, free of curios and personal souvenirs, but, as he told Zaida, Mariyam's faith must be accepted. It doesn't do to challenge the devotion of excellent cooks. So he muses while dislodging with a toothpick gritty sesame seeds left by his sister's halva. The best. Nobody makes halva like Halima. Despite Mariyam, he isn't putting on weight. 'A wife's cuisine,' Halima likes to annoy him, 'will get rid of your gangly looks!' He shakes his head. He's not a man who swaps wives like hookers. At any mention of Zaida staying, sister and cook exchange knowing glances, as if a man can't look after a girl.

He pops in a large date, fleshy and moist. Zaida has inherited his build and his love of aromatic food. She doesn't let herself starve like so many sad girls of her age. Mariyam showed her how to make gooey *gh'raybeh* and Allepian almond cookies. The two had fun speaking gibberish over the stove. She loves grilled lamb, stuffed vegetables, pomegranate juice and mint lemonade; homely food that he took for granted as a child until England, where his mother cooked only dull smelly foreign food. 'Why smelly?' Zaida asked. 'Fish and chips, fried onions? Boiled potatoes with no herbs! I'm telling you, we children craved for mezzes laced with rosewater and spicy lamb balls.'

He made the migrant story light and short, sparing the child and also himself the harrowing truths. It would have been too distressing to explain how his mother's grief over Seema's suicide became palpable in lumpy dishes and, later, in her refusal to go out, and finally lung cancer. How could he drop explosives onto a child? Ignore the tragedies. Talk about the survivors. The two youngest, fresh from Koranic classes in Leaford, acquired veils, husbands and a passion for Indian and Pakistani food. Her Aunt Halima followed Grandad Abdul back to Hama where she married happily into a Sunni family.

This is a truncated family story. Plenty of time to fill it in. He has such faith in Zaida: uncorrupted, provocative, easy to be with. Dressed up with elaborate kerchiefs and full make-up, the girl now looks much older than her years. A Barbie doll for Halima. He mustn't let his sister spoil her with old-fashioned girlish ways. He wants to be a modern dad. But how? Just a moment ago, he was caught out. Zaida, petulant on the phone, furious with her grandfather's refusal to let her go out to the Mak'Ha Internet Café with her male cousins. 'You see, Hama's an orthodox town,' he found himself insisting. 'A dodgy bar full of men eyeing you up is no place for you!' In Syria a man's honour is to protect women. Her presence is interrogating him already. How to be a modern dad?

He still finds it hard to believe she has made it to Syria. How did she manage to persuade her mother? She wouldn't explain it. She threw her head backwards in Virginia's gesture of denial, then said darkly, '*Iaa Afham* you, daddy.' She doesn't understand him! Because he doesn't sweeten her mother up? He shrugs. The girl has strong principles and a zest for life. She also won Mariyam Ajemian's heart by visiting not only the Ummayyad Mosque but also the holy chapel of St Anania: Christos be praised. 'It's close to heaven,' Mariyam approved. Closer than the Big Mosque? He winked.

Of course, she'll stay as long as she wants; they have so much to do and share. Her three-week visa will run out but a renewal will raise no problem. No doubt Virginia expects him to remain as reasonable and meek as ever, but why toe her line now he's back with his own folks? Many times she mocked him as a weak man under tribal pressure to return, but this time the joke will be on her.

They are having a great time. When they toured New Damascus, Zaida dismissed it, like him, as any dreary new city catering to the rich, though this one was safeguarded by uniforms armed to the teeth. She loved exploring the old city, intrigued by the paper notices of the dead posted by Christians with little black crosses at street corners close to Bab Sharki. Why trust walls to spread news better than newspapers? He didn't point out the dismal list of disappeared people pasted in full view of the mosque. Inside the old city gates, where traders have outlived ruler after ruler, there are enough memories of protest to provide the agents of order with jobs for life – a never-ending story he or Abdul will tell her one day. When she's older. She is staying.

He slouches down a few steps to get a carafe of icy water from his latest purchase, an American style fridge-freezer, all steel and shine, 'bigger than a coffin,' Mariyam tutted, crossing herself for good measure as she swept her black skirts away from danger. 'Superstition,' he mutters under his breath, changing his mind in favour of a beer.

Back in the yard, he sits straight on the edge of the shell-shaped fountain, smart in a white short-sleeved shirt and blue tie, looking like any other aspiring businessman except for features that make him less banal – unruly jet-black hair curling around his ears, owlish eyebrows and a deep terracotta complexion.

He cocks his head, listening to furious squabbling over a football coming from the back alley. The harried look gives way to a grin, happy to be on his own until the early evening meal: lamb with a red cherry sauce, another Aleppo speciality which Mariyam lavishes with herbs.

At the muezzin's call, a quietness as doleful as an English mist fills the house while boys, water-sellers and sock-pedlars pack up their wares. He ought to dismiss the chauffeur on time for the communal prayer and then savour the opportunity to hear himself think, relieved of office staff and agitated relatives.

His uncles chant in clannish unison that he is spending too much time on his own. To their minds he is soft, an ignorant Brit, wet behind the ears about human rights. He is too open, too trusting – on the internet, at business meetings and official soirées. They deride him for refusing kickbacks, a sure sign of his lack of common sense. But still, he's one of them and they will fix things up for him. Their condescension gets on his nerves. In Britain, he was respected as a lawyer and a man with brains.

Yes, he is beginning to tire of constantly watching his back. Professional people are treated like children here; whatever their trade, they have to play by the rules. Worse still for Sunnis in Hama. The Al-Sayeds still find it difficult to obtain passports in spite of promises made in London when they were discussing arrangements to return. It is so humiliating having to fork out bribes to lackeys every time you want to go abroad.

However, he does not resent his relatives having chosen for him this discreet, well-hewn stone house. Latticed windows looking onto the Christian quarter, hidden in a side street behind modestly high walls on three sides and cheek-by-jowl with knife shops on the other. Zaida loves the place. Conveniently, Abdul hired the servants from the previous owner, an exuberant Shia whose main political affectation was to employ people from different religions: Mariyam, the Christian cook, and Walid Hadidi, an Alawite Shia who has chauffeured for him this last year on a part-time basis. Why change sensible arrangements?

He is startled by a clap of wind rattling the shabby sheets of cloth stretched above the courtyard three storeys high by a system of ropes and pulleys. He enjoyed explaining to Zaida how the wobbly roof works, remembering his own excitement when he was first allowed to open up the sky at his father's house. Before the walls were full of bullet holes. It is too early to open the roof. Pouting, he scratches his scalp, dimly aware that despite one or two extra pounds, he has not lost the hungry looks endearing him to Muslim and Christian matrons keen to match him with a virgin.

A rich man, although not as rich as Zaida assumes, he is not short of marriage proposals. He gulps down the beer, impatient with the bitterness clinging to him. He used to have a loving wife. He looks around, sensing his solitude, suddenly missing the talk that nurtures a marriage of equals. Virginia. He had been devoted to her. Good luck to Virginia and her parents. They have taken good care of his daughter. But now, for as long as she wants, it is his turn. The Sharia Court would vindicate him!

Long ago little Zaida – gusty and quick, light and movement – had struck gold in her Syrian family. The djins burst out from Abdul's stories, real to the fascinated child. Her grandfather, incorrigible and doting, encouraged her to think that he travelled in the Middle East to track down the few remaining flying carpets, immune to rot and mice. The adolescent continues to be transfixed by tales of any kind, joking that the Arabs should put Death Knights on their magic carpets and send them against the Americans. 'Stop it,' he'd said. 'War-speak is too ugly for my girl.'

It is only now, in this house, that he will gradually grasp the essence of his daughter. This is her Syrian home. Secretive, lofty and, like the souk, mixing the old and the new. Not so grand as to invite misfortune but comfortable enough to foil the heat. Cool back rooms with high painted ceilings and flagstone floors. Zaida clapped at the wide screen installed in the smallest sitting room. They enjoyed viewing together, although there was nothing much she could watch apart from a soap about a Cairo dynasty. Straining to understand, her face creased like a silk purse.

He had to hide his feelings more than once. The second evening she stuck a dozen incense cones in the niches made by jutting stones in the walls, skipping around the fountain in a display of gaiety and grace. The way she held the matches, absorbed by spurts of flame and wistful at their demise, brought Virginia back to him: the night they moved to their first home in Leaford. 'Anxious and light-headed,' she said, and he watched her pacing the rooms gingerly like a fennec exploring a rival's territory; then he clapped as she rushed to set up fairy candles; dozens of small kisses around their bed.

Khalid slaps the handset back onto the Bakelite telephone someone brought back from France in the 1950s because of its additional mother-in-law earpiece. Damn that Mustapha Al-Dari! How dare the minister, an obnoxious Alawite, call him in at one day's notice to review this pipeline business at the Ministry of Petroleum and Mineral Resources. 'In the national interest we require solid advice before negotiating our contracts with international oil enterprises … independent, irreproachable advice … Like yours. I'm told you've got a good nose for a Brit. ' Really? He can see the bullying through the flattery. Solid advice indeed! Does that lead eventually to a personally profitable deal for the minister? He imagines Farouq, his favourite cousin, sneering at the summons: 'Grow up quick or you'll dance to their tune.' Will they play foul? Will it be all kisses and smiles, clapping each other on the back, smirking at the other buggers who aren't as clever or ruthless? In London, you have champagne and peerages laid out on the table: seeing the cards you have been dealt, you celebrate with a £10,000 bill at the Savoy. Here you make your moves in a mirage of tea and water, hoping for something far more precious than honour and money – your safety, maybe, or the lifting of travel restrictions.

Perspiring at the thought of the forthcoming manoeuvres, he wipes the palms of his hands on his trousers, raw with cunning. If Zaida is staying, that's another reason for him to get something for himself. But how? He could be forced to do business with Uncle Omar, devious enough as a Sunni to become a Ba'athist town councillor waving the banner of modernity in Hama – the old tricks of ruse and greed.

In a falsetto voice, he bows to the phone: 'Yes, Minister, our family is committed to supporting your sound and ambitious strategy. Yes, Syria's sole interest lies in laying down new gas and oil pipelines from Iraq and Eastern Syria to the port of Lattakia. By the way, are you finding serious investors?' He stops, deep in thought. With the occupation, Iraqi production has declined sharply and low oil prices have less to do with sound business or state-controlled markets than the Americans' evil presence in the region. Mustapha Al-Dari will like that line, hoping to drop it into the President's ear. And now that Bashar Al-Assad has nailed his flag to the free market, the minister will play new investors against each other – Russian, Indian and Chinese – and all against the Americans. A win-win situation for backhanders. And for the Al-Sayeds? Self-mocking again: 'Sure, Minister, it is my job to write the contracts. But, with respect, corruption gives Syria a terrible name.'

He is too much of an international lawyer not to recognise the jackal behind Mustapha Al-Dari's toothy grin and this realisation rekindles his susceptibility to official threats. You can buy some measure of freedom, but is that enough once you are a family man?

Hitched to the stone walls with flimsy strips of wire, the ropes of the roof clatter as if a storm is gathering. In October one expects warm asthmatic puffs, not gales. He should have the roof seen to, care for the house; Zaida's home where she will test the recipes of a grandmother she has never known. Never mind Mustapha. He shouldn't let politics spoil his enjoyment of having his daughter here.

She's only been here a few days, but her questions dredge up a whirlwind of emotions. How much can he share?

He was the boy shovelled on sinuous mountain tracks into an open truck filled with dogs and goats, hair full of dust and droppings, sick with the odour, bruised by each bump and turn, hugged by Seema, his clever and beautiful sister. She kept a little blue bottle of lavender oil to massage his temples and prevent his headaches, reassured him with stories of children loved and protected by Allah who would punish the spies and criminals crawling over Muslim lands. Oh why did she take her life that revengeful September in 1982? To shame the Christians in front of the Prophet, her mother believed. And now her father is finding his martyred daughter in Zaida. Even Virginia was happy to call her 'the Fortunate One'. But if he drifts into trouble with the regime, she will need more than a talisman to protect her from evil.

He brightens up at the whiff of charcoal curling from the basement, carrying tangy odours that take him back to his first summer in France when, beside camp fire barbecues, he discovered the terror of falling in love: holding Virginia's hands, desiring her lips, touching the web of her fine hair, drowning in her moods, transfixed, his passion unstoppable as a nosebleed.

Time, not just Syria, has come between them. He had to do what he did – be a son, a brother, make money, eat the soggy bread and butter puddings his mother refused to mask with rosewater and cardamom. Immigrants often inscribe their lives in food, to hold on to fading memories, but not his mother. Isolated, suffocated by grief amidst Leaford's blandness, she faded away. It's no surprise that he married straight after graduation into an insanely normal English family. The Franklins gave him comfort and escape from his befuddling heritage. But far too soon there came the years when he had to justify himself, mortified at the erosion of Virginia's natural generosity, her suspicion at yet another call to Syria, her fears. She thought him responsible for her sexual coldness and drifted further away. Be that it may, now, sifting through his images of her, he can touch the lush breasts, the pale glow of her skin, or smell again the sour drugged-up breath the day their baby was born. Once they could reach each other.

Zaida is the age when she can meddle in her parents' affairs and she will rub their noses in it! 'Why don't you want to see Mummy?' she pestered him just before leaving for Hama. 'Dad, I understand things you don't see. Mum doesn't hate you. On the contrary.' He looked at her blankly, afraid of taking advantage. She ran out with her suitcase.

Is she missing her mother already? Why not invite Virginia to Damascus? It is not too late to see the sights, to enjoy Zaida mixing with girls of good families, educated girls learning French and English. Silly, Virginia won't come. Too busy. Her old French friend, Marianne, is prowling about, Zaida said. He has always disliked the French, too clever by half when they ran Syria. And Marianne is a lunatic feminist to boot!

Walid Hadidi is trying to get his attention; he must have lumbered into the courtyard a while ago, waving his basketball cap as if to catch flies two feet in front of him. Not saying a thing. Surly. Doesn't like speaking. Must be a spy. Khalid slaps the man on the back.

'Time for you to go home unless you want to share my meal.'

Silently laughing, Walid rolls his eyes to refuse an offer only made when the master is dining on his own.

Khalid doesn't twig. Besides, he has never seen Walid eat or drink a thing in his presence. Perhaps he's the kind for whom eating outside the family is an indecency. And he may be one of the many 'heretics', the people who report back to the police – a Damascene mockery underlining ongoing struggles for power! In this so-called secular state, a cynical regime has drawn in more Shias from outside the country to offset *them* against *us*. His thickset jaw belies a quicksilver mind. Whenever Khalid gives him instructions, he lowers his head respectfully, grateful, wide-eyed. To give his Salam, he flatters the Al-Sayeds, to whom 'Allah will send rain in abundance to increase their wealth and protect their children'. Such a humble man! A bastard paid to bless as well as to spy? Unscrupulousness and love of manipulation are not in short supply in Syria – how else would the Al-Sayeds have survived? – but does Walid Hadidi have the slimy blend of instinct and cunning to betray? He will have to enquire, keep an eye on him. And speak English when the man is hanging around.

The two birds flap and flutter. There are a few pellets left but no water. He rinses their tin cup and fills it with water. The wire cage needs to be covered with a cloth to let them rest for the night. 'A three-floor house calls for a wife,' his father nags. True. Loneliness beckons unless he marries again. But Zaida's questions have rekindled memories of Virginia. He is confused, feverish, almost embarrassed. 'Stop your family interfering,' she'd say. 'Ignore those calls. Living under Sharia law is not for me... I'm a free woman...' etc, etc. They became what their love at first had refuted – the Oriental and his insular Brit. He never forgave her refusal to attend the re-burial of Sunni martyrs whose heads had been scissored to prevent their identification. For her, digging up gruesome remains was unintelligible, sick. For him, naming the victims, burying them in the family mausoleum, was a necessity, and the ceremony of remembrance, however harrowing, would ensure that the younger generations would never forget the violence they have so far been spared.

Another call. Uncle Omar.

'Is Walid Hadidi around? It's urgent. Tell him to come and see me today.'

'Is he working for you? I didn't know.'

'Everyone working for my family is working for me, my boy! What you do or don't do is my business. By the way, I had a word with Minister Mustapha Al-Dari.'

'Thanks. He rang me up just now. I've agreed to take on the oil and gas contracts.'

'Top marks. But don't spoil it by causing a scandal. Stop going out to that grubby coffee house in Sharia Sobhi.'

'I haven't been for ages. Only musicians and old doffers! They do no harm.'

'I've a different story.'

'From Walid?'

'Don't play the fool. Those idiots in the Democratic People's Party are banned. You'll drag the family into the fire!'

Omar hangs up.

What does Omar fear under Assad II? Could the family be expelled again? He paces the room, fists clenched, resolute to act sensibly but miffed at being patronised. God! He stopped meeting that bunch of reckless democrats some time ago. Syrian politics are so volatile.

Omar, Mustapha Al-Dari, Walid – they have got to him. He climbs two steps at a time to reach the upper terrace leading to his rooms. The last slivers of red and pink fuse sky and city into one sorrowful embrace, then tatters of darkness rise from the horizon. He changes into his jeans to greet Karim and Yasser who would otherwise chaff him for keeping on his suit for a quiet evening after prayers drinking beer. Should he tell them about the two calls? But what for? They are cautious family men who would fear for him. Better say nothing for now. Tomorrow he will talk to the Kurdish friends on his maternal grandfather's side. But whatever Omar's accusations, he does not regret helping them out with false identities after their release from a Turkish high-security prison. Old divisions are bubbling up, they claim, in Northern Syria. But one should never forget the shame of mass graves. Every man's death, rich or poor, Muslim or not, deserves a blessing and a name.

– 2 –

The Clinic

PERNICKETY AS A STAGE MANAGER ON A FIRST NIGHT, Virginia Franklin surveys her treatment room while waiting for the first client. Today its serenity is broken, not by patients' miseries, but by her own nagging at the *hows* and the *whys* which have taken Zaida to spend half-term at her father's. At reception, Gwen, her mother, is checking the list of today's clients, ready to welcome them in the hushed voice appropriate to the solid respectability of the Franklin Acupuncture Clinic founded twenty years ago by Walter in a disused bicycle workshop. Most of the time, the modernised building exudes a tangible atmosphere of calm efficiency with its natural light and soft colours, reassuring Virginia that she had been right to come back to her parents'. But this morning she can't stop churning odious thoughts. Why had she let Zaida go? Everyone knew tug-of-love disputes between divorced parents separated by national frontiers. She should have stood up to Zaida's pleas and Khalid's constant calls. On the walls, the watercolours he gave her in better times seem less restful than usual: an ice-bound Loch Maree and a Cornish harbour, Newlyn, also in snow. She pokes at the harbour accusingly. Was he buying her off? Her index dislodges the nail and the frame drops onto the carpet.

'Oh! Heck!'

'What's going on? I heard some shouting.'

'I knocked off one of Khalid's pictures. A bad sign, Mum. I can't find the nail.'

'Oh! Nonsense. It isn't broken.' A matter-of-fact authority permeates the room as Gwen moves the picture onto the shelf holding catalogues of interest to acupuncturists. 'Here you are. We're back to normal. We keep telling you, he's no baby-snatcher!'

'You didn't always have a soft spot for him. "Don't marry a Muslim!" Remember?'

'Let's not bicker! The past is past.'

'In her last email,' she wails, 'she didn't say anything much. Too busy. They are all… wicked. It drives me nuts. Who was it who raised her, for God's sake?'

'We'd better get a grip before our first patients, dear. I've to go now and register them.'

Virginia tightens her tummy muscles and breathes deeply, trying to let go of the tension, eyes closed for five minutes; to focus on Zaida enjoying herself in Syria. And that's how it should be, of course. More cheerful now. She should have gone too. Zaida begged her to accept, but how could she, as the old wife, watch him gloat over his new life in Damascus, a slim mistress at his side?

A small table has everything she needs: a lighter, packs of the Chinese herb, a red and white china tray, patients' files, boxes of stainless steel needles – not the stone or bone of the long distant past. The needles are fine as hair, pliant but unbreakable, topped with a spiral of finer steel.

Everything is in order. Reassured, Virginia listens to people talking in the corridor. Her father is walking into his room, ready to start; her mother is sorting files for today's clients.

She examines the needles, smiling at their simplicity, her mission renewed each time she picks one up. With the needles she travels through time, safely. The perfect tools, signifying both tradition and modernity. She has never been against 'tradition' – which did not stop Khalid rebuking her for her attitude – how could she be, as an acupuncturist?

Unrolling a sheet of soft tissue paper over the couch, she smacks the pillow into shape, wondering why he has not yet remarried – and with so many adoring cousins to choose from!

It is against her nature to be jealous and she can see how any child can be seduced by the Al-Sayeds' world; and in Syria more devastatingly than in Leaford, where little Zaida was already thirsting for her grandfather's Arabic tales. She smiles, looking forward to discussing things with Marianne who, as a teacher, well understands the power of words on children. How right she was to invite her to visit during Zaida's first holiday abroad.

Before kick-off, she has time to send a 'luv yu' message, hoping it will get through. She walks down the corridor, enjoying the recent makeover of the reception area: toffee-cream walls, apple-green upholstered armchairs, art-deco vases, unsullied magazines. Even the reek of new paint is refreshing. Treating may release for a while her own anxieties. A frail elderly man is slouched in a chair, lost in thought. Patrick Brookside seems ill at ease with himself – has he got worse? He brightens up when she approaches.

Over the last five years, Patrick has shown a variety of symptoms: lonely, asthmatic, a scaly skin. Today, he shrinks into himself when telling her about kids chucking beer cans on his front lawn. 'Bastards!'

Lying on the couch in well-pressed corduroy brown trousers and a tartan cotton shirt, his frustration is palpable, his pulses jerky. Fixing his eyes on the ceiling, he grips her hand tight, watching her from half-closed eyelids veined and wrinkled like dry prunes.

Usually, he doesn't take to short, talkative women but she's the *crème de la crème*. A good wench. He likes the way she focuses on each gesture, a hundred percent committed to the job, immaculate in her clinical overcoat, chestnut hair pinned neatly up each side of a smooth, reflective face.

Patrick's cracked lips part slightly to let out a puff of contentment, no more solid than a snowflake, but real enough. Virginia thinks to herself – do not rush the treatment.

'You've gone through a lot, haven't you? Your wife's illness, now those kids rampaging around. Let's see what we can do today. The right-hand pulses are still a bit too cocky. I'll try the left.'

'Aye. Expect you like them two sides to be even. Makes sense to me. I'm a military bloke.' He speaks with detached precision. She taps him on the arm.

'Well done, Patrick.'

He murmurs as if talking to himself. 'I should've re-married. To a lass like you.'

She takes her time marking with a biro the points which should release the left/right block. Fortunate Patrick, who has no kid to worry about.

'You aren't too bad yourself. Look at this flat tummy. What's your secret?'

They grin, enjoying the banter. Her father likes to say chatting to the patients is part of the treatment. Gathering her energy, she inserts the needles, turns them clockwise and removes them immediately, each time glancing at Patrick's face. Painless. She checks his pulses. The block has gone. So simple. He follows her every move expectantly, an old spaniel, head down, ears flat, dejected yet hoping for more of her touch. She must consolidate the pulses. With her fingertips, she cajoles dried herb into little cones before lighting them. The five cones on wrist points take time to burn, but the moxa usually works for heat-deficient patients like Patrick. Yes, he is responding beautifully. And now for the needles again.

The following four cases are familiar, trusting patients who do not require the same focused attention as Patrick. In between the last two, she gains enough time to glance at the phone. Marianne is confirming her time of arrival tonight.

It is half past one, too late to walk across the garden and have a proper meal at home. Today she can have the kitchenette to herself. The October buzz of trainees has not yet arrived to hang around catching up with news of their trade, bitching, collecting miracle treatments and wetting their troubles with bottled water. Munching through a stale egg and bacon sandwich, she has little time to ponder over Zaida's grievous silence. Patients shouldn't have to wait.

There is a new wiriness in her as she deals with another four people during the afternoon. The last case, a new one, overweight and squat, lasts nearly one and a half hours before Virginia brings the consultation to a close. He made her talk about her training and the cases she had treated. She pretended to be as good as her father.

Roger gone, she is checking for news from Zaida, when Gwen peeps in. 'They're starting the meeting. Have you forgotten?'

'Drat! We also need to be at the airport by eight. I hope Marianne's on time, or I'll cave in. I'll be with you in five minutes.'

Still no email. When she slips into the conference room, they have already approved the minutes of the previous month. Chaired by Gwen, it is open to all the practitioners using the Franklins' centre. One item which raises eyebrows comes from a national newspaper suggesting that control over acupuncture should be moved from the self-appointed body of traditional acupuncturists to an official quango.

'I'm afraid the negotiations with the Department are going to break down again. Medical doctors are better at lobbying than us.'

Walter restrains himself from adding that the profession is, in any case, far too divided. And there are too many poorly trained guys offering acupuncture in beauty salons, hotel spas and massage parlours.

Sue Benning intervenes. 'Let them fail again, the fools.'

Virginia bobs her head at the freckle-faced woman, a longstanding friend who still practises two days a week. Recently widowed, desolation camouflaged by tweed suits, her curiosity for every therapy under the sun has taken on desperate overtones.

Listening to over-familiar arguments, Virginia's mind drifts back to today's patients. Above all else, there is this prodigious sensation; a caress, unique, which connects her to them when the needle hits a strong point, pulling the energy tight, deep, vibrating slightly. Maybe like a harp string. She looks around. These people have taught her everything. How could she have abandoned her profession, as Khalid demanded, and left them for Syria? There is her father, of course, and next to him, the same age, Andy Gibson, his closest associate. Born in a Yorkshire mining village, Andy has kept the mildness of the self-taught. As a girl, she used to seek his reassurance – more comforting than her father's. Once, she sent her brother to play on the slide, a flimsy thing, which their parents kept in the back garden. Some time later, she found the little brat lying on the grass, white as a sheet. She ran to the clinic, 'I've killed him!' Andy, bless him, rushed out. 'Help us, child. Rub his shoulders and hands.' Ian wailed: he was alive! She was a magician, hands full of tricks. Much later, a pubescent, prickly Ian hated her when she gloated about saving him. Pimpled, loathsome, her brother talked rubbish as usual.

She had not run away that day. We can take responsibility. Save ourselves. Act. It is a simple truth; unoriginal certainly, but also unyielding. She guards it fiercely in a corner of herself. Would Marianne guffaw at the thought?

'Virginia, are you with us? Have you noted we have very few trainees registered for the next six months?'

'Sorry, Father.'

Andy hands over a schedule of the weekend training programme. Despite a forbidding skull, he is a reliable man, with easy manners and an old-fashioned politeness streaked with warmth that endears him to colleagues young and old. Ironically, acupuncture has failed to prevent the shining baldness.

When Andy reports their accountant's view that the fees they charge for the seminars are too high, Walter is quick to close the meeting: 'Given the late hour, let's have a special session when we have the accountant's annual report.'

Walter and Andy, the only ones who know how serious the situation is, exchange a glance. If the business does not pick up, the extravagant revamping of the buildings may cost them dearly.

Meeting closed, the Franklins excuse themselves. They have to run and grab some food before fetching their guest from the East Midlands airport. Virginia dashes off another email: "Dearest, please get in touch."

Throughout the flight from Charles de Gaulle, Marianne Castagou fends off appreciative glances from her neighbour, an excitable, portly professor from the University of Birmingham returning from an international conference on the future of Romance studies. With stale breath, chivalrous, he says that her sing-song English is "superb". She answers politely, trying to ignore the plump, ringed hand pawing the armrest. Yes, she comes from the Midi, Montpellier to be exact, he is right about her accent. Yes, she is on holiday. Yes, primary schools have a mid-term vacation. She will be staying in Leaford. Yes, she has been before, many times.

She straightens her shoulders, turning her head away to study the dense patchwork unfolding beneath them in the evening light. Such a small island! Will more Brits cross to

France to escape the overcrowding? They won't drown. They will fill our markets with Marmite and cheddar cheese and tell us how to privatise our public sector. No, she doesn't dislike England. Far from it. Her thoughts drift to her 'English cousin' who will be waiting for her at the terminal. Why did Virginia suggest her visiting now? She will soon find out. They last saw each other four years ago at the funeral of her godmother. Virginia came to Chateau Mourel knowing that the death would trigger, for her friend, a long period of mourning.

'Are you alright? Afraid of landing?'

She opens her eyes, realising that her sighs have alarmed her neighbour.

'A little but I'm alright. Thank you.'

She tinkers with her handbag to reassure herself. As a little girl, she lost her adoptive parents in a car crash. Her godmother took her in, her sister's adopted child, and raised her single-handedly while running the family estate.

The plane, ten minutes late, is getting closer to East Midlands Airport. There is a battered power station, cockroach-like, smudging the horizon. Sixteen degrees on the ground. Passengers smile at each other. Not bad for mid-October.

'I'm glad you're feeling better.'

After a slight bow, the professor hurries off, having wiped her from his mind as soon as he reaches the bottom step. Marianne gets out her identity card. She resents the long queue, roped-in cordons snaking round to an overzealous immigration control: "UK and EU citizens", "Foreign passport holders". Why should she fear any of their glaring signs? This is not Sangatte with its barbed wire, dogs, traffickers, shacks, doped girls, hacks photographing the 'sans papiers'. Nonetheless, the shame of entering Britain seeps through her bones, triggering the memory of other equally humiliating queues. For six cold years at boarding school, the invasive anonymity of a military discipline claimed her as one of the inmates marched between dormitory, classroom and refectory in sullen files, stripped of their own wills.

At the final gate, a familiar voice echoes through the hall, teasing, 'Hello super, super frog! Ha! Ha!'

They burst out in giggles. Walter, a giant of a man, a mop of silvery hair coiffing a yet-unwrinkled face, arms outstretched, grabs her by the shoulders and jauntily butts his forehead against her cheeks in four successive hits, bone against bone, then wet lips smacking hard against hers. She staggers at the impact and before she fully recovers from this 'French' greeting, Walter leaps back to take a look. Satisfaction spreads across his face, charming and confident of her affection: a response he unconsciously expects from all the young people he likes to have around him. Maybe, for the insular English male, assaulting French women in public fulfils infantile desires. Relieved when Virginia goes for a softer approach. Dwarfed by her father's athletic figure, Virginia cuts a less impressive shape – short, a shapeless blue cotton shift over layered white skirts. But beneath the indifference to fashion, there lies a feline, nervous vitality that the long garments cannot disguise. She moves gracefully, free of constraints and conventions. Rarely abashed, she inspects Marianne openly from head to toe at arms' length, the light colour of her eyes deepening with emotion. She takes in Marianne's tall figure, the beige linen outfit, the loss of weight, the puffed-up eyes and, under the tan, the blood-drained patches of dry skin.

'You need a treatment! Sorry, Marianne. That was rude. Give me a hug. I'm chuffed you're spending time with us. But you do need a rest, don't you? Teaching can't be that good for you.'

She gives another squeeze. Marianne feels grateful for the Franklins' welcome, her apprehension vanishing. Virginia has not changed, unmade-up, loud, oblivious of disapproving looks, her voice painfully posh, bursting with energy, out of proportion to her size.

She climbs into the Rover, hoping that her friends have not felt her stiffness. She is so fond of them but what a strain! They speed down the M1 unaware that sitting at the back makes it difficult for her to follow what they say. Her English must be rustier than she thought. How will she cope under this onslaught? Maybe she has lived on her own for too long. They are nearing Leaford. Walter winks at her in the rear-view mirror:

'Famous battles have been fought not far from here. I was born near here, in the middle of England, in a Saxon village called—'

'For God's sake, Dad, she's just arrived!'

Marianne smiles indulgently, sympathising with Walter's passionate feelings about the heart of England. A large flock of gulls scour a just-harvested field, a squabbling playground. She likes the idea of Walter being born in the 'middle', a private spot he can fill with his own fancy.

Leaford announces itself: two towers dominating the city centre, the same red-brick-and-glass feat of 1950s engineering which she had glimpsed as a teenager travelling by train from London abroad by herself for that first holiday, dreading mint sauce or cucumber sandwiches! Since then, things have moved on. Even Leaford University has brash mission statements on the lampposts.

'Like a business park,' Walter scoffs.

Virginia shrugs. 'Universities need to get the punters in, no matter how… degrees in media and sports, you name it!'

'France is no better. Students drop out like, what do you say, Virginia, those…?'

'Flies?'

'*Oui. oui.*' Marianne looks around. She understands well enough what is going on, in England as in France. Mix-and-match cultures where, insensitive to local craft and custom, IKEA's blue and yellow dwarfs the universities. As they pass the station, within walking distance of the university towers, she recollects her first impression of the building, grand and prim, the expression of a proud Midlands Railway, toiling for Queen and Empire, delivering people and goods on time. She was just fourteen then, with more spots than confidence, intimidated by Ian waving from a Hackney cab as shiny as a scarab beetle.

'You won't recognise the city centre,' Virginia persists, 'it's now littered with beer bottles, plastic bags and private contractors. That's Labour for you.'

She does not fully grasp how Labour alone has polluted the city, but she is too tired to find out. They must be getting near. Walter negotiates the busy traffic, at first along a sumptuous leafy street bordered by stately Victorian houses built with the profits of industry. As they move further from the city centre, the ancient trees thin out and the street now opens to gusty winds and the homes of wealthy Indian traders expelled from Uganda in the 1970s, illuminated by dainty cast-iron street lamps, fussy neo-Gothic facades glistening in the dark. Walter, Virginia knows, instinctively calculates the price of each house as he points out "For Sale" signs, like a dog sniffing a bitch.

'Dad talks about selling but he has a real horror of moving. He's a limpet – he wouldn't budge even if you paid him a million pounds!'

'Where would we go? I've been happy living in this part of town since I married your mother. What's wrong with that?'

'Forty-five years in South Leaford! I hope I never match that!'

'Why not?' Walter asks gruffly.

Marianne is puzzled at father and daughter, both with the same fleeting irritation on their faces. 'How is Zaida? Is she enjoying her trip?'

'She's having a ball. They're spending a fortune for her cousin's wedding. Did you ever meet Zaida's grandfather? When I was living with Khalid? No. His father has been orchestrating the whole caboodle of the nephew's marriage for months. Khalid tags along. They've been preparing food, hiding whisky bottles, hiring people in, getting new clothes, choosing presents. What 12-year-old wouldn't love it?'

Seeing Virginia's eyes watering, Marianne says tentatively: 'You are not cool about it?'

'For Zaida it's great, it's her first time, but I hope it isn't the biggest mistake I've ever made.'

'She'll be back soon,' Walter chimes in.

'You understand, Marianne, they could keep her there.'

'No, not Khalid. And she's got her return ticket in her luggage.'

'Drop it, Dad. I can't bear us arguing again.'

'I'm sorry I miss her, she is grown-up now.'

'I'll show you plenty of photos if you want.'

Closing her eyes, Virginia leans back into her seat. Such a long day. Too whacked to explain. Her friend will have to wait.

– 3 –

Leaford

WALTER MANOEUVRES THE CAR INTO THE ASPHALT driveway lined with conifers and rhododendrons. A large front lawn announces an imposing property. There are blue signposts to the acupuncture clinic in converted outbuildings at the back. The three floors are brightly lit. Gwen Franklin hurries along the ornate balcony spanning the sitting rooms, and down steps bordered with deep blue flowers in square stone jars.

'Welcome, dear girl. Your hair – what have you done to it? Is it much shorter? It suits you, of course.'

Marianne laughs. 'I had my hair cut years ago. I look less virgin, better for teaching. Your agapanthus! They are flowering!' Only good things have happened to her in Leaford.

'Virginia's taking your luggage to your old room. Nothing much has changed there. You know the way,' Gwen says.

Unlike her daughter she speaks softly; and yet, physically, she is her spitting image, short but attractive, with brisk movements, chestnut hair parted on the side, compassionate eyes. In contrast to Virginia's shapeless dresses, she wears a tight skirt and jacket, or an embroidered cardigan over linen slacks, revealing a sense of what is proper while understating the certainty that none of her Welsh relatives will ever find fault with her. Good wives indulgent of male passions, yet comfortable with young females, wet behind the ears, dazzled by husbands.

The Franklins beam their appreciation as Marianne unpacks modest presents to be stored in the fridge.

'Isn't she clever, Mother, to bring everyone's favourite?'

'Not Ian's.'

Virginia should have kept her mouth shut, as everyone silently registers the absence of the sweet Brittany pancakes that Marianne used to bring. Ian loved them. It is typical of her parents to pretend they've not heard her remark. Christ! He left for Canada ten years ago, in a tiff, she isn't sure what about now, but that's water under the bridge. Irritated, she is trying to find room for the packs of French food in the overfilled fridge. Ian was always a selfish brat, too pretty for his own good. But Dad would hear nothing against him.

'Any news from Ian? Still living in Vancouver?'

'Seems contented enough over there. Off you go, you two. I'll see to the rest.'

After shuffling them out of the kitchen, Gwen turns round to stack what is left of Marianne's presents. She breathes slow and deep, back in control. Her son couldn't wait for the pan to sizzle. Lips pursed, giggling at his prowess, he'd toss the wafer-thin pancake and pat it into four folds before adding plenty of sugar and lemon for his dad. Zaida is the same – they always serve Walter first. What's so wrong about that?

Forgetting the clinic, her husband is in his element taking Marianne around the house. Unperturbed by the late hour, he whispers a joke in her ear, giving solicitous explanations about home improvement, pecking her cheek for a kiss, all signs of a prudent foreplay which Gwen puts up with, knowing that he has always been an unrestrained flirt. He will emerge from each trivial indiscretion shining, revived, the bouts of irritation gone, his energy rekindled. There is never anything improper, she is well aware of that, and Marianne still has that *something*. Must be such a gift for a teacher. She ought to show her Zaida's schoolwork.

Tea is served in the less formal of the reception rooms. Marianne looks around with pleasure. Where else but middle-class England would you find such high ceilings, intricate plasterwork, silk wall prints and rich William Morris wallpaper framing the high sash windows? There are shelves with Chinese vases, Inuit bears, dragons made of jade, family mementos and glossy books. She recognises the aspirations that float in this room. They are not unlike those in Chateau Mourel, although the décor at home is less urbane – walls teeming with antlers and African masks. Both places share the delusion that time is held at bay by unbridled comfort and expensive acquisitions from exotic cultures.

On the Victorian mantelpiece, an alabaster male figurine, about thirty centimetres high, attracts her attention. It is exquisitely carved, standing upright, mapped in ink with lines and points. The acupuncture meridians?

'It was used to teach acupuncture many years ago. Chinese students learnt by following the lines with their fingertips. Nice.'

Marianne familiarises herself discreetly with the room, remembering fondly how Ian taught her to polish the parquet floor by dragging two woollen pads with her feet. What fun it was sliding like tipsy swallows through the tang of wax. The Franklins were like family to her then.

'How old is Zaida here? About 12?'

'Spot on.'

The woman-to-be in the child stares back at her with searching dark eyes, an inhibited smile, mouth wide open – a child caught in a moment of mirth, repressing her laughter for the photographer while cuddling a tiger to her chest.

With a twinge of indignation, Marianne realises that the room gives no sign of other children having lived there apart from the framed photos of Zaida. There are no pictures of Virginia and Ian as children.

'Have you contacted your solicitor?'

Virginia leaps to her feet, skidding across the floor to pull the long velvet curtains across.

'I thought we were not going to raise this now, Marianne's only just arrived.'

'Anything new?

'Mother, don't, not now, it's late in Syria.'

'We've been on edge for months. Virginia didn't want her to go, but Zaida took no for an answer. Understandably, of course.'

Marianne is taken aback by the bickering.

'I understand, Gwen. When did you hear from Zaida?'

Virginia presses her lips tight, unwilling to respond.

'I wish I have not come. I am in the way.'

'Don't be silly, darling. We're really glad you're here, as you well know. We'll have a long natter tomorrow. I miss Zaida terribly in the evenings. And it's Halloween soon.'

Gwen gets to her feet to grasp Marianne's arm.

'Don't mind our grumps. Anyway, time for bed. Sleep tight, dear Marianne.'

The wrong time to come. With her door closed, Marianne is relieved not to have to speak to anyone till morning. Virginia is a pack of nerves. She will have to find ways of talking to her. Why is she in such a state? Spending time away from home is usually for good for teenagers. And Zaida will be getting to know her dad as a real person, not someone imagined in his absence.

She will take her time unpacking, but there are birds everywhere! Since her last visit about ten years ago, collections of birds made of wood, clay, one material or another, have moved in, covering shelves, bedside tables and mantelpiece. She had forgotten Gwen's passion, 'a bug', Walter says, which his wife inherited from her Welsh grandmother who had a keen eye for ceramics and pots. Unable to blank the birds, Marianne winces at the privilege of wealth, erratic and wasteful.

Apart from the bric-a-brac, she is pleased to have been given the old guest room. Ian used to have the bedroom above hers. Across his landing, Virginia kept quiet, although she knew. She was 18 when they made love. *La belle affaire*. And Ian, 17? Had Virginia heard them roaring with laughter when Ian dangled a smelly rubber thing in front of her, equally ludicrous as a *capote anglaise*? It wasn't really love that kept them awake but the narcissistic need to go beyond childhood, to explore sex safely, to get her virginity over with without humiliation, and with a gentle partner.

She chortles. One night she told Ian how Proust's neighbour demanded the picture of her own father to be placed on her mantelpiece to assist her mildly sadistic games with her lady friend. Ian required the same chastisement under a photo of Walter. The transgression brought them renewable pleasures when literature and living fused into one. Nowadays, her night performances are less exquisite. As the years went by, sex began to lose its exhilaration, slowly tarnished with introspection and fears. Is she now romanticising what happened that first time? Over twenty years, memories of sex have piled up in her brain like dead leaves, packing in layer after layer, mostly buried: why dig up her first love?

She pulls a face at the dressing-table mirror. She has little in common with the girl Ian knew, apart from still reading novels, but she is good enough. A grainy skin, mousy blond hair, no wrinkles, approaching forty. She is glad to be back but too drowsy to think of how to help Virginia.

The following morning, Marianne runs down the stairs to catch Virginia, who is about to walk across the yard to the clinic.

'Tell me, any news?'

'No! Little Madame is too busy.'

'Don't take bad what I say. You're a loving mum. She needs to spread her... wings... without you.'

'How do you know?'

'I can see kids at the school. And my friends talk a lot about their children. They say... to give space is difficult but the right thing.'

'Heck! Can you hear the rain? Let me find my coat.'

Groping coats, jackets and rain gear, she steps around a majestic Victorian coat-hanger spreading its arms above their heads.

'That's mine. Thanks. I understand what you're saying. But she is so far away, out of touch. Anything can happen.'

'Why worry about things that have not happened?'

Virginia gives her a hug.

'You're so French!'

Both laugh.

'You are positive with your patients. You know it matters, why not in your own life?'

'Good point, teacher. What else do you want to tell me before I get drenched?'

'Zaida comes back with opinions that surprise you. Not the stories of Mum or Dad. That's good for a teenager.'

'Spot on. She wanted to see Syria with her own eyes, she kept saying.'

Although she has no fresh news, Virginia steps into the practice feeling light-hearted, reassured by the brief tête-à-tête. She smiles at the irony: the apprehensive mum, drawing comfort from a childless unmarried woman.

She has no worry about the first three patients – routine cases. Unlike the pretty British-Caribbean woman she treats just before lunch. This is the third time she has seen Mary Angel, who owns a successful cosmetic shop for black people in the city centre. Married, no children. Today, she presents the usual story.

'I feel shit, really. Everything is a struggle, I'm always knackered and I don't know why. Money isn't the problem. I bought the shop four years ago and now we're thinking of franchising it.'

Eight pulses are all over the place and, for such a well-built woman, pretty weak, deep and knotted. While she prepares moxa cones on the tray, she seeks to engage Mary about the shop. Mary remains impassive; she has not come here to chat. Virginia is quiet too, enjoying the moment when, virgin needles at the ready, the room brims with unspoken expectations – the patient's and hers. She tries to imagine a woman's life without children around. Such an emotional desert. Whatever, it is safe to treat her on the arms. The room is getting stuffy. Mary sits up, glaring at her.

'You aren't getting anywhere, are you?'

Virginia, unnerved, jots down more pulses. Too much yin.

'Ouch! Go on. Turn me into gruyere.'

Mary has stopped fidgeting. Her pulses are still wiry but steadier.

'If there's anything which bothers you, tell me. It's alright here, quite safe. What are you missing?'

Her face turned away, hidden from Virginia, Mary's voice croaks, choking with tears and anger.

'I can't come. I've never enjoyed sex. It hurts. That's why I don't have any kids. Can't be normal!'

She stifles, furious for speaking against her will, arms clasped tight on her chest. Virginia is stunned. The needles have released the energy to the point of brutality.

'Thank you for telling me. I've treated a few patients with that problem, it isn't uncommon. Do you want us to talk about it?'

Mary swivels her head back, brimming with hostility. Handing her a box of tissues, Virginia represses a feeling of self-congratulation.

'You are my last patient this morning. If you don't want to say any more, that's fine too.'

What causes sexual blockages in women? Maybe she should use the Eight Principles, and not just the Five Elements. Better not tell Walter. A fuddy-duddy, he doesn't like mixing the two systems of acupuncture.

'Where's the pain exactly? Describe it for me.'

No story of abuse. Normal doctors – would you believe it? – recommend herbal tea! Humbled by the woman's trust, Virginia books her for another appointment, free this time, later in the week. But will she come back?

Late for lunch served in the Victorian conservatory, Gwen's pride and joy, Virginia throws herself into a robust rocking chair, wondering how much the fact that she is missing her daughter helped her to uncover Mary's problem. Sex? Child? The parallel's absurd! But self-rebuke won't help either. She rocks the chair roughly, like a swing. Gwen jumps to its rescue.

'Be careful! Marianne, can you see the carving at the back? Look! A bearded little man sitting in an oak tree. A story-teller. My father. That chair was made for him. Quite phenomenal! Have the soup, dear.'

Virginia wolfs down the gazpacho and fresh granary bread before turning her attention to Marianne.

'How was your morning?'

Marianne, wearing a loose wrap-over dress Virginia wouldn't be seen dead in, smiles back.

'You make me feel bad, you are working hard.'

'What did you do?'

'I walk the riverside. I follow two big girls, 15, maybe. Pink sandals, white leggings. Pink tops. Pink hair things. And their mobiles, pink too! *Mon dieu*!'

She stops talking, realising that Virginia is not interested in her babble.

'When is Zaida due back?

'November the 7th.'

'I'll miss her. What bad luck!'

'You would've liked our heroine. We'll send you piccies of the wedding Zaida is attending.'

'Is she good… travelling?'

'I told her to hide her passport and return ticket somewhere in her bedroom. Just in case. I briefly explained why. She didn't bat an eyelid. She said OK, she would, but I've no idea what she made of my advice. I'll show you her bedroom if you want.'

Walter, resting from the chat, pecks at a bowl of nuts and seeds his wife put down beside him. Clean-shaven, vigorous, he does not look like the man who has gone for a half-hour run at 7am and treated five people in the morning. He sits astride the chair, legs apart, exposing the bulge of his genitals to the women, back straight, an adept of pilates and self-discipline, confident of his place in the world.

There are tense lines around Virginia's mouth and her eyes are clouded, the heavy lids cloaked. Something else must have gone wrong this morning, he thinks, giving her a sharp look.

'Tough morning, Virginia?'

'A new patient is niggling me.'

He asks a few questions, keen to eliminate false tracks. Both anorgasmia and infertility can be a long haul.

'Well done, girl. Keep her trust. If you want, I can help you with your treatment plan.'

She remains in awe of her father's experience. Forty years! Would he have done better this morning? Yet why not let her try the Eight Principles approach, and not just the Five Elements that they practise here? Needle points directly linked to dysfunctions? She could follow the new course at the college in Reading, but Walter would see such a move as a betrayal of his life's work. At times, it isn't easy to remain a faithful daughter. She stops rocking. Is Zaida having the same thought?

The light lunch over, Gwen snaps as her husband helps himself to another thick slab of Roquefort. 'Your diet, for heaven's sake! Did you take your vitamins this morning? And the statin?'

He concentrates on the moist mushroom flavour with the attention of an addict. Gwen backs off, not wanting an argument in front of Marianne. The bloody doctor can't even look after himself. He won't take the medicine prescribed by the hospital. High cholesterol is not critical, he says. All he does is talk, talk, talk.

'Mum, look! Can you hear him?'

Tap. Tap. Tap. In the glare of the sun, a great tit is pecking microscopic insects from the glass panes of the conservatory.

'I'll tell Zaida he is back. We need to run. Enjoy your afternoon, Marianne.'

It has been a good day for the Franklins, happy to chat around the evening meal. Gwen has excelled herself with a fine fish pie, one of Marianne's favourite English dishes. With the addition of soya milk, the potato mash is light and creamy; the hake, moist. For dessert, there is Marianne's lemon tart, sharp and sweet, to be topped with low-fat Greek yoghurt. You can hear the family purr.

It would be perfection for everyone, Virginia thinks, were it not for Zaida's silence ringing in their ears. But it is fine to be lazy after a good day's work. There is a light knock on her leg: Marianne kicking her under the table with repressed mirth.

'Look at your father!'

'Don't take any notice.'

Chin resting on his chest, Walter nods off. Virginia and Marianne exchange a look of complicity. Women rarely expose their features to other people like that. Only men feel safe enough, or are thick-skinned enough, to do it. He slouches further into the chair, head slumped to one side, mouth dropping open; a faint snoring. Gwen, frazzled, exclaims, 'Marianne, darling, nudge him!'

Marianne and Virginia quietly dissent. They enjoy the sight of Big Walter at rest, half-consciously expecting the conversation to take a new turn, a feminine agenda this time, until the moment, all too soon, when he reclaims their exchange as his own, setting its pace and topic, leaving the women to chip in with those signs of affection – a smile, words of encouragement: Brilliant! Do go on! – that men so fully deserve.

When they entertain, Gwen likes to watch her husband, a leonine presence. Even now she is surprised at him occupying the opposite side of her table. Marrying him had been her lucky break. Her Baptist mother died young and her father remarried within the year, leaving her angry and hostile to the new wife, a Quaker. She was just 8. Wrapping herself in a coat of self-reliance and detachment, she transformed the unspoken loss into a desire to be moderate in all things for fear of worse to come. At Liverpool University, she smiles to herself, she developed an eccentric interest in collecting. Her room, said Walter, had class with its watercolours and a small bird cage, empty, the door open, propping up books. Her only love understood and never queried her gentle passion. She chuckles to herself. Although a flirt, he would never set out to harm her.

Checking that he is still asleep, she says, 'It's refreshing to sit here for a while. Now the practice is so large, we rarely have a break during the week! Not that I'm complaining.'

'Poor Mum! We depend on you so much! You like it really, don't you? Maybe not.'

With a pang of envy Marianne watches mother and daughter, Virginia falling into the odd habit of answering her own questions, Gwen patting her arm. Her godmother was not the sort you could get close to, even when she became fatally ill. Intimacy frightened her adoptive mother. Women's needs were so hushed! Marianne sighs. She never had a flowing, cosy relationship with her or with anyone else. Virginia raises an eyebrow.

'What's wrong, pet?'

Marianne cheers up; nobody has ever called her that before.

'Would you prefer "What's wrong, duck?" "Chick?" Or "What's wrong... guy"? It's trendy. Take your pick, sweetie.'

Such joking mellows the home. Gwen leaves to make more herb tea.

Quietly, respecting Walter's doze, Marianne attempts to probe her friend's fears.

'The Khalid I know years ago never try to hold Zaida against her will.'

'But he's not the Khalid you knew. He's back home. Things are different there. Other pressures, other loyalties. You know, when we were married, his father, Abdul, sometimes came to see us. After the meal he'd get a map of Syria and tell us the Golan Heights was their land. Hammering the table. For Jews, Christians and Muslims, the land is blood. And blood is religion.'

'But they didn't say Zaida is a Sunni Muslim?'

'Never as such. We told them our future kids would be taught no religion – let them decide for themselves when they grow up. Abdul, the hypocrite, interfered later! Although he himself had broken ranks by marrying an Alawite. I tell you the truth, for him, our pact was galling.'

'Galling?'

'Exasperating. Annoying. He wanted to name my baby "Seema". A girl who was raped! How to explain that to her later?'

'Shush. Don't wake him up.'

'Our baby girl, in spite of her fair hair, "looks like her ". That's what he said. Spooky.'

'Spooky? I know… in the books for children in my room.'

'Clever you! Abdul called the baby "Seema" a few times – not on purpose, of course. We had to laugh about it. When Zaida was about 6, he sang her bits of the Koran. We let him. She's pretty modest. She never dresses in see-through tops, belly buttons, you know how they do it now.'

'Sensible like her mum?'

'I'll show you the family tree she's made. Decorated with arabesques, Syrian stars, very glitzy. And she's got a nose for bargains just like Abdul. But have no fear – she's an English teenager through and through! Worries about her thighs, her little boobs. Hates salad and beetroot, that sort of thing. Not that interested in Twitter. Prefers to play on WOW. You see, she's a pretty normal kid.'

Gwen bustling around brings Walter back to them, stirring, shaking his head like a seal coming out of the sea. The women, protective of him, are grateful for his clowning. 'I've things to do!' He leaves the room, followed by Virginia. Five minutes later she bursts back in.

'Listen! I've just received a long email. I'll read it out to you.' Her face lights up as her voice gathers strength.

I met the new bride. You couldn't see her face because she had loads of make-up. And she is old, cousin Ali told me. He dances like a ceb. People want to take my picture when Dad tells them I am visiting. There was a man who wanted me to marry his son. Dad got cross. I am enjoying myself, Mummy. Don't worry. They bought me new dresses. Pretty scarves. Gym shoes. Nice bracelets.

Marianne interrupts theatrically, applauding until Gwen hushes her. 'Do go on, dear!'

Did Dad tell you we were going to this huge fair on top of a hill? He said it would be a break from Damascus. I could not ring you. There were loads of monkeys in a cage and men racing on white horses. We visited a huge citadel with

*big towers inside. We did not see any prisoners. Am so tired I
can't write any more. They are calling me. I love you so much
Mummy. And Grandpa and Granny. Your loving daughter. Ta
ta.*

'Let's call your father and drink to that!'

Virginia kisses Marianne on the cheek, whispering, 'Zaida
is doing well on her own. You were right, you know.'

Marianne is doing her utmost not to look triumphant as
the family celebrate Zaida's feisty spirit. Eventually, Gwen
retires to bed, soon followed by an exhilarated Virginia.

'Stay, Marianne. We'll watch the 10 o'clock news together.
It's on in five minutes.' She strikes Walter as a woman of a
fierce independence – quite startling, given her conservative
upbringing by a Languedoc family. How do they take to her
being unmarried, with a teaching job and a crumbling estate to
run? He has never poked his nose into the Hernandez business
although the two families have met over many summers. With
her electrifying energy, Marianne has always been good for
Virginia, especially now. She worries too much. He can't share
her distrust of the Al-Sayeds. He always had a soft spot for
the man – dignified, warm, ebullient, sympathetic. And such a
devoted dad. It can't be easy keeping contact with your child
on Skype. They mustn't forget that. And remember what
people said of Abdul. Such a good GP.

How can these decent people harm Zaida? Their older
girl was raped years ago in a Beirut camp. The four children
were hunted down by a gang of Maronite Phalangists out
to kill Sunnis. When Abdul told him what had happened to
Seema, he felt honoured to be his confidant. He and Abdul
were close to tears. The families are bonded, divorce or not.
So when Khalid asked for a loan to support the expansion
of the Al-Sayeds' business, he didn't refuse, although he was
never quite sure what the new project was – transporting
Iraqi oil to Syrian Mediterranean ports? Restoring pipelines

for the government? Anyway, a little money goes a long way over there. Khalid paid the loan off with interest when the clinic needed to expand. A sensible affair on both sides and a nice little secret.

Walter works himself into a surge of self-satisfaction. The Al-Sayeds are resilient people, tested to the edge of sanity by vicious conflicts. It is preposterous to believe Khalid and his father, who, he suspects, are still grappling with memories of persecution and imprisonment, would keep Zaida against her will – a child, so full of beans and funny ideas, well able to speak up for herself. You can see it in her email. His mind at rest, he wanders across the room to shut the curtains. The little monkey is enjoying herself at her dad's, but come the 7th, she'll be on the plane.

On the screen, an American expert talks of the crash. A tsunami. Banks will need bailing out worldwide. With billions from taxpayers. Will that be enough? Stock markets continue to decline; countries cannot borrow.

'Brandy, Marianne? All this news about bad debts and sub-prime mortgages is so depressing. Speculators owe billions! And shirk responsibility! Our City people were up to their eyes in it too.'

He serves her in a bulbous glass, taking in his breath as he stands close, blocking his nostrils for a split second out of a professional habit to assess her body odour: sweet and bitter like chocolate. Suddenly, the day takes its toll. He feels jaded. Bankers do rob people. Children do not return. Marianne draws him out of his dejection.

'I hear Andy after the meeting. On the phone, very loud: "Walter is hiding his head in the sand." What does it mean?'

'Did he say that?'

Hiding his irritation at the indiscretion, Walter switches off the news. Making light of the situation, he explains how the clinic's cash flow problems have been made worse by the renovation. It is a temporary problem as new courses will increase the clinic's reputation and bring in more patients.

'Don't talk about this to Virginia or Gwen. They have enough on their plates at the moment.'

Marianne steals him a glance. 'I have money from my godmother. You get 20,000 euros now and pay later. I don't know when you pay. You are family, you see.'

There is no response. At the sight of his bushy eyebrows going up and down she stifles a smile.

'How generous! What can I say?'

'Please accept.'

'It's very tempting.'

'I am happy you accept.'

'Sorry, dear girl. I can't accept.' He slows down his words. 'I am most grateful but I can't be sure we can pay you back, do you understand me? More debts won't solve our long-term problems. And no offence to you, lovely friend – you're not family. It's a family business and I want to keep it that way.'

She waves her arms around, testifying her good faith. 'I don't want to run your place!' Seeing his startled look the blood rushes to her face: 'OK, you're right. More debts is not good.'

'Many, many thanks for your offer. I'll never forget it.'

He gives her a hug. Catching a whiff of her perfume, he hesitates, and with a slight effort becomes sure of himself again. 'Goodnight, sweet friend.'

He sags into his chair, staring at the now blank screen. What a relief she's gone! For a split second, he was ready to be seduced. He refused for many reasons, but mainly because he couldn't be sure of repaying any loan. The news has darkened. 'Scoundrels!' The slump has taken 20 percent out of his savings. He groans. His boy had seen what was coming. He abandoned us. What's he up to now in Vancouver? He wishes he hadn't had the second brandy. He's unused to drinking on his own. Abandoned by the young – Ian, Khalid, Zaida. Like so many of his patients, he needs reassurance about the future. But who will give it, apart from Marianne?

He stands up, tottering because of a new pain throbbing down his left leg. Christ! The boy should be here when the family is in such a pickle. That would be the natural order of things. Would it be irresponsible to ask him to come home now? He looks at his watch, calculating the eight-hour difference. There are moments during a treatment when, foxed by sinking pulses, he acts on gut instinct. For Ian, he'll pick up the phone at the proper time. But what about Khalid? He is a sort of speculator now, isn't he?

Twenty minutes later he squeezes into bed, trying not to stir Gwen. The old bird would peck at him until he bleeds. He has emailed Khalid: lend the practice £25,000 to cover temporary cash flow difficulties. Gwen will not see the sense of this, although he put it diplomatically by stressing no offence would be taken if Khalid cannot help. And another clever move, an afterthought: he would try to make Virginia see sense and let Zaida stay a bit longer.

At last, he falls asleep torn between self-delusion and self-congratulation. Khalid is still family.

– 4 –

Damascus

Since her return from Hama, Zaida's presence is undermining Khalid's solitude – for the best. Breakfast is not at 7am anymore but much later. They take their time. Her chat competes with the budgies, diverting his energy away from work. Zaida insists on eating on the top terrace, now flooded by a soft light diffused by the roof screens that she loves to manipulate. He is happy to join in the fun by adjusting the angles of the canvas sheets hooking each sail, calling out 'hi ho!', much to Mariyam's amusement. Sharing a meal brings more satisfaction. He rejoices Zaida is not a fussy eater anymore. What else will he discover? Such a tall girl. She sits back straight while they play at being attentive guests, unhurried by the demands of the day.

'Will you hand me the bread basket, please?'

'Dad, tell Mariyam this is the best breakfast I ever had.'

They savour bowls of spicy hummus and eggplant caviar, creamy yoghurts, a tomato and parsley salad and their favourite halawa, the sweets made with sesame paste.

'I love roasted aubergines. Much nicer than in Leaford. Why is that?'

'Can't you guess, my pet?'

She screws up her nose. 'We aren't in Leaford?'

'May be. Tell me, what would you like to do today?'

'Go to Palmyra!'

'No. It takes two or three nights to do it justice.'

She slips back into the chair, rubbing her eyes with her fists to hide her disappointment, a child again. He stretches his hand out across the table to tap lightly the sweet dent on her chin. 'Knock, knock, who's there?'

There is a petrified child running wild around the chairs. 'The big bad wolf! Help!' He catches her, hugging her close, sniffing her neck – milky and fragrant, his baby girl. She wriggles out of the embrace and, facing him at a safe distance, waves a challenging index finger.

'Why do you have big ears? To listen to me! Tell my mum I am staying until Christmas.' Khalid's voice rises with an unquenchable frustration.

'You listen to me! Virginia cannot trust me – never, never! You want a proof? Two years ago, they arranged for a 'port alert' in case I whizzed you out of Britain without her consent. As if I have no honour—'

'Sorry, Dad, I was only teasing.'

'Under British law, the mother knows best, never the father!'

Zaida's eyes filling with tears deflates his anger, leaving him feeling guilty for weighing the girl down with unsolvable conflicts.

'I am sorry to drag you into this.' He stretches out his arms to catch her, growling, 'I am accused of bad, bad things... like eating you up!'

Zaida pushes him away, pleading, 'Why can't you try? She won't bite you!'

'Let's see what I can do. But don't let it spoil our fun, my love.'

She runs into his arms again for another cuddle on his lap. 'What are we doing today?' Neither of them moves.

'Not the big mosque. Grandad said he'd take me. He is a better guide than you! That's what he said.'

'Fair enough. I've plenty of time. We can walk to Azm Palace, through the souk. The smell of spices and soap will make you stop at every stall. We call it the smell of Damascus. There's no other place like it.' He can't help his voice ringing with an infantile pride.

'Have you been homesick?'

'A bit.'

'When you were with us?'

He strokes her hair back from her forehead. 'You'll see for yourself. Don't bother clearing up. Let's go down.' She counts in Arabic the steps to the ground floor. 23. Loud and clear.

'I can count to 50.'

'Pretty clever. Who taught you that?'

'Grandad, yesterday.'

'I've told Mariyam you'd be happy to feed the birds. We do it before we go?'

Up and down the ornate cage, there is a flurry of anticipation. A couple shuffle to the perch the furthest away from the intrusion; two others move to the right corner, close to the feeding tube.

'Look at them! The greedy ones! You'll soon recognise them.'

'I'm no good at birds.'

'Have a go!'

'Can I stay, Dad?' She fills up the little plastic cup with seeds and nuts. 'What about the water?'

'It's pretty full. We'll do it tomorrow. Check the door hook is on or else we'll be in trouble.' Zaida blows kisses at the closed cage.

'You like them being in a prison?'

'No! I don't! They were given to me by one of my Chinese partners who thought I needed company.'

She closes the plastic container storing the bags of seeds. 'Where do I put it away? I don't know your house yet.'

'*Our* house. When you are 18 you'll stay for months at a time. Would you like that?'

Smiling, she collects the few grains that have spilled on the floor and, cooing like a dove, holds a hazelnut between the wooden bars. No bird bothers to move. She turns back to him, discouraged.

'Teach them to sing, whistle, talk…. I haven't had time to try. Have a go!'

'How long am I going to stay?'

'Depends.'

'He says I look like her.'

'Sorry?'

'Grandad, you silly! My dead aunt.'

'What did he tell you?'

'Do you think I look like her?'

'I don't remember much. Sorry!'

'*Your* older sister!'

The indignation catches him off-guard. 'Seema died in Lebanon. We were refugees.'

'I was little when Mummy told me. Grandad has a big hole in his heart.'

'What else?'

'Not much. The camp was a prison, dirty, with no proper food. Seema was very ill, they couldn't help her. How terrible!'

Well catered for, the yellow budgie launches a long series of chirrupy sounds, which are soon repeated by its partner. Zaida skips around the fountain and claps until Khalid, diffident, resumes the conversation.

'We all missed Seema terribly. Me and my sisters. She was like another mum, she spoilt me; I was her baby brother. She taught me old Arabic proverbs to make me laugh. Curiously, they come back to me when real Damascus people talk to me.'

'Try me!'

'Wait a minute. I've to translate it. Listen. "The camel is lame because his lip hurts." Meaning?'

'Don't know.'

'Something small can hurt the whole person, or something like this.'

'Like a bad dream?'

'Why not?'

'I'd love to see your photos. With your sisters.'

'Ask my father. Now get ready, you little chatterbox.'

Two hours later, on the way to the Azm Palace, they sit down at a café in Sharia Al-Mir that the Al-Sayeds frequented when he was a boy. The same family runs the place. For some obscure reason this discovery makes him light-hearted.

'The same Bidiri? No kidding?' Above her glass, her eyes, burnt chestnut, enhance the colour of the mango juice. 'The Umayyad Mosque is round the corner, isn't it? I remember this tall wall at the end of the street.'

'Right on!' She is bright. She had coughed out the odd Shemi words like "pistachio nuts", which made traders drop their price and fill her hands with sweets or crystallised fruit.

'I won't forget that souk. It's so cool. I'll get Aleppo soaps for Granny and I won't forget... can you guess what?' He shakes his head. She continues, 'The sexy lingerie... Sunnis – I saw them buy it for their women. Under those awful black gowns! What a laugh!'

'Shiite pilgrims to be precise, not Sunnis. And they come from Iran.'

'Tell me, did you buy red knickers for Mum? From this souk?'

Shocked, he stammers, 'Such trash? Never!' before concentrating on his drink. He won't look at her, feeling priggish and cornered by her intuition. Black... they were black. On his first trip back to Damascus. From one of the cheap shops you find on the way to the mosque. Old Damascus

47

is an eternal present. Virginia refused to parade on her high stilettos, claiming that'd be too demeaning. Her love had already gone toxic. Did he reply, 'You said alright in that hotel in Albi, why not now?' He sighs.

'What's wrong? Can't I say anything about Mum? Mum doesn't hate you,' she says softly.

'I wasn't irritated, just amazed. Give me time to get used to your cheek.'

From the pavement table, they watch a swarm of dark Iranian men shuffling past them, shepherded to Al-Husayn Shrine by dignified white bearded clerics.

'Dad, how many buy saucy bras?'

'Drop it! We'll wait until they've gone. OK. Let's go before another coach load fills the street.'

She takes the map, wanting to find the way by herself. He walks a few steps behind her, certain she will get lost before long. Her changing moods, which were at first disconcerting, now warm him. She is so different from his sisters. Fun and self-confident at home and outside. She expresses herself clearly and with conviction. That's good. That's the ways the Franklins brought her up. He'd love to tell them his appreciation. She should learn classical Arabic in Leaford – or, much better, here. Damascus has famous *madrassas* where all sorts of subjects are taught.

'Talking to yourself again, Dad!' Zaida is triumphant. 'We've arrived. I heard a group saying they were going to the palace. And I can read the map.'

She has taken over. 'Did you know there are famous places which teach Arabic to students from abroad through the year? Watch out for the gate.'

There are mostly Arab-speaking tourists for whom November is a popular month after the summer heat. From the grand inner courtyards, the crowd slowly moves into the sumptuous reception rooms decorated with painted panels, colourful tiles and star-studded ceilings.

She gasps. 'It's... a magic lantern. I can't take it in. The women lived in there, all their lives you said? Like budgies!'

'Hand-clapping budgies, clogs dancing on the floors. Can't you hear them sing?'

Playful, father and daughter leave the central pool to get some fresh air under the trees, where they find an isolated marble bench. In search of a toilet, Khalid excuses himself.

'*Amrikan? Swidsh?*'

She nods. No.

'Good. *Swidsh. Welkum.*' The shorter man sits down on her left, the thin one on her right. She averts her eyes, fixes the floor, timid and flattered, sweeping her hair from her face. The spontaneous gesture triggers baffling comments, all flying over her head.

'Butifell.'

She is sweating. Why isn't she wearing her Hama headscarf? Where is her dad? She can't shout for help. They are doing nothing wrong, just shuffling their bottoms closer and closer. Is her breast being touched? In a flash!

'Daddy!' The men melt away.

'What's wrong? I saw two boys running off. Did they bother you?'

'Boys? No. No boys.'

He seems to believe her but she does not calm down yet. What really happened? Did she imagine it? She'd better forget it. She holds onto her father's hand throughout the visit, pretending to admire every exhibit.

'I hope you didn't give them your address!'

'I'm not that stupid! My school told us about sexual harassment, you know. Nothing like that happened. Gosh! Dad, I don't know my address. If I lose you, what do I do?'

'What was I thinking of, sweetheart? I'm still learning to be a dad again!' They hang close to each other, sailing through the exit gate into the street throng.

49

Disregarding the budgies' excitement, Aunt Halima and Zaida collapse into each others' arms, hugging and laughing. Her aunt is impressive. A round pleasant face; an authoritative figure, bulkier than her brother, wrapped in a fashionable *abaya*, black and gold; long hair tied up at the back in a single knot underneath a shiny shawl.

'Let me look at you properly. God bless! You are a beauty.'

She launches into a song, high pitched, hips swinging, arms raised until she realises Zaida's astonishment.

'Sorry, baby. There were too many people at the wedding. Let me celebrate you, my beautiful niece. That's our way.'

'What's the song about?'

'It's a popular love song from Damascus. "Your black eyes made me sing, your black eyes make me forget mother and father, and when I am…" wait… "in deep sleep" – that's the line I like best – "a vision of you comes to drive me crazy."'

'You teach me it?

'Another time. We've so much to talk about before Khalid comes home. Let's go and sit down in one of the *iwans*.' Acting the hostess, Halima places Zaida on the elegant settee in a raised alcove set in the furthest wall. An opening high up in the arched roof gives enough mellow light to outline Zaida's face. 'Good. Here I can see you! Traditional houses are so dark but Khalid won't move to the new city!'

Tugging her legs together, arms around her knees, Zaida tries to ignore her aunt's ferocious scrutiny. 'Your English is brilliant. How come?

'It's not a big deal. I was 13 when I arrived in Britain. My father took me back with him when I was a young woman. And I completed my degree at the University of Damascus.'

'Were you happy about… coming back?'

'I had no choice. My other two sisters married British men and I was the only daughter left. I loved teaching English until

I married. My kids? You know them, of course. They leave me enough time now to work as a translator.'

'I like Lilleth very much.'

'Good! What about you? Aren't you bored? I've long lists of stuff to get for that other wedding. At last it is the end of the season! Come out with me tomorrow. New Damascus is so much better than Hama for shopping.' She embraces Zaida again. 'It's a marriage of love this time. Fancy that!'

'Is that unusual?' Zaida, assaulted by fast-delivered lines, finds Aunt Halima's enthusiasm nearly intolerable.

'For our Hama relatives, yes. They met as students at our university. The bride, one of your third cousins, is a young, modest and beautiful girl.'

'Naturally!'

Halima, who is so keen to enlighten her protégée, misses the ironic tone. 'Yes! It's the best day of her life.'

'Were you never as happy?'

Halima chooses not to hear the challenge since the poor girl has no mother to help her understand women!

'You'll see the bride with pearls all over her dresses. We'll dance in circles with Bakaza in the middle. Your heart will burst at the singer! Just like that wedding in Hama.'

'I wasn't really dancing.'

'Practise with Lilleth first. Sway with the band. Our joy is irresistible. One day you'll be feted as much as Bakaza. You see, in our culture, every bride becomes extraordinarily beautiful.'

Bored with the lesson, Zaida points to the luggage Walid has quietly brought to the courtyard. 'So many bags for just two days!'

'We'll fill them up, I have a long list. Go and ask Mariyam to bring some tea. And say I want a quick wash before Khalid is back.'

Zaida leaves her bossy aunt, relieved to hide her ignorance of things Damascene girls should know.

Exchanging compliments about their good health, brother and sister settle into the sitting room. Halima serves the delicate cups of an Assam rose-tinted tea.

'She is a pet, Khalid. I love her! *Inshalla*, I'll teach her our ways as I do with my daughters. But you listen to me! Wearing a pair of skinny shorts in front of a chauffeur is indecent. She'll get a bad name.'

'For God's sake, she's just a kid!'

'And stop giving her cuddles, she isn't a baby any more. She's got bigger breasts than my youngest girl. Look! She'd better go to the evening prayers on the women's side.'

'Honestly, you are being fussy!'

Halima puts her cup down, staring quizzically at her brother who grins back in an attempt to get off the hook. 'Sister, why are we speaking in English?'

'We always spoke English in Leaford. That was Dad's rule. "Children, speak in Arabic to Mother and no-one else." Do you remember talking a funny mix of Alawite and Arabic to annoy him?'

'I don't remember.'

'You remember Seema? She looks like her!'

'Not sure. Be careful as to what you tell her.'

'Wait!' She pokes inside the canvas handbag lying at her feet and, with an expectant look, straightens herself to hand Khalid a tired-looking photograph with torn edges. Very small. Stained. Faded in places.

'My God, where did you get it from? Dad?'

He holds his breath. A girl getting water from a rudimentary tap over a pile of dirty tin saucepans in the foreground. In a long shapeless cotton gown. 'Seema in that camp!' Her face is slightly out of focus as she had turned her head away from the camera to watch the pail filling up. The urge to cry is overwhelming.

Halima also blows her nose. 'Isn't she cute? Dad carries it

in his breast pocket. I must give it back tomorrow. Is she about 11? The same oval face. The nose. The tense smile.'

'I beg you, don't overdo it. Promise you won't show it to her?'

'Why not? These two look like – what's the phrase? – two peas in a pod!'

'No! No! One is dead and the other is alive! God! They are not alike! And I don't want Zaida to know too much about Seema. She'd be devastated, though she is pretty clued-up for her age.'

Halima sniffs back her tears. 'Can you see those rotten camps? Us kids scavenging for used batteries, shooing off the rats? And later, in those few months we had left together, can you see our big sister, so lost in that horrible distress, her hands shaking, her eyes accusing? Our ruined Seema. When Dad—'

'Shut up! I can't bear it! Promise you and Father will never tell the whole truth. She thirsts for ghastly stories about refugees, spies, massacres. They poison her mind. And she is too young to understand why Seema ended her own life! Seema died of malaria. Promise me you'll stick to that?'

Tacitly, they share the same subterranean pain until, after clearing his throat, Khalid breaks their mourning. 'I'd like Zaida to stay with us until Christmas. I'm not sure how but I'll work it out. I don't want to tell anyone yet, not even her. Can you help me look after her?'

'I will do anything to help. Just ask.'

'It is not easy for a dad to take a pretty girl out. Men look at me as if I have no morals.'

'What else do you expect?'

'On the way to the Azm Palace, we stopped at Hammam Bakri. Zaida found the black and white architecture interesting but once in the courtyard, she wanted to join the queue of foreign and local women getting tickets for the main baths. I refused. She wouldn't speak for a whole hour! You see what I mean? I don't know her well really.'

'Do parents know their children?'

'Do children know their parents?'

Brother and sister share a fragile certitude: we all muddle through, groping for each other under layers of unintelligible thoughts and feelings.

'A last favour. Can you take care of her when I go north overnight to Qamishli?'

In spite of her impressive size, Halima ejects from the seat in a blink and, standing up, confronts her brother, shouting down at him, 'No, I won't. That's out of order. But we'd be only too glad to have Zaida at other times.'

'Why not?'

'Too much risk. Father is begging you to be more cautious. Uncle Omar has warned him too. You must stop seeing those Kurdish people. That's also why I've come today. To tell you how anxious we are.'

Khalid defies the confrontation by stretching out further into the cushions, yawning with feigned boredom at the rant. 'My dear sister! Thank Uncle Omar for his blessed concern. His beloved nephew is not a hero; he only meets a few evicted families wishing to regain their lands. Surely this is still within the laws passed by young Al-Assad three years ago.'

'Khalid, don't mock!'

– 5 –

Tugs of Love

OVER THE FOLLOWING DAYS, MARIANNE SETTLES DOWN TO a morning routine. She is an early riser with plenty of time to brush up her English before breakfast. She reads anything: bulletins of the *Acupuncturist Association*, *Rural England*, children's books belonging to Zaida. Thrilled to share them with the girl, she is swept along by the tales, unflustered by the occasional obscure word. When she trips over in conversation, the Franklins rebuke her gently like a sick child. Sticky tenses bother her. Always the teacher, it annoys her to take so long to work these things out. Better stick to the infantile present and forget the "have beens" and "might have beens". All malignant traps! "Zaida should be with us on Sunday." Is that different from "Zaida ought to be back on 7th November?" And what about the future? "Will she? Is she?"

Stacking newspapers and books into neat piles by her bed, she wonders when she last saw Zaida. In Chamonix, a puny 8-year-old, trailing behind on her sledge. A funny girl. Quite brittle and shy, resistant to physical exercise. Short-tempered, she had brightened at the mention of computer games, or shopping for her father. Hurt that he had just left home, sorting the good from the bad, she had pushed Virginia off: 'I don't do hugs anymore, except from Daddy.' Soft as a kitten at the sound of her dad's evening call. Two years later, he moved to Damascus. The girl had had to toughen up.

There is much to understand about the Al-Sayeds. Thankfully, Walter was forthcoming. Zaida is discovering a thousand relatives, not all of them Sunnis. One great-grandmother was an Alawite who had grown up among impoverished goat farmers, on the margins, like most Alawites at that time. A maid in Sunni Hama, she learned the Koran by heart. Piety and beauty did the trick, and she married the younger son. A mixed marriage, Abdul had explained to Walter: for his own people, Alawites were beyond the pale of Islam, like pagans. By good fortune, the bride-to-be agreed to practise as a Sunni. Walter went on. One daughter killed herself in a camp before their escape to Britain.

Romance and tragedy! Two poles that would prick Zaida's curiosity for days, especially as her grandfather is a brilliant man, they all say. In the 1950s, he completed his training in a Lebanese French hospital. Later, with Nasser in his sights, he got interested in politics. A liberal family, Walter reckoned, opposed to the dictatorship of Hafez Al-Assad. One of Abdul's brother was killed in door-to-door fighting and two others murdered in prison.

Zaida's life springs from the Franklins, rooted in green Middle England, and the Al-Sayeds, rooted in the red earth of Middle Eastern tragedies. A fragile graft, according to Virginia. Maybe not if the child is allowed to grow by herself. Something both parents should understand eventually, with a bit of help.

Khalid is a caring man, aware of the brittle destinies of migrants. How could he cut Zaida off from the Franklins?

She has crisp images of that first time they met in Albi, the Cathar town manicured for the summer – the homeless, winter weeds, plucked out by the mayor – on the Pont Vieux over the Tarn where knights and thugs had assembled for the liberation of Jerusalem. In the photos she took that afternoon, *le petit ami* is attractive, tall and troubled. He glared at the crowds, shouting something which stuck to her brain like… there are .. 'plenty of guys who fuck us up again'. Pressing her breasts against him, Virginia had kissed him on the mouth, in the full view of passing cameras. A scandalous couple with faces high on hope and misunderstanding.

Naturally, she was jealous, but not for long.

Over coffee, he had talked fast. His engaging grins belied a tormented past, fists clenched. He'd never go back to Syria; it was a dump. Virginia believed him, too intoxicated to understand the shards of terror at his very core. He'd survived the shelling of Hama by hiding underground near the ruins of a museum, scavenging for food at night. Memorable stories. Among shattered bodies and cement slabs, he stumbled over a clay pot left untouched by the bombs, the size of a watermelon, sealed: a funeral pot – baby's bones inside. He cried, starving after three nights. It had been an all-out war among brothers, complicated. His father, at first, had backed Hafez Al-Assad but changed sides after so many deaths. He had a dream! To help refugees. That's why he was studying law. And he will never go back. The boyfriend was dark and idealistic. She was won over as well as Virginia.

She slips on a thick woolly jumper. However much she likes England, she can't bear the burial-chamber feeling of its autumns. The boy refugee, too, had felt the chill… and the uncrowded streets, the measly fruit, the stench of wealth.

She can't leave her bed unmade: the Egyptian cotton sheets have to be tucked underneath the mattress and each corner folded in envelope pleats. A way to pacify her nights and think her own thoughts.

In the last five years, people like the Al-Sayeds have returned under Bashar Al-Assad. Syria is healing, that's why Zaida can be entertained by her successful relatives.

The Franklins have a lot on their plate. How can she help apart from offering money? Mildly despondent, she looks around the room for a lead, startled again by the clutter of china birds. Gwen, Walter said, became obsessive after Ian left. Ian indeed! She has to put sexier times out of her mind to concentrate on Virginia and Khalid! The present calls her.

Zaida. What else does she know about her? Only a couple of close friends. She rarely chats online but is hooked to an online strategic game, which is quite unusual for a girl. In World of Warcraft, she plays as a healer, not in the elite guilds class yet. Needs to test herself out of her comfort zone, that's what the boys say at school. Impressive. More mature than most, she'd guess. Yet Zaida was never allowed abroad with her father. Virginia's solicitor set up a 'port alert', ensuring that he couldn't take her out of the country without her mother's consent. Why does Virginia see Khalid as a Death Knight? How galling for him!

She would have played it differently.

As she pulls the bottom sheet tighter, she muses about the explosives separation leaves behind. Any teenager worth their salt could stir the feud between the families, enjoying the full assault at Level 80. Play for real, full of hurt and anger. An inchoate love. For Zaida, does Syria seem like WOW? Indubitably, a far cry from the miserable Cornish B&B where she faced an uprooted father during their annual one-week holiday. Her first days have embellished Syria. Everyone is beautiful, especially the bride – an oriental princess, polished and shiny.

A cushion slips off the bed. She tidies the room, oblivious for once of the birds flapping on shelves. She saunters down the swirling oak staircase with its fluted spindles; strong enough years ago, she remembers, to let her and Ian slide down the banister, going off into peals of laughter, their adolescence erupting in blurted-out confidences, mean and generous in turn.

She sees very little of her friends after breakfast. She will walk into town, maybe along the canal, grateful for the long hours stretching in front of her. Above the hall mirror, one of Gwen's birds returns her stare like an antique dealer appraising an object overvalued by its owner, assessing age and detail.

She turns the corner into Friars Street where a secondary school has mushroomed in less than two years, designed by a friend of New Labour, which runs the town. Walter is one of the governors, oddballs with whom French schools do not have to cope, *Dieu merci*. Her mobile rings when she reaches the canal.

'Sorry, Virginia, I do not listen...'

'I thought you'd be happy to know my brother is arriving three days before Zaida. It's mad. Bye for now.'

Struck dumb by contradictory emotions, she hurries past the first row of boathouses glistening with gloss paint, announcing the tail end of the white middle-class zone. She will see him. The joy of it! She has never fully understood why he left. What ghastly timing though. Will Virginia feel displaced yet again? What will he make of the situation with Khalid?

Look! Fish jumping, silver specks in the sluggish water. She takes snapshots of warehouses, empty of wool, boarded-up; old engineering factories now making pork pies, sausages, *walahi* lunch boxes, crisps and pizzas. The British diet!

She is nearing an area optimistically called Green Park: an ill-tended lawn embellished with the odd carrier bag and a few strays eating their own shit. She finds an empty bench. Should she take a picture of three large bouncy dogs, coats shining, held back by two down-in-the-mouth, moth-eaten, skull-shaven white youngsters slouching past her, obviously smelly and louche?

Ian could become some kind of ally but she doesn't yet know how. He won't convince Walter they could borrow from her. She fidgets with the camera bag, clouds of anxiety enfolding her again. *Faute de mieux,* she could leave Zaida a "welcome back" present. What exactly? Virginia, so full of her daughter, has given no clue apart from Zaida's love of shiny knick-knacks and Bollywood movies. By rooting around the right shops, she should find something. And a present for Ian.

As she stands up, someone coming from the back jostles her, trying to snatch the leather bag strapped over her shoulder. She fights back, screaming at the top of her voice as the dogs bark at her French. The attacker runs. 'Dirty cunt!' the youngsters shout at the vanishing figure while patting their 'boys' to calm them down. She leaves the park, annoyed with herself for sitting in such a desolate place. Better get the presents later.

In the hall, she bumps into Virginia huddled up on the bench close to the massive coat hanger, head buried behind a curtain of coats.

'What's wrong?' A few sniffles. 'You crying?' More groans. 'Please come out. I can't see you'.

Virginia pokes her face out. 'I've just had another email … Don't tell my parents yet.'

'Why? Tell me.'

'I can't believe it!'

'Let me see!'

'It can't happen to me!' Wiping her eyes, she lets Marianne sit down next to her.

My Dear Mummy
Don't be cross with me but I don't want to come back so soon. Dad will pay for a teacher to teach me Arabic. There are many people in the world who speak Arabic. Much better than learning French. There are no French people I can talk to in Leaford so what's the

point of coming back early when I am learning many more things here? My teachers will understand. Now I want to learn a language, why stop me?

'You see! I told you! I am losing her.'
'No! You are hysterical.'
'The cheek!'
'The point is valid.'
'Don't start!'

Dad said I should make things clear. I stay until the end of the month or I leave. I don't want to yet. Mummy, I won't see you for another three weeks. Can't you take a holiday in Canada and see Uncle Ian? Funny Mummy, you wouldn't like it being so crowded but it's OK. Grandad took us to see a film – it was on a huge screen and the sound was horrible. I couldn't understand the story but I loved the clothes and everyone sang. They chat during the film, they spit seeds on the floor and other things... I don't know. Oh. Time for my first lesson. I am a bit worried. This serves me right, I know, Mum.

Feeling self-righteous while making an effort to control it, Virginia pours out her misgivings. 'Why is she doing this to me? I don't believe they have no working phone yet. Don't be taken in, Marianne, by her babble. She is lovely. But remember what's happened. Fact one: the Al-Sayeds took Khalid from me. Fact two: they can hold onto Zaida as well, easy-peasy. Fact three: he adores her, she adores him. Fact four: she has her own passport! I hope I'll not live to regret it. See what comes next.'

Dear Grandpa and Grandma

I am sorry I am being a trouble to you. I promise I'll cook lovely kebabs when I am back. Don't worry like Mum, I'm nearly a teenager now. Grandad is calling me downstairs. We are going to a festival. It is not a Muslim festival but it is OK. He says they dress up like a dragon and Saint George will kill it from his horse. You see, I'm good.

Your loving Away Princess

Hot cheeks, Virginia stops glowering, stirred by her daughter's warmth. Marianne hugs her tight, allowing herself to express her opinion.

'What intelligent child! Listen! They do not betray you. They are open with you. They love to be together. She wants to explore! Good! Khalid is a nice man. An exception. He has made a success of his life two times. Be happy for her. She has a... exciting father.'

'True enough! But I'll be without her for another three weeks!' Unexpectedly, a snap memory takes her over. Khalid, head bent under pouring rain, running from their front steps to his car having just dropped Zaida at the agreed time like a recorded delivery parcel. He turns round to wave to Zaida, watching from the porch. Wipes his face. Aching as much as she is now. She should show the same dignity. Marianne is right. Khalid will let Zaida come back. She ought to do the same; let go of that bad energy polluting her heart.

'Feeling better?'

'Sorry for the fuss.'

'You are not... at war!'

Marianne stands up. Noting her impatience, Virginia seizes her wrists and pulls her towards her, scrutinising her face, searching for a common ground. 'My special friend. Do you mind me being over the top? It's good I can let myself go in front of you. There's no-one else. Even with Ian, I can't share what I share with you. You understand? You have a beautiful faith in humanity. I am taking in what you've been saying. OK. I'll let Zaida enjoy herself a bit longer.'

They walk upstairs to their rooms holding hands.

– 6 –

Troubled

WHY, OH WHY IS HE FLYING BACK? JUST A FEW CONFUSING emails from Father and Khalid and here he is! To be fair, Walter didn't ask directly although he said he was beginning to feel the weight of running the clinic. And there's Khalid turning up on Facebook, out of the blue, fretting about his rights of access. Zaida is in some kind of trouble, they say. How funny! It's her turn to upset the apple cart. *Famille, je vous hais!*

Five hours left. The romance of flying worn down by soiled newspapers, spoilt immigration cards, fouled toilets, jaundiced kids. Air travel should be rationed. The sooner vouchers are introduced to cut out the plebs, the better. Ian sits stiff, indulging his wave of disgust at other mortals, fearing meeting his relatives in the flesh. How can he open the inviolable space he has created over ten years? Virginia, but not his parents, figured out why he left: to forget the piquancy of Brighton air mixed with spice and grief.

Vancouver was the place to do business, whatever its nature. He started a posh practice, close to downtown, in a street flush with funky bars. The place became his. With Clint at his side, he loves running early morning in the nude on Wreck Beach, leaping over tree trunks smoothed into giant's fingers by the strong ocean currents.

They met coming back on a ferry from an early hike to Mount Seymour. Ignoring the turbulence of Howe Sound, Ian worked it out. Clint was among the children who, twenty years ago, were compulsorily removed from nearby reserves to be placed in infamous orphanages run by predatory missionaries. He got himself a Christian name when he went to Seattle to study Western art and cinema. Eastwood, of course, was his god then, until First Nation art became fashionable.

How thrilling it was to be told much later the secret tribal names. Contentment fills him, a peculiar sensation like a swelling in the tummy or a cramp in the leg – something physical that doesn't belong to him and shouldn't be there. With an unsteady hand, he takes a few sips of water, disregarding the shuffles and sighs of fellow passengers, his mind filled with beautiful illustrations. Clint completed the book at the Children's Book Co-op. He found it under their pillows for his thirty-fifth birthday. Six double pages mixing traditional and modern styles. At the time, he was upset by the title page "The prodigal son". True, he had rejected the Leaford inheritance because of twisted love between parents and son. Stunning pictures, though. On a pebbly beach, the son, a sad white youth, and a new dark friend are invited to join Nuu-chah-nulth teenagers in a game of football. He likes that drawing. The white line of the surf underscores the horizon.

Until he received the book, he had never really considered going back, although recently he had been having disquieting dreams of Leaford, triggered by his father ringing to talk about liquid assets – an obvious ploy to lure him back home. Yet, he did not recognise himself in the child at the end: two pages contrasting the sunrise with the bluish black of an eagle dragging a little boy across the sky to an oak tree bursting with fairy tale birds, its roots forming the British isles. The final prediction pulled no punches. In the sunset, shadows of people stand in a circle of broken totem poles. The feather of an eagle protrudes from a tomb slab. They talked about the story: prodigal sons survive by destroying the law of the fathers. Clint's intuition relies on distant memories from cultures where sons call on fathers' fathers to renew their strength through songs in which whales bring sons back and bears dance with wolves to announce the end of time. He has been so privileged to get a glimpse of Clint's origins. Maybe soon the two of them will be taken to the ocean village where fathers still carve long canoes from cedar trees, to get his father's blessing. Walter won't kill the fatted calf! Why should he?

Here comes the steward, British with a posh accent and stoic patience, who removes his tray with casual accomplishment over the heads of an American couple with no appetite for idle conversation, their eyes glued to the screens.

'Finished with the whisky, Sir?'

'Yeah. I'll try to get some rest. Unless you offer something else.'

'Beg pardon?'

'Only joking, man.'

Funny the way things work out. He still aches at the thought of Britain, remembering how he dreamt of leaving long before the summer of 1998 when Canada did not ask too many questions. British, aged 27, self-employed, sponsored by friends living in British Columbia. Born Leaford, 1971.

Since adolescence, he had reached so many lows. Everywhere you looked, you saw the same fucked-up kids, white or black, clutching sculpted hair, betrayed by futile back-to-work-schemes. Leaford was getting too dangerous at night and, in the day, too familiar. Too well stocked with folks like his parents, chuckling at exploding house prices, swaddled in comfort, untroubled by horses crushing miners. They found one excuse after another for every mess, big and small – war in Kuwait, a shattered windscreen – "we've done our best, dear".

Why did the old man cajole him back home?

They used to row, but in the end he did what was expected. A levels, a summer fling with Marianne, an acupuncture licence in a college chosen by his father. For Christ's sake! He had to leave.

With his sister he shared a few laughs at Leaford. White people who believed in thrift and family as well as warring St George; grubby plaster divinities offered for sale; orange-robed geezers on smoking terms with Vishnu. The dome of the mosque glistened with tinsel like a brothel. As the Tory virus became more aggressive, they plotted: they'd set up their own clinic on the south coast, wave to France, sell out and travel before Armageddon.

Caught in the games of prey and predator, the wider world was equally tragic. AIDS killed silently. Young enough to be arrested, he chopped off his long hair, aping respectability.

Timid in sombre parks, he became eloquent in public. Put an end to the arms race. Waste not our natural resources. Lower the age of consent to 18. It was not long before street agitation had little to offer. In this state of mind, acupuncture was also losing some of its appeal. There was no scientific evaluation of treatments. This bothered him deeply. For his father, the patient was the best and only judge. That attitude seemed tacky and dictatorial for a guru. He was in his twenties, still looking underage, wishing to get away. He considered switching to journalism. A hack or a quack?

Damn! The couple is watching *American Body Shop*, laughing, nudging and making loud comments. They're getting on his nerves. He searches for the earplugs he keeps in his breast pocket. He ought to fly back first class. That can't be too soon!

His parents had put travel and adventure behind them, clinging to a future in which their two children would run the clinic. Virginia capitulated. After falling for Khalid, the turncoat hankered for respectability and a baby – only an amateur at women's lib.

If only he could catnap!

Didn't Walter say Marianne might be around? A generous girl, first class, glossy as a queen. They were a giddy pair! His parents believed in their good fortune but he broke it off. Sooner or later he would have to come out, not wanting to give a childhood friend a bad time. At Victoria station, he told her. There was a long pause, followed by a tornado of reproaches until, the fit over, she went icy, vengeful. Friends! Never! *Hypocrite*. The lashing stripped him of any affection for Leaford.

In London, he was never short of small change as he serviced people with his acupuncture needles. This went on until he moved in with Martin, a one-time war correspondent. Martin thought Brighton would be better suited to his convalescence. An intense town where seagulls bickered over ice creams, kids over pebbles and adults over sex. They talked of surf, books and miracles. With redundant needles by the bedside, there was no cure. The injustice bonded them beyond the indignities of the dying.

'Do you want an extra blanket, Sir? Blue or red?'

He wraps his shoulders, trying not to disturb his old neighbours. They are asleep, heads sloping towards each other, holding knotted hands. Quite touching. Untested. Until their feelings for each other fade away like family photos pinned to bedroom walls.

He takes a sip of water. His parents are ageing too. He has never given much thought to it. The last time he saw them was so painful! Exhilarated by his imminent departure for Canada, he unravelled his life at their feet. He was a dickhead! Mother was worst – still-love-you sort of thing. Father was sanctimonious, as ever the bleeding doctor. What else did he expect? Had he really told them about Martin? No matter. He is not so needy anymore. Hopefully, they'll manage to talk of his life with Clint. Maybe that's why he's going back. What about Virginia? Were they that close? Anyway, he'd like his people to know about Clint. He was made by Clint as much as by Martin.

The drone of the plane lulls his mind. Images of inscrutable ice caps permeate the reverie. In Canada his hunger for rebirth was inexhaustible although he had no wish to forget Martin. He travelled, walked and watched. He sold his practice – perhaps as an impulse to tell the old folks of his liberation, like a joke they would understand. Also, he had had enough of palling up with sick people! Patients, like lovers, can be hopelessly clingy. He had saved enough money and could at last try his hand at journalism.

That's enough. He needs to rest.

Blast! He sits up, gripping the armrests. Was he that four-year-old whining at Marianne and Virginia who wouldn't let him onto the swing, intent on torture? Closing his eyes again, wisps of memory from the Languedoc cling to him. He could have the swing back, they promised, if he caught three or four of the beasts, bigger than a chestnut though the same colour, spilling horrible sticky trails. *Mission impossible.* It was so unfair! He jerks his head on the pillow. There was a family photo – or did he invent it? – showing the criminal girls dressed in white shorts, hugging the ropes. Maybe the snap was taken another day. But one afternoon, a bucket full of snails was brought in. Incredulous, expecting to die, he watched his father drop the grotesque thing into his son's palm. At the repulsive, slimy, cold contact he grasped his little dick, thus discovering how anyone, good or bad, can find comfort as well as despair in the most testing moments.

Laughable, really! In his thirties and still blaming the old man! Better to spend the time watching the stewards, but these days they're piss artists with the sex appeal of a lunch box.

3.15am. Get some sleep! It's no good working over old stories. Virginia will vouch for the parents by claiming they didn't treat the siblings differently. As for Walter, he will resist sneering at journalism, a lightweight profession, when seeing that the boy, still bubbling with cheek, has a fat bank account.

— 7 —

Damascus

IT IS A FREAKISH SULTRY DAY FOR OCTOBER. STRONG LIGHT shafts cascading into the courtyard stir the birds whose cage is now hanging from the corner of the main arch, low down, so that Zaida can clean it easily. She tackles with zest her morning duty while trying out new songs on her recalcitrant pupils. Today, *London's Burning* is faring no better compared to the fresh seeds which Tom and Jerry gobble up while the other two sit safe on the highest perch.

'You silly!' she shouts, and stops. 'OK, that's not fair, I'd be bored to death too.' She lifts out the most colourful one and, cooing and stroking, puts him down on her left shoulder. 'You're a sweetie.' Gripping her top, his bright red claws scratch her slightly. Mesmerised, she doesn't move. Will Pip fly off? Will she lose him?

'Dad! Dad!'

Her father, tousled, tumbles down the iron stairs, alarmed. 'What's wrong?'

'Dad! Look at Pip! He doesn't mind!'

'Sweetie, don't cry wolf, please!'

'Why is Pip so tame?'

'They were born in a cage! Bred as pets. To be handled by people.'

'Pip has been in prison all his life?' She takes her time to return the bird back and when she faces him again, she looks sullen, mouth pinched, oddly grave.

'What's wrong now?'

'Grandad showed me a photo of Aunt Seema in that camp! I don't look like her, no way!'

'You don't, that's true.'

'Swear it?'

'Come here, my pet.'

He whispers sweet reassurance while keeping for himself the volatile signs which have enchanted him since her coming home: the same grin, the same twinkling eyes, the same jaunty shrug; but how can he be certain of such resemblance? These traits are not rare among young girls. And memories are made as much of imagined things as of lived experiences. This is why, maybe, Zaida's edginess and fleeting moods also bring glimpses of Virginia.

Wriggling out of his arms, Zaida opens the cage, her voice challenging. 'Why can't you tell me anything? Did you starve?'

'No! Nothing like that! Listen! Why upset us now? We've just come back from the wedding; we had a great time, didn't we?' Pangs of anxiety engulf him, difficult to control. They could topple him over into the crippling world of jaundiced memories and fears he has attempted to escape since boyhood. Shell-blast, he clenches his fists. He can't let Zaida stab him again out of the blue with her crude questions. No way! Even for her, he will never be able to shrivel those horrendous times into smooth sanitised tales. His rage was too volcanic. He saw too much.

'Dad! Were there rats around?'

'Stop it! I don't want to go there. I've already told you it's no good. Nothing so terrible will happen again. And when he says you look like Seema, it is his way of saying he loves you as much as his lost daughter.'

'A funny way! Oh! Here you are!'

The raised voices have called Mariyam Ajemian from the depth of the cellar kitchen. Without a word, her bustling presence and severe looks express such disapproval that Zaida sheepishly removes herself to the *iwan* where she waits for her father. He remains talking to the cook. Dad was fobbing her off. But what are these two up to now? He is pulling out his purse. Why? High-pitched words hit her harsh and fast. She prefers listening to her Grandad, whose voice, when he reads Arabic, is magical – lower and softer, flowing with mysterious sounds. 'Because he is reading poetry,' Dad said. 'You would enjoy having a go if you stay long enough.'

Ouch! Her father throws a cushion at her before dropping at her side.

'A penny for your thoughts?

'What was that about?'

'She has a son who lives in Sydney. He's written asking her to get him a Syrian Christian bride.'

'Cool.'

'She needs time off in the evening to visit prospective mothers-in-law. It is a great moment for her.'

'Oh! Can you hear? Listen!'

'Dad! You silly!' The words, although screeched and croaky in turns, are clear enough. Zaida and Khalid are rolling on the floor, fingers on their mouths, silently shaking with laughter. 'Dad! You silly!' The rondo stops after four rounds.

'Unbelievable! Clever Pip! Clever girl! Here's my hanky to wipe your eyes. I haven't laughed like this for ages!'

'How long will Pip remember that?'

'Not long, I hope! Imagine Tom and Jerry picking that up.'

'I'll teach them!'

'You won't! Ah! I can hear Farouq coming in. I was waiting for him. Get dressed properly, will you? You can't swoon around the house in those pyjamas.'

Pretending not to hear the reprimand, Zaida runs to the newcomer emerging from the dark recess of the entrance arch.

She enjoyed his compliments at the wedding and he never treated her like a little girl, unlike her father.

'I came to see my beautiful niece.' Khalid observes his cousin kissing the adolescent on both cheeks with the precision and lightness of a man knowing how to flatter. Will Farouq ask for her hand one day? For his son? A rancid thought, although he has often relied on his cousin's warmth and integrity.

'Gosh! You do look awful.' Abnormally tall and thin, nearly bald apart from mean dark patches of hair above protruding ears, Farouq seems wan, ready to cave in. They were close when boys and then drifted apart. Injured by scorn and rejection, Farouq's life has been dominated by his father. Although he wished to study Fine Arts in Paris, Omar squashed the dream and instead he had to take up International Business Management. After years of practising in that corrosive milieu, Farouq has remained uncynical, unspoilt and trustworthy – a pearl of a friend.

'Two molars gone and a jaw aching like mad! I've paid that charlatan through the teeth... literally! Don't laugh, Khalid. I hate that man! Syrians are only good at hurting each other. But not you, Zaida'.

She agrees while trying to overlook the swollen cheek that makes his English sound really funny.

'Enough of my suffering. Zaida – welcome to Damascus. You'll meet again my son, Ali, as soon as he joins me in Damascus. With your father's permission, of course. We'll be delighted to treat you like Queen Zenobia.'

'What do you say, sweetheart?'

She chews the thick pad of her thumb, gaining time. There were so many Alis at that wedding! Dad is giving her no clue, looking awfully blank. She crosses over to the cage, ignoring Farouq, who refuses to be defeated.

'Let me explain. To say you are Queen Zenobia is... the best compliment paid to a young woman.'

Sticking her tongue out at the men, she skips upstairs chanting, 'Dad! You silly!' The cousins laugh heartily until Farouq moans again as the pain assaults him with a vengeance.

'Wait! I need to take my tablets or I'll be in deep shit.' He searches his pockets while Khalid brings back large glasses of water from the utility room hidden behind a discreet curtain.

'Are you alright? Let's carry on in English, if you don't mind.'

Swiftly, Khalid lifts his glass to the light, swishes the liquid around and sniffs a couple of times before drinking. Farouq claps him on the back. 'Are you that posh you drink only vintage water?'

'How weird! Talking to Zaida has triggered something about the Shatila camp. I mean... my big sister was... raped by those Maronite bastards! I wasn't aware I'm still doing it!' He hides his face in both hands, full of grief.

'Sorry for teasing you!'

'No harm. You see, Father wouldn't tolerate any impurities in our drinking water. No rotten smells either. How many times did I spit it out just to please him!' He shakes himself as if waking up. 'Enough of that.' He walks to the bottom of the stairs to make sure Zaida has retired to her rooms.

'She's having a shower.' He squeezes Farouq's shoulder with affection. 'I just want to say, don't harp on about Ali! She is too young, and in any case, she has strong feelings against marriage. When Father urged me to get a new wife she locked herself in the bathroom until Abdul persuaded her he'd been joking. You see what I mean?'

'Come on! She'll change her mind if she stays long enough. As her guardian, under Sunni law, you can promise her in marriage... in a couple of years, perhaps. She is such a dazzling girl she won't be short of offers from honourable Damascene families.'

Irritated, Khalid waves away Farouq's simple-mindedness. 'Kill that stupid idea of marrying her off! And don't tell me where I stand with regard to our laws and customs. You are too naïve! The law is unhelpful. I have turned to Syrian laws, international agreements, British court cases – I know them all, believe me! Nothing helps me find a way ahead that does justice to all parties—'

'That's never been the job of any justice system, or else there'd be no job for lawyers.'

Too tormented to combat the unexpected derision, Khalid continues. 'I long to care for my daughter in my own home but what about her mother and her parents? They love her to bits as well as me, they'd give their life to her, just like me and Father. And what about today's Syria? Is it the right country for my girl? Will she have to become a fully fledged Muslim to marry into your family? And worse, to live like you and me under the screws of a stinking dictatorship?'

Farouq, in a petulant tone, enjoys the rare opportunity to give his senior a lesson in generosity. 'I'll forgive your insinuations, but what's wrong with my family? Like yours, we go back to Prophet Muhammad. Peace be upon him! Of course, you've no respect for our religion!'

'I meant no offence! Look! Zaida isn't like our Syrian girls. See the insidious ways in which, in our daily life, repression and religion are twinned. They feed our veins and our souls, whatever our beliefs. Sure, she'll adapt, her appetite for instruction knows no bounds! Sure, she'll applaud our First Lady, the patron of her school, in front of the president's portrait. She'll be happy to throw sweets to unmarried wedding guests, appreciate Arab architecture, recite "Mashalla" to confer Allah's blessing, cook white food for luck on New Year day, bake *brazig* cookies for Ramadan or greet guests with joyful "zagharid". But despite all that, will she ever feel a genuine Sunni niece of yours? She'll remain at best an exotic stranger – in her own eyes and yours – constantly on the lookout for her *faux pas*. Her life, a never-ending struggle to perform correctly. Her vivacious spirit – squashed.'

'Is this why you came back?'

'Come on, I could kick a ball and show I was one of the lads. And she will be even more lonely than I was if she balks at our sectarian violence.'

Farouq lets a few seconds pass until he feels able to defy his friend. 'You're hopeless! You dug a rat-hole for yourself with your ruminations! There are many thriving communities who pull out the best from cross-cultural junctions. Zaida could invent a fantastic adventure, enjoy life to the full. Why have you no faith in her? No faith in us? No faith in the Franklins? And, I bet, no faith in international law. Your confusion is beyond the pale!'

'Listen! Mariyam told me a Damascene proverb: "Is the tree in the courtyard for me or my neighbours?" Do you know it? Traditionally, it is just a question.'

'What was she on about?'

'Muslims worship in her church. John the Baptist as Prophet Yehia. He belongs to both communities, she said – that's the only way to live.'

'I agree! That's my answer too. The tree can grow for both. Isn't it what Zaida wants?

'Her generation has more balls than us. They'd be happy not only to live but... to let live.'

'Let's drink to that!'

They hold onto their glasses, enjoying the coolness slipping through their throats.

'Tell me, Khalid, why do we stick to English when Zaida is not with us?'

'Walid Hadidi, my Alawite chauffeur, may be spying. And he understands no word of English.'

'Seriously?'

Khalid sighs. 'Don't know. Zaida has seen him going in and out of my rooms where he has no business to be. He could be planting mics and cameras, you see what I mean? I've checked my papers and made sure there are no tricky files left. She is as sharp as a weasel! I tell her there is nothing to fear but, honestly, I know little about him. He was hired by your father before I moved in. Can you find out what he says? Be discreet. Say nothing about me.'

'OK, I'll find out. We're not on best terms but recently he's been less impatient with me. He's getting soft.'

'Good!'

'He isn't that keen on Alawite staff. He has just sacked an aide for that reason.'

'Why?'

'He is up to his ears in deals for the Assads! Naturally, he is attacked by jealous cadres in the Ba'athist party who won't let the grass grow under the feet of overconfident Sunnis.'

'Is Walid a member?'

'I'll see what I can find out, but Omar isn't happy with you. Stop your trips to Qamishli, that dung-hole.'

'Is that why you've come?' Khalid spits out the words, refraining from yelling for fear of alerting Zaida. Both men know that Qamishli has been a sore in the eye of the regime since the violent repression that destroyed the Kurdish elites in 2004.

Head cocked to one side to keep the pain still, Farouq snarls back. 'Aren't you helping people who are trafficking weapons? Don't they launder money for kalashnikovs and that new Democratic Union Party?'

'Honestly, I wouldn't tell a damned mole!'

'You'll sink our families deep in that shit. The buck won't stop at you.'

'I've done nothing the Hague courts would condemn. They won't arrest me, I am such a small fry. I swear I'll keep my head under the parapet so that no-one can shoot me down! Tell him! I intend to be extra cautious and I won't risk any restriction of our movement. In order to stay, Zaida needs to feel we're both safe, as snug as in Leaford, you understand that?'

'Three years ago, that was fine, but it is madness today. Fact one: the Damascus spring ended years ago. Fact two: young Assad is a wolf in lamb's clothing, my father says.'

Subdued by the claims, Khalid promises to warn again his milk brothers in Qamishli.

There is a regular thudding coming from upstairs followed by snatches of *Bleeding Love*. Intrigued by Zaida's music, they stand up – frail and resolute in their friendship.

'God! You look awful! Go home to Zeinab now.'

A few minutes later, thankfully, Leona Lewis has stopped singing. Khalid climbs up, jumping two steps at a time, consciously imitating his daughter, refraining from rushing into her room. Her presence makes him feel the particularities of the old house. From the top floor, it is cut off from the outside world, apart from the light pouring below him into the fountain courtyard linking water, stone and a square blue sky void of any malevolence. There is no sound except the odd chattering of an iron shutter. A fortress that encases his own miraculous survival. He takes a deep breath, resolute – never let rogue wolves destroy it!

Zaida does not yet feel comfortable. Her room is for adults only; it is filled with old-fashioned brown furniture, a far cry from her white, sunny bedroom crammed to the ceiling with toys, posters, CDs and books. The huge bed is so high that her legs don't touch the ground. It is always in a semi-darkness. The high oval-shaped window has frosty panes. Women should not be seen! At times, she feels too young for Syria. Her dad can't really help with women's things. She throws a pair of jeans back into a monstrous wardrobe. Choosing clothes without her mother is a chore.

'You should knock on my door, Dad! Tell me, have I got the right clothes on?'

Colourful dresses and skirts, long and short, are lying on the parquet floor. She understands the enquiring look. 'I'll tidy up later. I'm not sure I have got it right for tonight.' She won't tell him how much she is missing her mum tonight. She has a few tummy cramps; that should go away. And her aunt has already told her off for wearing clothes that are too short for a girl from a good Muslim family. 'Should I wear a headscarf?'

'In Damascus? Wear what you like, my love. We aren't going to a mosque! You look great in that pink dress. And if you don't mind me saying it, you look like your mum!'

'Really? Aunt Halima doesn't think I do apart from the hair. She's funny though. "You should lower your eyes when men look at you… or they won't marry you!" But I want to study.'

'Fine. Are you ready? No bag?'

She blurts out, 'Dad, Walid has a secret.' Khalid represses a smile, sitting down. Theatrically, in a well-rehearsed line, she spells it out, index finger raised. 'Walid has got a gun. Is it to protect us? Why?'

'Why do you say that?'

'I saw it yesterday night. He dropped us at the door. You were in your rooms. I went back – I had left my camera on the back seat. He was holding a small gun, here – I mean, on his lap. I startled him and he shooed me away, hissing rude words.'

'Are you making a mistake? Was he holding a camera, a box, who knows what? Anyway, thanks for telling me. I'll talk to him and to Uncle Omar. OK, love?'

'He gives me bad vibes.'

'Don't be silly! After their military service, quite a few people like handling guns at home. That's dangerous but that's how it is in this country.' He jumps to his feet. 'Time to go! Look, girl, don't take so many pictures when we are out.

You, blonde and pretty at my side, and me, dark and ugly. That draws attention.'

'What? Mummy was right then? Syria isn't safe?' she asks, wincing.

'Not as bad as she imagines!' He laughs her off, pushing her out, making light of the situation.

'Let's go to that picnic! Your cousins are impatient to spend more time with you.'

She screws up her nose, a baby again. 'Where?'

'At the Kirsh source. Near the beautiful orchards the family has owned for generations just outside the city, with wonderful views. We have ancient fruit trees – figs, pomegranates, black grapes. You'll love it. It has a special place in our hearts. Attracted by the sound of water, families climb up the hill with huge baskets. Mariyam has packed up salads and *kibbi naya* – cold ground meat and spice, and the sweet pancakes you like. You can ride the swings from that walnut tree of ours with Ali and the other kids. You'll see where my bum has polished the bark sliding down. Come on, we say summer comes back in November.'

− 8 −

Waiting

Gwen cannot help complaining as husband and wife are getting dressed for the day. 'Why not tell us sooner he'd be back? He's in debt and needs bailing out. And poor Virginia! I bet she hasn't slept a wink. What will she do?'

'You're running round like a headless chicken!' Walter snaps, offended by her reluctance to rejoice at seeing Ian. 'Don't fret! Zaida just wants a good time with her dad. Fair enough. She's been waiting long enough for this trip. It's only natural, as Marianne said last night.'

'Her place is here, not in Syria. They didn't bring her up, we did.'

'Don't get into a state! The law is behind us if they fight over the girl. But it won't come to that.'

'Not theirs! You're so naïve at times!'

'Shush, will you! He won't keep a troublesome adolescent for long.'

Quarter to eight already! She tries to control her rage. Their little girl, abducted, jailed by barbarians in a remote cave, married against her will at 15. Why hadn't they realised that Khalid would want more time with his child?

'Khalid. He wouldn't hurt her, would he?'

'What on earth are you talking about?'

'Nothing. Awful things happen to girls anywhere.'

'Jesus!'

Walter, in vest and pyjamas, strides into the en-suite bathroom, blinking angrily at the bright Spanish tiles decorated with dolphins – a rejuvenating folly of Gwen's. He slips on the wet floor, knocks his head against the glass of the shower, swears.

'Hurt yourself? Let me see.'

'Don't fuss!' He rebukes himself silently for shouting.

'Who got up on the wrong side of the bed, then?'

'I emailed Khalid and I'm not sure I did the right thing.'

'What do you mean?'

'Money to tide us over. Don't scream! I'd pay him back of course, as soon as possible.'

'For God's sake! Without telling us? Begging for money when they're holding Zaida? He'll laugh at you…Wait! What's happening at the clinic?'

After the ensuing row, Gwen is downstairs, banging pots and pans around, full of a deadly energy. As the head of the family, he said, he had the right to contact Khalid when he saw fit, and, after all, he had asked only for a few thousands to tide them over. She was blazing: without consulting the seraglio? He admitted he'd been rash and confused, worried about new expenses to cover for lawyers. What a moment to upset everyone! The ass!

Pray Khalid won't be offended.

She'll battle it out in her own way! Chain herself to the British Embassy in Damascus, shame them all. Marrying outside your tribe is trouble. Full stop. Damn PCness! Zaida will be pushed into the women's corner, slaving over stoves. Nothing makes sense.

At sixty, she still feels bouts of yearning for her father's ordered life: the Church music, the wobbly organ, the self-effacement. As a mother, she has failed to instil this need for selfless order in her children, each in their own way unpredictable. Ian is the more outlandish of the two but nobody should underestimate the passions that can engulf Virginia. Leaving her studies to travel, marrying Khalid out of the blue, having a baby far too young. And now take Zaida, a chatty child yesterday and, today, hours on the web, as self-absorbed as the young Ian. His email has rattled her – he seems as insouciant as ever. Surely she loves her two children just the same?

There are moments when she wants to shout out loud. Just one glance at the papers tells you of the sheer madness since the Icelandic debacle. Receiverships spreading like a forest fire. Banks in the dock gambling with fake money. And the clinic? It isn't just a hiccup, or Walter wouldn't be begging Khalid. How could she trust his crooked judgment? Wives should not question husbands' business sense! The thought makes her boil. You don't need a diploma to know that people don't pay for funny therapies when cash is short. Nor do they wire a few thousands out of the blue to ex-fathers-in-law. Walter is muddled. She nods to herself while taking the wholemeal bread from the tin. Why mix dirty linen with clean napkins? Better sit tight in the short term – but beyond that? They have enough on their plates. Zaida will always want to have her cake and eat it. Like Ian. How could she not worry?

Calm down, woman! She sees to a washing load while listening to Walter stomping around upstairs. Now he is in the shower. Slouching. Hairs on his back bristling. Swilling his cock. Is he thinking about sex? Has he any idea of this drying-up inside her, this encroaching emptiness? Does he, too, miss them tasting each other to the full, wet and holding? My God, what's happening now? There is a loud chitty-chitty-bang-bang as the machine shudders to a stop. The sheet has got entangled… in the dishwasher, not the washing machine! Can she be that senile already?

Gwen waves to Andy and Sue walking past the windows on their way to the extension. Time's up. But why is her boy coming back? This morning is exceptional. She doesn't mind being late, sorting out the post and reminiscing. He has no idea how much she missed him in the first years, going back to his bedroom, picking up his things and putting them back in the same place, mystified by her incomprehension, displaced by objects sketching out a life that she hadn't loved well enough – so he had shouted. Later, when the clutter stopped leaking accusations like a burst drain, she stacked cardboard boxes until the room, clean and harsh, bereft of Joe Orton, Leonard Cohen and Elton John, allowed her to give the things away for jumble. It helped, though her boy would never change. His email is typical: "Back on 10/08. Heathrow 6pm. You'll recognise me, won't you?" Casual and cheeky. Prodding the lean and fat of friends and foes alike without thought of the offence it might cause. She hasn't forgotten the pretexts he deployed to leave the practice, each one a slap in the face. These are ugly thoughts. Naïvely, she had half-expected that he'd help to run the business. He has a good head for figures and is a better organiser than Virginia, bless her.

How can the same parents do fine by one child and not the other? There was an incident over an air rifle he got hold of. She didn't let him keep it. 'You never trust me, but you trust Virginia.' Something like that. Enough to hit the bull's eye. To love, and not to trust who you love, destroys you. How could he know that already? They told themselves 'let him live his own way, have his affairs outside'. Why his anger? And now here is Zaida threatening to walk away too.

It is during a break, when Virginia is getting the couch ready for the next patient, that Gwen hands her a fax from Khalid:

Zaida does not want to return to Britain now. Don't panic. We'll book another ticket soon. We are off to more celebrations at country relatives for the next few days. Zaida won't be in touch before we're back to the modern world. Sorry for the concern this may cause you. You know I will never hurt my daughter, or go against her. Please understand Syria is such an exciting place for her. Take care. My best wishes to your parents.

'That's it! The son of a bitch cancelled her flight! She won't be back on the 7th. I knew it, I knew it all along!'

Gwen took her sobbing daughter in her arms, stroking her hair, repeating, 'Zaida is in safe hands, Khalid is not an abducting father. Come on. Wipe your eyes. There is a patient waiting. Zaida is having a great time. She'll be alright. And we've got Ian to think of as well.'

Wrenching herself from her mother, Virginia sniffs into a hanky, hiding her annoyance at the suggestion that Ian matters as much as Zaida. Throwing her white coat onto a stool, she storms out, back straight, repressing a thousand questions. Is Khalid trying to soften her up, email by email, with his honeyed tongue? What is Zaida looking for in Syria? Are her hands tied? But Gwen is right. They have loads to do. Ring her solicitor again. Get Ian's bedroom ready for Sunday. And now Marianne talks of leaving earlier to give space to the family and Ian. Is she afraid of seeing him?

One hour later, Gwen, pale and dazed, hands Virginia another fax.

Dear dear Mummy

Dad told me to send you a fax. I'm fine and nobody is forcing me to stay. I'm having such fun with my new family. Loads of them and great music. I've learnt a few dances. I can't move my bottom and my shoulders like they do, they say I dance like a pigeon! I can say a few things in Arabic. It makes Grandad Abdul laugh to tears, I hope they aren't rude words. I can do a few clicks with my tongue and they clap. Mummy, don't be cross with me, rich people here laugh all the time as in the films. The women have lace, jewels on their scarves. The food

*is fab. They say we are going to another wedding in the
country. Yippee! I love you, Mummy, and Grandpa and
Granny. Dad will fix my ticket when we're back. It will
be cool when I go back to school. Love you, love you.
I can make basboosa with honey and lemon, almond
rings and a bean dish with currants and cumin. I have
written the recipes for you. Your loving daughter, Zaida.*

'Reassured, darling? She wants to stay a couple of weeks
longer, that's all.'

'Mother! You don't think she wrote it herself, do you?'

'It sounds just like Zaida.'

'OK, she wrote it herself, but are they tricking her into
thinking she'll be back? Oh, how I wish I could go there!'

'Maybe one of us should go.'

'What about Ian? We must be here for him! God, why is
this happening to us?'

Leaving Marianne to clear the lunch and Virginia to take a call
from her solicitor in the hall, Walter and Gwen have their coffee
in the William Morris room. Walter conceals his thoughts
behind *The Independent*. There is no word from Khalid. Their
favourite Duchy Originals untouched on a tray, husband and
wife, hardly on speaking terms, stare into cups decorated with
cheerful peacocks untroubled by the strain. Virginia comes in,
her soft features creased into a grimace. Gwen rushes to her.

'Darling, sit down and tell us every word of it.'

'Under English law, Zaida is old enough to be asked her
preference and motivation for overstaying. You see what I mean?
Teenagers can arbitrate between parents, it's monstrous!'

'What else?'

'Her usual line, "keep things in perspective". But Khalid
knows the loopholes in domestic and international law well
enough, I'm sure of that.'

'What can he do?'

'Ask for permission not to return the child. The English court will reject his case and order Zaida to be sent back to Britain where she normally lives, but the Syrian family courts will be on the dad's side, especially if the child wants to stay. Angela says her job is to consider the worst-case scenario. I can't bear thinking about it. I can't, I can't. I don't want to.'

'Angela's awfully clever.'

Virginia sits cross-legged on a chaise longue, skirt tucked beneath her knees, leaning her head back, rubbing her eyes as if full of sand, not wanting to know anything. But is there a coconut smell, Zaida's hair, coming from the upholstery? Her baby is now a big girl, she's getting breasts! Can she be allowed to decide things? It'd be an outrage!

Her instinctive faith in people is dissolving at the prospect of the battle ahead. Could she trick Khalid? She loved tricking Ian. Once walking a tightrope between the two apple trees, he annoyed her by inventing acrobatic games she couldn't do. Out of sight, she shook the main branch, which knocked him howling to the ground. A puff of wind, she claimed. When Zaida is back, she should find a way to shake Khalid off for good. Get him banned from entering Britain. The law will be on her side, Angela says, but on whose side will her girl be? Drained of energy, she crouches forward, hair drooping over her lap.

Walter twiddles with the Chinese figurine and absent-mindedly traces out the acupuncture points as if they were prayer beads. Keen to nurture an illusion of normality, Gwen hustles in and out, tidying up or briefing an over-solicitous friend on her mobile. 'Yes, we've got to be patient.'

'Nice coffee, Gwen. *Merci beaucoup.*'

Marianne takes a couple of biscuits. How can a loving child not understand her family's misery? Has Zaida been plotting with her father for months? No-one speaks. Bold flecks of colour from the garden, framed by the large bay windows, distract her attention from the turmoil of the room. She is used to the grounds around Chateau Mourel, bare most of the year, all burnt sienna and scorched oaks. In England, she never ceases to admire the romance of gardening, the idylls of order and luxuriance that generations, irrespective of wealth, aspire to. A mild autumn brings apple-green lawns, riots of dahlias and roses, begonias, late-flowering creepers.

A tinkling of spoons brings Marianne back to her friends. She has offered money – what else can she do? She has read Zaida's odd blog. Nothing. No clues. That should comfort Virginia. But there is a gap, she realises: no-one knows anything about the Al-Sayeds' businesses in Syria. Who are they mixing with? How safe is Zaida? Leaping to her feet to check a potential lead online, she knocks to the floor a porcelain box perched on a side table by her armchair.

'Oh, my Limoges piece!' Gwen looks at Marianne coldly, the corners of her mouth turned downwards. The carpet has hardly softened the blow to the lid. Shining with brown and green glazes, the two wrens no longer coo, one of the tiny heads rolled away inches from its slim body.

Scarlet, Marianne cringes. 'Oh I'm so sorry. I'll pay for it!

'You won't. No, leave it to me!' Gwen prevents anyone from collecting the fragments. The leaf clasp is not working. The perfect fit has gone. Kneeling down, she cups her hand to hold the head as if alive, examining it for more damage.

'Can it be... stick?'

'Too many of these crazy things around if you want my opinion!' Walter grumbles as Gwen goes for the dustpan and brush.

'She'll get someone to glue them back.'

Reduced to whines, Marianne moves to the other side of the room, away from the table where father and daughter lay minute fragments onto a sheet of paper by the decapitated body, glossy eyes interrogating the future.

At breakfast two days later, there are traces of sleepless nights. Nobody listens to the radio droning on. The real news comes from Virginia. There has been no response to her emails; Zaida is now cut off, as Khalid warned a few days ago. Virginia's solicitor is sending him a recorded delivery letter instructing Zaida to return to Britain by November 7th to be met by her mother at Heathrow. And, after that, if there is no voluntary return, Angela Wright will start legal proceedings for the wrongful retention of a child. The fresh scent of jasmine tea envelops the family as she unfolds the plan.

'That should scare him. I feel more confident. Zaida should be returned to her "place of habitual residence". I'll spare you the jargon. Britain is her home, Angela says – there are no two ways about it, he should send her back.'

'I'm not with you. Have you started... what's the word... a process in Syria?'

'Not yet, but we are putting things in place in case Zaida isn't back on the 7th. The bad news is that Syria hasn't signed the Hague protocol, which deals with transnational cases. If there is no immediate return I'd have to hire a Syrian solicitor to appeal to a family court, under Sharia law – the Al-Sayeds are Sunnis. And that could be dreadfully expensive! Thousands of pounds.'

'What? Come on, Virginia, isn't Angela Wright making it up as she goes along?'

'Cost depends on each case and how long it lasts. She refuses to go into detail.'

'I'd like to know more about *your* legal costs.'

'For God's sake, it's too early to worry about that. One thing at a time.' Gwen glowers while pouring him more coffee.

'Angela knows her job. It was good to meet her yesterday for the first time.'

She had taken to her immediately. On the phone, the posh voice suggested glitzy offices in one of the towers thrusting glass and wealth into the Birmingham sky. So she was caught unawares by the crammed rooms of a bleak community centre housed in a disused chapel where Angela ran her surgery next to a Refugee Council soup kitchen. What bowled her over was Angela herself, a graceful Hindu in her thirties, strong, open, a beaky nose under a red dot on her forehead.

Virginia turns towards her parents, repeating how much she trusts her solicitor. 'I've already phoned the helpline she recommended. Reunion, they are called. They advise parents from any country in the world. There're loads of us in the same boat! With partners from abroad, families splitting up, mums going back to parents with the baby, dads not returning kids from vacation, you name it!'

'Terrible! But also reassuring, if you see what I mean, darling. Do you want more toast?'

'No, thanks. The Reunion man advised me not to let my feelings play havoc.'

'How so?'

'I have plenty of time, he said, to think things through. "Don't give Dad hell yet." It seems there are ways to put pressure on him. I don't know how though!'

'Do you want me to take one of your patients so you can phone?'

'As you know, the patient heals the practitioner. I'll ring at 4, I've got a free slot. And I expect there's a lot to do before Ian arrives. There's his old room to sort out!'

'We've got four days left. I'll look for some nice photos of him for the sitting room. Will he care for our changes to the house?'

Gwen gestures to the enlarged bespoke kitchen they put in a year ago, an abrasive display of black marble and stainless steel. Ian may love the cold glamour, like his father who was unsentimental at seeing her old things being dumped: sky-blue cupboards stencilled with red flowers, 1920s flying ducks, egg baskets and dark-blue glass bottles collected from car boot sales – all banished. Homemaking is not the same, she feels, missing what Walter called her "airless cottage clutter".

Walter gazes around, bearing in mind the cost of the whole thing, pushing down Gwen's real question: how has Ian changed? She has always worried over him. Over-protective. And it has been the same with Zaida, well before the divorce, whenever the tiny tot stayed at her other grandfather's, wondering in case the Al-Sayeds were not up to looking after her. No reason. She was so cuddly, perky smiles bursting into little frowns when she was displeased. She has always had this stare, testing people out until she crumples into your arms, sticky as a lump of fresh dough.

He pushes the papers away. Headlines are all about bad news since 7/7 – suicide bombers, phone hacking victims, housing bubbles, cuts, and more losses in Iraq and Afghanistan. Secretly, Walter rejoices that his son will be back, however stressful. A journalist! They'll enjoy discussing the news, watching the BBC, switching over to football with beer and crisps. In an ebullient mood, he turns his attention to Marianne.

'Why change your flight? If you don't want to stay, we understand. But don't be shy of Ian.' Marianne looks bewildered. Walter acknowledges the gaffe. 'Sorry, none of my business! Sorry, folks, Andy wants a word with me.'

Walter saunters off, confident that Marianne will forgive his *faux pas* – so will Khalid – and also reassured by Virginia having hit it off with her solicitor. Moving in harmony, their energies will feed a single purpose. Gwen hears the optimism in his steps and resents it since such foolishness prompted him to pester Khalid. And annoy Marianne?

'It is sweet of you to suggest you leave earlier. There's no need. The house will be full, but we love having you here. And Virginia needs you to talk to. But it's entirely up to you, dear.'

Marianne hears the stress in Gwen's voice – the tension is taking a toll on a woman who habitually makes a cult of reticence. She folds her napkin into a neat square, saying how much she enjoys sharing a family breakfast, a rare treat for a single woman.

'I'm clearing up this morning. Off you go, *Mesdames*.'

Doors slam upstairs. They'll be late. Most unusual. What did Walter mean earlier on? She sweeps the terracotta tiles and makes a show of two Victorian vases, filling them with roses. She raises her eyebrows at the mirror. *Pas mal*. Safe in French, asking the daft question haunting her since the news of Ian's homecoming. Had he not been gay, what would have happened? She tests the sentence again, this time in English. She fumbles for words, not familiar enough with the bloody language to interlock hypothesis and conditional, but old enough to know that such entanglement is the stuff of regret for anyone, whatever the grammar.

Virginia catches Walter alone in the clinic washroom. 'Dad, this isn't the best moment, but have you been thinking of my suggestion – you know, me registering for a new course?'

'You know what I said. Traditional Chinese Medicine is what I learnt years ago alongside Professor Fosmey, I'm proud of it and it is what we do here. Nothing else.' Walter snatches the nail brush from her to scrub his fingertips furiously. 'Thousands of generations have lived by the Five Elements. Haven't we got the same bodies, the same basic emotions, the same blood, the same organs?'

'We can't be blind to other therapies on the basis of ancient teachings.'

'Aren't you proud of what we've achieved here?'

'I am, but can't we do more?' She holds her ground, her anger resilient at not being taken seriously.

'Is Mary Angel giving you trouble?'

'Maybe the Eight Principles will treat her better.'

'What if the unbalance is deep down? Have you tried what I suggested?'

'Nothing has been released. She can't have sex because of the searing pain, and she is hysterical at the prospect of never having a child.'

'Remember Joyce Sweeny and Kirsty Shears? Two breech positions you sorted out. Why are you so defeatist? There is no such thing as a bad patient.'

'Her pulses are weird. Choppy. She panics and she's very angry. Like me about Zaida. I really want to help her. I have a kid and she hasn't.'

'I know, love, how tough it is for you. You can refer her to me or Andy.' Avoiding Virginia's face, he turns to place the towel back on the rack, giving her time to respond.

'Sorry, Dad. No, I must get through by myself. Somehow, it keeps my mind off my little devil!'

− 9 −

Fish in a Bowl

PLACING THE PHONE BACK, IAN FEELS LIGHT-HEADED, tired of harping on at Clint. As expected, he has been walking on quicksands these last few days, struggling against waves of disappointment, confused as to how to handle people. Keyed-up parents, a dispirited sister and, on top of it all, Marianne to deal with.

No. 12 hasn't changed that much: books on Zen and leather-bound Dickenses; insipid watercolours of Snowdonia and Kathmandu; hideous brown furniture; macabre birds; and in his room, there are left two Mods and Rockers posters which were already out of fashion when he put them up. Maybe as a teenager he was an oddball – shy, parochial and self-effacing – and not the rakish, dynamic townie he likes to imagine.

Like a cat watchful of the precarious balance, he sits down gingerly, wary of the rocking chair. Grandad's. An affair of solid oak and carving on the uprights, which his mother waxes with a sickening polish. Can he slip away from the party she has organised at the clinic to celebrate Walter's acolytes? Not really.

Everyone appears straight enough. Andy has acquired slouching shoulders and an aching back – 'the acupuncturist's badge,' he jokes, hugging him tight, radiating warmth. The red-skinned face has retained, beneath extravagant eyebrows, the kindness and modesty of a natural listener. As for old Sue, her feverishness has slowed down with the passing years; no longer taking his pulses, she scans him up and down to check he is not dying.

'Sorry, Ian, I must go. Andy, why don't we introduce Reiki to the clinic? It'd do no harm.'

Andy steps forward. 'I suppose, now that you're a hard-hitting journalist, you've forgotten all these sorts of things?'

'Is she serious? Is Dad for that claptrap?'

'Don't mock, my lad! To make ends meet, the clinic may have to open up its range of therapies. We are about £30,000 in the red. But let's talk about your work. What's your biggest scoop?'

'A couple of years ago. Uncovering a mob of forestry barons selling native lands to Seattle and Alaskan firms mad for oil. I came across grizzly bears but not Sarah Palin.'

'We can't match that! I still think, though, it's a privilege to practise acupuncture. See our AIDS survivors. Or cancer patients.'

'Sorry, acupuncture no longer works for me. A placebo? Maybe. No offence, folks.'

Walter ambles across the room to join Ian's group, loud, punctuating his words. 'Get real, lad, people heal in all sorts of ways, including odd ones. When I was a boy, GPs prescribed "the mixture", that's what they called it, syrup in reddish bottles. For flu, coughs, bones, chest pain, epilepsy, you name it. Isn't it true, Andy, people felt better?'

Disinclined to listen to yet another lecture, a few people leave while flimsy tops moulding generous cleavages rush closer to witness the fracas. Unable to resist an audience, Walter acknowledges vigorous nods from old and young.

'I'm far from saying acupuncture is just a placebo, but, as you'd expect, the mind plays a crucial part in healing. Today's patients want their complaints to be understood as events unique to them, both disastrous and meaningful. Well… no, enough of that now. Let's have another drink.'

Wishing to end his spat with Ian, he gets a glass of Chardonnay. The boy's cheek is still formidable. And on top of that, he exudes a kind of charm, cloying and sweet. People hang on his every word. Gwen remarked the day after he arrived, 'Marianne is eating from his hand already.'

It has been a long day. No reply from Khalid who hasn't bitten the bullet. The sod! Walter swears, wiping his forehead with a paper tissue. There's also the strain of having Zaida's defection on the brain. And Ian's quibbles hurt more than he'd like to admit. He shovels in a last lamb samosa. Too bad for his cholesterol, but Gwen is right to patronise Indian shops. Then he takes a bottle of tonic water and a tumbler, hoping to sit down in a corner, rest and avoid Ian, who is helping Marianne circulate trays of nibbles.

Virginia is coming back to the party, mobile stuck to her ear. Any news? She shakes her head and leaves again. He has left no stone unturned. But women don't understand the world of finance where to ask for money is reasonable. When Khalid needed to fund his export business, he had no qualms. Helping out a third-world country was as natural as plucking an apple from a branch. Under the young Assad, new technologies of which he knew nothing were at hand over there, with better trained brains than here. He made his investment on the quiet and Khalid paid back on time. Pessimism has been sapping this country's energies for far too long. Khalid would still be living here had he been able to borrow from a bank, and yet his was a good idea – a British law firm dealing exclusively with immigration from Muslim countries. Khalid had to leave. He was far less shocked than Virginia when her ex did not return. Khalid would be a winner. Not a child abductor. But his silence about the loan is blunt. He deserved a polite response. Something else must be going on. He isn't so sure about Zaida. She is too young to tell, but there is plenty of grit in the girl. Virginia shouldn't get on her high horse, just send affectionate, funny letters. Zaida, bright as she is, can make her own choices. And if things work out for the worse? Heaven forbid! He allows himself to sigh loudly without fear of being overheard.

Someone bumps into his chair. Marianne, grasping his lapel to coax him back to the party. He bends his head towards her, eyes nudging her breasts. 'Super frog! I'll do anything for you.' Uneasy, Ian watches the stilted pantomime. The old-timer is back to his tricks, but the performance somehow lacks conviction.

Walter glances at Ian. A funny lad, his boy – wiry, with sparks of anger exploding at random, telling hammer-and-tongs stories about corrupt oil barons and the abuse of first-nation children. Can he tell him about Khalid? Gwen, dressed in a frilly top that he shouldn't fail to compliment, catches his eye and waves discreetly. They should let people understand it is time to depart by collecting trays and platters.

From the corner of his eye, Ian sees his father, six foot two inches, flawlessly working the room to say goodbye. Flowing white hair. A diamond pinned to the left ear, he sails forth, showy with *savoir faire*, right ear cocked towards the last speaker, registering skin colour and the quality of the voice. A real pro!

The washing up done, Ian reclaims the rocking chair for himself. The party hadn't been that awful, but he wishes they hadn't rowed. His dad is quite a decent guy. He pushes back the chair, which swings violently before gently coming to a stop. Mouth half open, he marvels at its moods: movement and stillness born of each other in a single sweep, like love and anger.

Another day. A sturdy rain cloaks the Scots pines relentlessly, cutting out a walk with Marianne. Ian roams from room to room, idle, disoriented by the churning of return. He is unable to read the paper. English news is provincial. Glazed-eyed birds cramming the room yap away, cantankerous. What is the story? 'You'll never grow up, kid, never. Look at that gold chain round your neck and that tattoo! Showy and selfish, that's what you are. For you, we're aged and baffling but we, old birds, love you all the same. That's enough, isn't it?'

As a boy, he was in awe of the athlete in Walter who could, without much training, run a marathon in four hours to raise money for Shelter. At the party, he recognised the old feeling of insignificance standing next to Muscle Man whose strides used to leave him panting. Not for long. He has just learnt that the giant strutting at the party suffers from the wrong cholesterol and works backbreaking hours to save a shoddy business at an age when other people think of retirement.

Stupid rain swirls outside. Another wasted day, making him long for Clint. When Marianne asked about adoption rights in Canada – they are pretty straightforward – a stomach cramp flashed through, a surge of a possibility. Is it that strange? It's the old place that does it. Once full of his adolescent yearnings, it is now bursting with Zaida's. But he will never be a dad. Selfish guys, balls packed in tight jeans, live with insouciant men and have no kids. Why the cold sweat, then? He presses his back against the caned back of the chair, spreading his gangly limbs, pushing with his toes at every move, rocking hard, a fractious tarantula ready to pounce.

He peers at the garden, listening for the first clap of thunder that will bring another gale. He enjoyed his father asking for his advice, but was Walter being overdramatic? Should they replace the clinic accountant, an old friend with no incentive to stir things up, with a new firm keen to make a name for itself? That would set alarm bells ringing and worry everyone, staff and family. Business will pick up before Christmas. Meanwhile, getting Zaida back is their top priority.

Is there something concrete he can do? Help with the clinic where Dad still behaves like the Messiah? Gwen never complains. She has awful warts on her neck and hands and she walks funnily when she thinks no-one is looking. As for Virginia, he hasn't made any progress with her. She shores herself up with ironic smiles, slipping away whenever he asks how he can help or giving him accusing looks, proprietary over her grief. 'You don't know Zaida.' Christ! How could he? Though, he supposes, the child is of his blood too. He has never considered the fact, and Virginia knows this. She frets like an eel caught on a line, heroic and helpless as if her girl has been kidnapped. Overdramatic! He remembers her antics all too well, having never forgotten the only time they went out to the Athena Club. He shoved her off as soon as they walked in. The following morning, she was found slumped into ecstasy by the Patels' corner shop off Victoria Road. The fuss filled him with resentment, disfiguring her in his mind.

He sits upright. After a long absence any child faces the relatives' blessing and disorientation, the memories and the loves in need of repair. Clint said the same on the phone. 'Be patient, prodigal son! Help out.' Easier said than done. Gwen has refused to let him replace her at the reception desk and even if he wanted to, he can't take on any of Virginia's patients since he isn't insured to treat anymore.

Marianne is so determined to help. He will seek another conversation. This perks him up. Right now, he can shop to fill up the fridge.

– 10 –

Damascus

Tireless, Zaida has asked to be taken out at night to a place where young people hang out as they do in Leaford – 'I mean, without a chaperone.'

'We'll try downtown, sweetie. And it'll be fun to walk.'

In daytime, Zaida skips ahead through the maze of souks. Tonight, in Al-Bzouriyya, feeling a bit sickish, she sticks close to her father. Most of the shops are closed behind ugly iron shutters, and the light from the ancient chandeliers of the few traders still offering roasted vegetables and nuts is too feeble to dispel the deep gloom. In the old days, Dad says, traders with donkeys brought onions, sweet potatoes, beans, fruit and gas bottles to every house through these narrow alleys all day long. People and animals knew each other while affecting disdain towards the strangers squeezing past.

'How d'you know? You're not that old!'

'My little finger!'

Joking all the way, they reach a grand square fringed with imposing buildings, restaurants and falafel sellers sitting cross-legged on pavements of blue and white mosaic. They have booked a splashy place, recently restored, spreading over several levels. At the top, delighted, they take in the minimalist black and purple décor broken by huge mirrors and windows overlooking the marble-clad fountain of the square.

'An internet café-bakery and bar called "Sweet and Spicy", or "SS". Clever, isn't it? Sorry love, there's no mango juice left but it's an Edfina juice. From Egypt, they say.'

She screws her nose up at the banana smoothie, changes her mind and sucks at the plastic straw. 'That lemon tart is French?'

'You're wolfing it down! The French occupied Syria not that long ago. There are still several excellent French patisseries and restaurants.'

They glance around. There are no wooden panels. No carved ceilings. No floor rugs. The severity of the modern is broken by splashes of colour from cushions stacked in angular steel and white leather armchairs; and in the far corner, there are the predictable computer desks where people perch their laptops and ambitions for a Syria connected to the liberal West.

'Dad, look at them! Over there!' Controlling her excitement, she discreetly scrutinises two elegant young women with glittering jewellery, strutting on high heels in search of a quiet corner. Tight black dresses. Animated. No chaperone. Neither knees nor arms are covered. They settle down at a coffee table nearby, chatting, taking for granted stares from men and women alike.

'Dad, how old are they?'

'What if they understand English? Shush! 16 or 17. With all that kohl they look much older... I don't like it that much. What about you?'

Zaida, feeling plain and boring with her Benetton jeans and a tacky Miss Selfridge blouse, is mesmerised. With her long sleeves, she looks like a granny, resentful of her mum who doesn't care a pin for fashion. Khalid smiles at her, happy to share her fascination. The pair are so striking, confident of their looks and opulence, unburdened by wealth gained by blue blood families from... Syria or Qatar? Kuwait? Rolex watches.

Yves St Laurent handbags. The older one holds the menu card with red-painted claws. She has an expressive high-cheeked face under a thick coat of powder that does not mar her pale looks. Her jet black hair drops onto her shoulders. The other also has pouting vermillion lips. The perfect oval of her fresh-skinned face is encased by a purple and gold scarf underlining the harmony of her features. They could be models for *Vogue* – he registers the image while repressing a sigh of disapproval.

'Can you see yourself made up like that?'

She mulls it over. 'Mummy wouldn't like it but Aunt Halima would!'

'How is that?' he asks, hoping that both women would object to such ghastly masks.

'It's obvious, isn't it? You don't know anything, Dad! Time to grow up, you know.' Her bubbling laughter comforts him. She is the best teacher he has ever had about women's things. This café is a good choice for tonight. No-one is harassing the posh girls – about whose conversation, out of earshot, he can only speculate. Zaida, losing interest, leans over her seat to contemplate the floodlit people milling around down below. His heart swells with pride. His little girl is so mature, soaking everything up. But he must never tell her too much; she can be far too perceptive. Behind her questions about him as a boy there still lingers this unhealthy curiosity about his dead sister. Anyway, he can't even share his happiest memories without—

'Dad, look! I've just seen Walid! He walked into the music store with CDs and books outside. Can't you see? I called you but your eyes were on the women!'

He shrugs off her tease. 'It's his night off. You could be right.'

'Could be wrong. Forget it. Look at those crowds; it's so busy. Why?'

'The Christian quarter closes late tonight and sells alcohol.'

'Come on, proper Muslims don't drink!'

'Walid can. You see, Alawites don't observe the five pillars of Islam. That's why many Sunnis and Shiites don't like them... cut them off.'

'What?'

'They've been persecuted for centuries—'

'Like the Jews?'

He nods. 'Outlawed for being devoted to Ali, Muhammad's son-in-law.'

'Where does Walid live?'

'I told you already, in Jaramana. The suburb we drove through on our way up to Mount Qassioun. Above Damascus. With stone houses clinging to each other? Some with collapsing roofs. With loads of kids. You remember? You want another juice?'

'No thanks! There were funny houses, we went up and up and the streets became so narrow! I was scared we'd scrape the walls. And when Walid bumped into the woman in a black *djellaba*, didn't you see me blink like that?' She pulls a face at him which he ignores.

'He didn't run over her! He knew what he was doing. She was sitting on a stool. On her doorstep. It's what they do. Walid didn't harm her or we'd have heard her screaming! Her people would have thrown stones at the car or gone to his place to give him hell. Don't worry, love. Can I leave you a minute, to get another cocktail?'

Her dad drinks quite a lot. She chews over the other revelations she has to piece together day by day, patiently. He helps people to settle in Syria although he hasn't yet quite told her that. Kurds? That's risky, for sure. She has a fair idea as to why he helps. He can't forget the camps. She loves him more than ever. Because refugees live in bad places with bad food and bad health and they have nowhere else to go. And it is much worse for Jews and Muslims, she's done the research about ghettos and massacres. She can't ask, it's too painful.

'For you two to be happy together, don't talk about evil things!' That's what Grandad said, word for word. She said OK, but it isn't that OK! Adults are jumpy. Immersed in her thoughts, she hardly notices her father returning with a tray.

'Sorry, it took ages to get served. Wake up and help yourself.' He puts down a pink and orange drink full of fizzy bubbles arising from a lump of caster sugar and a plate of creamy sweets. '"*Qanafa madluqa*", can you say it?'

Her tongue chews the words like gum and finally twists them out sounding nothing like her dad's. She looks down, peevish.

'Not bad!' He pats her hand. 'You like them?'

'Tell me, where did you kids live in Leaford? On top of each other?'

'We were lucky. Soon enough my dad qualified, you know, as a doctor. And we moved to a splendid Victorian house. Not far from your place.'

'Oh! I saw it. Mum showed me where you lived before you got married.'

'Did she? Good of her! Let's walk back home.' He slips his wallet and Android into his attaché case, pushing to the back of his mind Farouq's email he has just read at the bar. Two of their acquaintances have been stopped and searched. Very likely he won't keep Zaida if the going gets rough.

Gobsmacked. Just outside their entrance, there is Walid again, crouching on the stone bench, muttering in Arabic, waving his arms around, overexcited. Smells vile. She can't really see his face because it is dark. Dad bends over. She can't see his face either but he doesn't sound amused. Was the horrid man waiting for them? He seizes her father by the hand and kisses it twice before collapsing against the stone wall, whimpering, recoiled into himself.

Now urgent, concerned, Dad whispers to her. 'Help me get him off the street! Before he gets arrested!' He shouts into Walid's ear. The effect is astonishing. The clown shakes himself and, hiccupping, stretches up onto unsteady legs as if walking on eggs! Then, hands gripped over his heart, he bends his head forward to salute them like royalty. He takes hesitant steps down the curve of the alley into the night, oblivious of the scents trailing over the neighbours' high walls.

Khalid pulls the iron bars, closing the ramshackle, worm-eaten door behind them. In the courtyard, released from street ears, they crack up.

'I'm in stitches!'

'What did you tell him?'

'What a fool!'

'I'll die laughing!'

The outburst over, they exchange a long, truthful, penetrating look before she asks, 'Was he waiting for us?'

'We'll never know!'

'Are you keeping him?'

'He is not that educated and he's done well to get where he is. He doesn't appear that clever. I like the fact he is an Alawite, like the president. But I could sack him any time. It's what I shouted! It gave him an electric shock.'

'Just words, no weapon! What a trick! You'd beat Voldemort!'

'Who's that?'

'Come on, Dad, the death lord in Harry Potter.'

'Dear me, what a compliment!'

Another giggling outburst over, they relax, enjoying the fragrant night. Mariyam has placed dozens of sweet-smelling pots filled with carnations and red Damascene roses on floors and stairs. Zaida tiptoes to the birdcage, sending silent kisses to Pip and his friends, huddled on the lower perch, asleep, colourful like toys.

'It's bedtime but let's sit a bit longer and have some flower water. You like it, don't you? Help me take this table to the corner Mariyam has cleared under the vine. Please don't wake up Pip and the other rascals! I couldn't cope with their nonsense on top of Walid's panto!'

'Can you really sack him for being tipsy?'

'I could, but why? He's got seven kids to support. Let him have a bit of fun. He doesn't drink that often. Don't you worry, sweetie.'

She leans forward, whispering, avoiding his stare. 'He pinched my bottom.' She pauses. 'When he helped me into the car.' Another pause. 'I'm not sure really.' Pause. 'Sorry, I'm wrong. Maybe...' Words stick to her like mud.

He is stung. What a bloody awful night! He wipes his forehead and neck with a tissue. She won't say anything else. She is sucking her thumb. Is she having him on? Flirting? With whom? Annoyed with her for getting him in a muddle, he snatches her glass away, hammering out every syllable. 'Listen to me. No joking. Tell me if anyone doesn't show you respect. It has to be real facts. Understood?'

She isn't dumb. She was serious, but she can't bring herself to argue, wishing them to be happy together again. 'Understood, boss!' She nudges him with her elbow. 'Remember the children in blue uniforms? They looked smart. Running around. Boys and girls. They waved to us.'

'Pouring out of that shabby school? In Mount Qassioun. One boy was carrying the Syrian flag. Security people guarded the road by Saghrir park – I don't know why.' He speaks dryly, uncertain where she is leading. Will that be another accusation?

'Walid wasn't drunk then.'

'Of course not! He was driving and—'

'He was really nice. He waved back out of the window. Said something funny – the kids laughed too. He looked really happy. Maybe... his own children were among them.'

'We've never talked about his kids.' An acute weariness comes over him imagining Walid drunk as a lord, dragging himself up terraces of prickly pears, hobbling over cobblestones, past the orchards to reach the slopes crowded with aggressive tower blocks and higgledy-piggledy houses with no water. In Al-Almara, Walid would pray no-one was watching before dropping into his cane chair by the locked door, hoping no child was waiting. For the first time, Khalid feels some sympathy for the man. It is hard work to be a father.

Zaida appears to follow his thoughts. 'You won't sack him, will you? Poor Dad! You're whacked!'

'Let's forget him. It's bedtime.'

Back in his bedroom, his neck and shoulders aching with fatigue, Khalid flops down after retrieving from the Persian rug the dark blue beads of a bracelet Mariyam must have dropped when cleaning. He will lie down a few minutes to think things through. Why did that creep get pissed? Why on our doorstep? 'I'll catch him!' he mumbles, jumping up, stretching out his limbs like a bonobo testing its agility in anticipation of an athletic leap. From the left drawer of the cumbersome Victorian desk, a reminder of his father's GP days totally at odds with the retro Cairo furniture he later purchased online, he pulls out a pad of A4 and switches on his phone. From his contact list, he selects a dozen numbers and jumbles them up with relevant international codes into a list of fictitious international contacts for Lebanon, Turkey, Egypt, Israel. He includes Amnesty International, Human Rights Watch and Refugee International. He writes on top in Arabic "to call again" before ticking a few numbers to show who he has already contacted.

Reaching the courtyard, he is distracted by the soft trickle of water and captivated by a first crescent moon whose light strokes walls and balustrades, fortifying his resolution. It should work. The prayer over, he scrunches up the coded page as if it has been taken out of a pocket before hiding it under the Bakelite phone on the leather trunk. Walid knows he can make the odd business call from the *iwan* after his office hours. He is careful to let the top part of the sheet stick out before taking a few close-up photos of the trap.

He kicks off his Turkish slippers and tiptoes back upstairs, savouring the thought of tricking Walid into displacing the paper and sacking him if he refuses to say who he is working for. The only thing left tomorrow morning is to tell Zaida and Mariyam not to touch the paper but without explaining why, so as not to alarm them.

On the last balcony, he stands still to enjoy the night scents – jasmine in particular whisks him back to his father; the word in Persian means "a gift from God" – to calm his nerves. 'As good as valium,' the good doctor would say. 'We were right to return to the old country.' Once again he is restored by the thought of his bastion being tucked away in a city with many faiths whose stones of worship and trade, dignified by time, will continue to protect the people. He lets the moonlight, moist with cooler air rising from the Barada, bathe his face while resisting the urge to ask Zaida to join him. Other rituals, less private, are looming up soon enough since the lunar calendar will bring the Al-Hijra festivities to the streets to celebrate its new year, on 29 December. Even if it turns out that Walid spies on his phone calls, couldn't Zaida stay until Muharram, the most holy month after Ramadan? Zaida would love the idea. Not her mum, though. But with regular contact she ought to be reassured. And what about Walter's ridiculous message – to exchange Zaida for £20,000? Crazy! Ignore it.

– 11 –

Old Flirts

When Ian is googling Beef Stroganoff for tonight's dinner, someone knocks and, in a characteristically French manner, walks into the sitting room without waiting for a response. He grins.

'I hope you do not mind.'

Marianne has lost her hungry adolescent look. Barefoot, she takes her time to settle among the cushions. A confident dresser. He smiles again. As for him, how does he strike her as he strides over to the quirky rocking chair? Effortlessly raffish?

'I'm sorry you're leaving so soon. We haven't had much time together, but you've been a wonderful support for Virginia, I hear. Any idea about how I can help?'

She enunciates each word as if transmitting a coded message over a long distance. 'I have experience of missing people.'

'How is that?'

'A long story. I've looked for my natural mother. I am adopted. You may not remember my grandmother?'

Ian stops rocking, injured at her suspicion. 'Come on! Remember us in that cool library? And her telling my parents off – "reading never hurt anyone". They wanted us out for another boring walk. She liked to shoo them off us with a flap, like waving flies off meat. True?'

An exceptional person, they agree. Outside, leaves glisten, an exalting moment between showers, fresh as the perfect love one never gets.

'Sometimes, I help people with missing relatives. Not for money, *naturellement*.'

'Zaida isn't missing, is she? Virginia has Khalid's home address and she's writing to her. Or do you know something we don't?'

Marianne feels wrong-footed. The room needs fresh air. As she struggles to open a sash window, it gets stuck halfway up. They push, two bodies pressing hard at the frame until it jerks free. They laugh, connected to each other, ready to spill secrets like dating people.

'Where does Khalid really live? Is it Zaida who writes? We don't know. Child abductors are clever. They lie. Easy. Very easy. Does your… penny drop?'

'Christ! You could be right, of course. What does Virginia say about this? If you raise the stakes, she'll flip.'

'*Pardon*? The stakes? Flip?'

'Never mind. I'd say Khalid is a good guy and he will respect the law – he is a lawyer after all.'

He looks inscrutable. Under his stare, she feels like a podgy, middle-aged woman. Better attack. 'We know nothing for sure. Virginia has never been to Syria. They can… fabricate many… histories. Were they really refugees? The family can spy for Assad. Abdul in Britain had occasion for a *mission secrète*. Sorry for my English… to be a doctor can be… a blanket.'

'A cover? Come off it! We all respected the man. I remember him well – he was genuine, and handsome to boot. And a good listener.'

'Obviously.'

They battle on. Like any insightful detective, she believes all scenarios should be examined, while he ridicules her portrayal of spies and terrorists swarming from the Middle East.

'Ian, don't mock. Who help Virginia? Courts take too long to get children back.'

'What else can she do?'

'*You* go to Syria now. Check their address in Damascus and Hama. See Zaida. You're her uncle. Get Khalid to trust you and find out what he is playing.'

Furious, Ian scowls at the woman: a fucking menace, scheming to send him on a wild goose chase. Just because, once, long ago, they had shagged upstairs. 'What about you? Why don't you go?'

'Relatives do better. And Zaida will trust you.'

'How do you know? And can you honestly see me? "Hi, I'm Zaida's uncle – yes, the poofter from Canada."'

He lets out a long sigh at the thought of complications ahead, feeling a pang of regret for the boredom he was fighting against a few minutes ago. But he will have to consider Marianne's scheme. She is as persistent as the rain.

'Listen. I've never been to Syria. I don't know how I'd cope.'

'You're a journalist!'

'Will they cope with me? Have you looked it up?'

'Yes, I'm afraid…'

'I get it. Homosexuality is outlawed?'

She recites, 'Carnal knowledge against nature is punished with one to three years in jail.'

'Could be worse! Suppose… I go for one week. I don't know a bloody thing about bloody Syria!'

'Ottoman palaces—'

'Jesus! Spare me the crap, will you?'

'Just a few days. Talk to Zaida and see what she wants. I believe journalists go for adventure.'

He is beginning to enjoy the game: she throws him up into the air and drops him gently, not quite letting go, not yet breaking his neck. A subtle change is taking place in him. Her idea isn't that terrible. What is there to lose? He could be back in Vancouver by mid-November. Could he play his cards right among people whose culture eludes him?

'Can't you see I'd put my foot in it? Forget it. I'm a selfish bastard. Find someone else!'

He resumes the rocking, sheepish at letting her down. Stuff the kafuffle! He deserves a bit of comfort at home and won't oblige the lady this time. He did 'oblige' out of bravado; his first time with a woman, a first for her too. He had warmed to a boyish body marked by infant breasts and a golden tuft twitching between long thin brown legs. For some time, he felt tearful afterward, dispossessed maybe, sad at clammy bellies pressing against each other, frightened by the intimacy he could not give women. He owed Marianne for this gruelling lesson.

'Please, stop that chair! Sorry, Ian, it's the noise.'

A hangdog silence fills the room. There is a raw edge to it, expectant and angry. Sitting up, frozen, Ian looks out of the window, pretending interest in the garden. Marianne concentrates on arranging cushions from a bygone world of women embroidering quilts and covers with herringbones and Basque loops. She pats a couple into shape while also thinking that the English never see disaster until it stares them in the face: Dunkirk, Northern Ireland, Iraq, Afghanistan, Northern Rock. The Franklins should take their chance and get Zaida out without delay. Or else, a drawn-out case costing thousands of pounds. Her friends' passivity is exasperating. Their financial situation is not as good as the house stuffed with antiques and the state-of-the-art clinic lead one to believe. They are so short of funds that Virginia cannot afford a private investigator to track Khalid's family in Damascus or Hama. Ian is free to travel. How can she persuade him?

He looks more reflective than during that fatal summer. Despite the cherubic face he was jittery, intolerant of other people's vulnerabilities, prone to fits of anger, mercurial to the core.

Life is full of incoherence, no matter the logic you weave between seasoned expectations. It will catch you off-guard, as it had that warm night when she lost her virginity. The exultation gone out like a candle, she probably opened the window onto the climbing roses, frozen to the spot, listening to the dawn, quiet traffic, a fox, doves already cooing. Flushed, she turns her face away briefly to disguise her longing, before staring back at him, taking in the sharp line of nose and brow, the high forehead, the full mouth – more sensitive, less willing to exploit his alarming good looks.

'I hope you don't mind my question...' Pleased to be let off the hook, he encourages her to go on. She drops the brisk teacher's voice for a softer tone. 'Why... you and me... that summer?'

Pleased to explain himself, he ventures, 'Things were different. Believe me. More fluid for young men. Pride wasn't asking me to support them. You understand?' Seeing the hurt look, the shrinking mouth, he pleads, 'I wasn't cheating, I was in love with you too. Very much.'

She shoots a perplexed glance. Is she thinking words in his mouth are easy and naïve? He has to persevere. 'We were all in love with you: Mum, Dad and Virginia. With you, of course, you are so attractive! And your godmother in that *chateau* was terrific. The Languedoc seemed made for us Brits. Honestly, for me, you *were* then that idyllic place. Take no offence. I was sincere.'

'Let's move on.' Does he still care? She must not look flustered. She shuts her eyes. He used to see through her. Such an intuition, brittle for men. They could work together, if she doesn't frighten him off. Get Zaida back.

They listen to the muffled sounds of rain and sorrow, the same furtive smile floating on their lips. Nobody knew of their shenanigans, though Ian wonders about Virginia – she's the jealous sort. Does she still take the mickey out of Marianne, mouth pinched like a chick's ass, clicking her tongue between the words, "ZoRRI... mON AngLICH"?

Encouraged by his attention, Marianne shifts the conversation back to Zaida. Yes, the girl sent a few photos – a dromedary licking her ice cream, souks, crumbling Roman temples.

'Zaida can be anywhere... east... after the Pyramids! Ian, please, will you go? Do you care?'

'Care enough? I don't know.'

Irritated again, they look daggers, a stale couple, each wrestling with the other's obstinacy. The thought makes her snap. 'I've got something on Khalid.'

'Go ahead! But before you do, tell me something about Chateau Mourel.'

He points to the family albums, carefully labelled and dated, in the alcoves by the fireplace. Yesterday morning, he leafed through them methodically. Unlike people who wolf down family photos like chocolates, he picked at them with caution, anguished by faces he should remember: Marianne's godmother at the piano; Grandfather's farm near Banbury, a frightening place – 'Get the boy onto the damned horse, or else he'll turn out a fairy!' Did someone say that?

'I've found quite a few snaps but there's one missing. Do you have it? You two girls, on the swings with a bucket in the front full of brown snails. Did I make it up?'

'No, I don't have a photo with swing. And we do not have brown snail in the summer, it is too hot. Sorry.' The grin fades out. 'This Khalid, there is more to him than... meet... the nose – is that what you say?'

Ian is baffled again. She is dangling him like a bloody mouse. She has collected information about Khalid with the help of a private investigator. What a fixer!

'I've got this man looking for Khalid. I mean, his business affairs.'

'What? How did you manage that?'

She hands him a memory stick. 'It's all there. Now Khalid has big money. I don't think Walter knows.'

'What about Virginia?' His voice is croaking as he slips the memory stick into his pocket.

'You are the first person I tell. John Norman gives it to me yesterday night when I meet him at the station. He works fast.'

'Not on his own, and at a price, I bet. How much did you pay for this service? We can't afford somebody like that—'

'*Chut*! I've got money from my godmother. It's a Christmas gift. The Al-Sayeds are now rich Sunnis, that's sure. The information is good. They have... diversified – can you say that? OK. They possess the Umayyad Import-Export Company; they sell carpets, textiles and chemicals.'

'If the Al-Sayeds own a string of businesses, how does that bring Zaida back? And—'

Marianne casts him a warning glance, stopping him in his tracks.

'The question is: what do they do now? Don't you want to know? Crude oil and gas pipelines from Iraq.'

'So what? Is that a crime? Jesus! I don't like it. You think Khalid is on Assad's side now?'

'The regime has Mafia methods – corruption, drugs and *assassins*. You see, you are the man for the job. You get a good story for your paper.'

'Christ! I need a stiff drink. Do you want one?'

When he returns, Marianne lights up at the sight of the blood orange Campari – he has remembered her favourite drink.

'You like adventures. Am I right? You will have fun. Better than stay in a cage – Leaford, I mean.'

'You have a point.' He pretends not to hear her triumphant tone. 'You're quite a schemer. Impressive. How did you learn such tricks?'

She blushes, flirtatious. 'Big heads think the same thing.'

'And you're leaving soon? I'll miss you.'

He bends over and kisses her abruptly on the cheek.

Marianne's conviction has stirred him out of his afternoon lethargy with buoyant images of Arab horses and minarets, mint teas and halva, and a page-boy to rescue. He will have to get a tourist visa as fast as he can. That shouldn't be a problem. In no way will he attempt to investigate the Al-Assads' business activities. How foolish of Marianne to suggest it! His head spins. Once you take responsibility for family affairs, the burden grows. One week isn't a life sentence, though. The point is to do the job. Check out Khalid. Bring Zaida back.

Maybe the idea of sending him off came from his father in the first place and Marianne acted as a go-between. Is that why she was pussyfooting around? Will his parents be glad to see the back of him?

He looks for clues around the bedroom, now refurbished with Welsh antiques. Despite the substitution, the room still reminds him of the unhappiness that filled him when waiting for a Martin, a Clint. There is the familiar crack in the glass of the grandfather clock, Georgian, heirloom from Gwen's father who died before he was born. What is most pleasing, though, is that its fastidious clanking came to a grinding halt the morning he flew back. 'Time stops when you are around,' his mother quipped.

He will be more comfortable in luxury Syrian hotels. The bed sits high on bulbous turned posts, complete with a sagging mattress that has consumed his relatives. In his turn, he will shuffle his back over the bumps while hearing voices from the Banbury farm. "The boy is a chicken", did Grandad say that? Bitterness seeps into his bones like the smell of naphthalene. He has to rescue a damsel from a dangerous country. Will he fail to bring her back? Marianne is right – the journalist instinct clinging to him, he won't lose Khalid's scent. What about Zaida? She must have quite a story to tell. He won't bring her back by force, of course not. Jesus! He's got another idea. So obvious! Ask Father to come with him! The Al-Sayeds will open their door to the older man, if not to him. And Walter will accept, suppressing a vague worry that his son might get trouble from the Syrian police.

He'd better check gay sites on Syria to see how bad things are. Doom swells in him at the thought of having yet again to hide who he is, act dull and conventional, waiting for the right girl to marry. What the fuck to expect? How will he take it? He's no chicken, he tells himself, raging against the bumps and holes that will give him a stiff back in the morning.

– 12 –

Damascus

'SHUT UP, PIP! STUPID BIRD. I CAN'T BE BOTHERED. Things aren't fun, you know. Dad is doing his best but he leaves me for hours with that Arabic teacher or Aunt Halima. I'm missing school. You see, when Dad is with his friends, he's rude. He forgets I don't understand anything. And Halima wants to be – you won't believe it – my mother! I choked. No way! She dresses me up to pass me around. No! No! I am not Seema. I am going mental. Pip, I hate Walid. He's a freak.'

She blows into his back wings, his puny head eyeing her, listening from the cradle of her hand while the others are pecking at the seeds. She loves his flame-orange patches. He weighs nothing; she could easily hurt him. He is so cute. She smoothes his wings. 'In Britain, they'd kick him out. They do that in films too, but Dad doesn't. He follows his uncle and cousins. I don't know what.' Once Pip is dropped into the cage, he hovers and flaps until the others shuffle along the perch to free his favourite space in the middle. She claps. 'You stick together!'

What is going on? High-pitched voices. Khalid and Walid in the dark corridor by the front door, shouting, bellowing in that awful language. She puts down the water jug and the cleaning brushes, listening to the onslaught, petrified until Khalid rushes out, squinting at the full light of the yard.

119

'What's wrong?' She runs across but collides with Walid, also dashing out. She falls onto her knees. There are more shouts as they pull her to her feet.

'Are you alright, sweetie? I am so sorry!' She shrugs them off.

Her lips are sealed – she won't cry in front of the man who keeps annoying them. She watches her father gesturing to Walid. The creep hesitates then leaves.

'Are you OK? Sure? I've to go out now. You're upset? Never mind. Syrians shout about nothing – over beans, peas, peanuts. I mean real peanuts. Listen. I'll be back early and we'll have a long chat. Farouq is calling with his son. Put your nice clothes on. For me, not for Ali! Bye for now.'

How childish he is. She gallops to her room, breathing fast, leaning her back against the closed door, needing to calm down before examining her knees. Dad is talking crap but alright, that's his business. Her knees are not bad. She sticks on an Elastoplast. Buoyed up, her attention turns to Ali. Does she fancy him? She's got an idea. She clicks an app. He'll see how much she loves playing demons, zombies, vampires… war games. That'll test him. But why bother?

Before dinner, she approaches her father who is standing on top of a step ladder in the sitting room opening onto the courtyard. 'You're back already. I didn't hear you come in.'

'I was worried about you. What about your fall?'

'Nothing much. I'm fine. What are you doing up there?

'Mariyam said the air conditioner has stopped. It'd be nice to have it repaired.'

'You'll sweat like a pig up there.'

'Pigs don't sweat, my love, though they have that reputation.'

'You want me to help?'

'I've just dropped a plastic container full of screws somewhere near the sofa. I can't see it from up here.'

The black screws have scattered like ants on the floor, where they have the decency to stop moving. Kneeling, she squeezes her forefingers onto each beast to fill the box. A good moment to get her dad's attention.

'What was wrong? You were shouting at Walid.'

'Nothing much.'

'Really?'

'Can you switch this machine on? It saves me going up and down the ladder. Look. The controls are over there, by that radio.' The conditioner does not start. He looks bothered.

'Poor Dad. You'll have to try again.'

'Can you hold the ladder for me? I need to reach that wire high up.'

She stands close to the bottom rung, holding the sides tight. 'I don't like him.'

'Christ! Let me finish the job!'

Chastised, she waits until he climbs down.

'I'll try and switch it on. We'll see.'

'Clever you!'

'I want to get a proper tool box, light, with drawers for storage. I could give that heavy wooden box to Walid, though it's Father's.'

'Spies are bribed with precious stones! Not junk!'

'What?'

'Teasing!'

'I won't sack him! You see, I much prefer to have him stay with us. We can keep an eye on him. And bear in mind his large family up Mount Qassioun – we can't be unfair, he needs the job. And I trust Uncle Omar. He said the man is loyal to our family.'

'Has he said sorry for being tipsy?'

'Not in so many words! Love, it's a question of honour; Syrians are proud men. But that's enough about him. Let's move the table to the middle where it belongs.'

The room cleared, they sit down by the antique radiogram. Junk to Zaida? The shiny fifties piece, with large white buttons sticking out of a squarish mahogany case, resurrects his father hanging to the BBC News in the early evenings. A Winchester given by a Leaford family devoted to the doctor for reasons he has forgotten.

'Have a look!' He reveals the record player underneath the top lid. 'Isn't that clever?'

She is astonished. 'You had… umm… plastic records when you were a kid?'

'Vinyl, they're called. A collection of our great classics! Umm… Kolthum Farid, Al-Atrache, Fairouz – all beautiful singers but, I expect, not for you! Halima's kids have a diet of Syrian pop bands.'

She giggles. 'Ali had me listening to Lena Chamsomething.'

'Oh! You liked her?'

'Very romantic.'

'Who? You two?'

He strokes her hair, happily listening to her babble. She had enjoyed herself with Ali, watching flocks of pigeons racing over Hama roof terraces while listening to CDs, not plastic stuff. The sight of the Bakelite phone breaks the interlude by bringing back to his mind his failure to catch the chauffeur. The test was too crude to prove anything. Walid played dumb – No! He's never touched or photographed a list of phone numbers. He claimed a pious probity: he doesn't take dirty money and serves only his good master – 'I pray, Sir, Ali to recommend you to Allah and do well by Him with a kind heart!' The sod was unflappable. He had the gall to refuse 500 dollars. Too cool. Too well-rehearsed to be convincing.

Zaida, fiddling with the radio, draws him back to her. 'Lovely, it stopped working ages ago. If you want, I'll find someone to see to it.'

'Don't bother.'

'Listen to me. As long as my uncle is on our side, Walid won't do us any harm. Things are too complicated to explain but, believe me, this is true.'

She gives him a kiss on the cheek. He clears his throat. 'What about you writing a proper long letter to your mum tonight saying why you want to stay until the end—' He is interrupted by the door-knocker, a rusty hand, Fatima's, which he has inherited from the previous owners to protect the house against evil intruders.

Zaida stands up to welcome the visitors, ready to bolt upstairs if Ali is with Farouq. No need! Khalid stretches out his arm to bar his disappointed daughter from retreating upstairs.

'Sweetie, stay with us. Omar Al-Sayed has come with Farouq to have the pleasure of meeting you. Wait while I bring some coffee and rose water.'

She steps towards Uncle Omar and stops halfway, overawed by his stiff military stance in spite of the crooked arm, the butchered face, the ghost of a smile. Repressing her dismay at his hideous presence, she forgets the Arabic greetings she normally masters. His mouth, a machine gun, shoots out jerky unfamiliar noises alongside oddly intelligible words – present, girl, happy – and then snaps closed, silent and offensive under his piercing stare. She panics, ready to run away. Looking diminutive, Farouq moves in between the two. Sensitive to his flourishing compliments, relieved, she gives him a radiant smile. In perfect English, he apologises at a great length for his son's absence earlier in the day until his inconsiderate father pushes him aside to give her something wrapped in a silk blue and gold pouch. Two rings with jade beads. What for? Too big for rings and too small for bracelets. Omar bends down and swiftly touches her ankles, smiling.

'Anklets, I see. Thank you so much.' No, she won't give him a kiss! How can she get out of here without being rude? As Farouq is encouraging her with a grin, she lets her hands be patted by the monster, fearing more displays of his good will.

When Khalid returns with Mariyam, who is sorting out the *nargile* pipes from their niche in the wall, he is dismayed to see his little girl parading two jewelled anklets – far too expensive to suit a young girl. What's going on? Omar welcomes him back, keen to honour daughter and father with celebratory gifts. A heavy silver ring carved with his initials. He plays along, slipping the Bedouin ring onto his middle finger, repressing a subterranean frustration at the timing of the gifts. Has Omar been alerted by Walid? Is he bearing gifts instead of bribes to teach the wimp a lesson?

He directs the visitors towards the grand *qa'a*. 'Zaida, help your uncles settle down. Not in the *iwan*, which is now too cool for our autumnal evenings.' She leads the way, happy to show off the magnificent reception room, with its painted wood and plaster decoration – the first time her father has entertained there since she has been.

Once they have settled on the cushioned banquettes, Mariyam brings in trays of coffee and sweetmeats. Zaida watches her arranging fanciful teapots, water jugs and pipes of all shapes on the mother-of-pearl-inlaid table. She has always loved the smell of strong mint tea. What is going on is fascinating. Her father is preparing what they call *shisha* tobacco and some charcoal to ignite it. The men chat by themselves while keeping an expert eye on their bubbling pipes until her dad asks her to open the sweet little boxes, he explains, for the guests to choose their flavour.

'Oh! It smells of apple. That's lovely.'

'Yes, *Nakhla shisha*. What about the *Al-Amir shisha*?'

She sniffs at the crushed tobacco a few times. 'Pass!'

'Blueberry. Sweetie, it's time for you to leave us grown-ups to ourselves.'

Khalid smiles to himself. Zaida should have left much earlier, but hopefully she won't tell the Franklins about their evening. Virginia's solicitor could go to town about the corruption of youth, but the British Council would not move a finger against him. Anyway, it is also good that Walter has been silenced by him not acknowledging his ridiculous offer to exchange Zaida for a loan! For sure behind Virginia's back. Quite a few Brits are nowadays losing the moral high ground! He chuckles at the thought, but enough of bad feelings. The three of them should now enjoy a perfect session and, all being well, even manage to feign some bonding. That's what the gifts are about – some truce for the evening; forget politics and spies.

'With respect, can I interrupt your thoughts? For no reason, I've just remembered my father often quoting a proverb... something like... "having faith in men alone, and not Allah , is like having faith that water will remain in a sieve".

'Typical of my brother. What's your problem?'

Farouq is as sharp as ever. 'That's obvious, Father. If godless men are sieves, there is only despair left. That's what bothers you, Khalid?'

'Something like that. Do we mostly act out of faith, self-interest or naivety?'

Father and son have, or feign, a mild interest in discussing the saying. To his surprise, they rapidly agree with each other: one must have faith in men if one is to move on in a godless world, or else life would be a daily diet of derision, cynicism and corruption. Khalid listens without interrupting, inhaling deeply, pushing to the back of his mind questions about Walid's loyalty. To Omar? Who else? Best to drop them. Enjoy the moment.

Much to her relief, Zaida has been sent to her room. Her mother would hate her dad smoking like an addict in front of a child! She kicks off the silly anklets. Will he come and say goodnight? To fight back a pang of loneliness, she slips onto her right arm the Hermione's charm bracelet her granny gave her for the journey. It's not too late to write home. She tears three pages out of her All About Me diary, which she ought to start one evening, but not now. Impelled by overflowing confusions, she dashes off a letter.

My Dear Mummy,
I am missing you and Grandpa and Granny. It is also true I love staying with my dad. Getting to know Aunt Halima, Grandad, cousin Farouq. Omar is scary but he has given me anklets and a big silver ring to Dad. I don't want to marry Ali. He does not talk but Aunt Halima says it is not a problem for married people. She wants me to morph into a Syrian niece. She never stops talking of weddings, dance, shopping, festivals, picnics. She is good though. She gets me long dresses to cover my figure. In Hama, she made a hullabaloo to celebrate my period! Can you believe it? She made special cakes for me and girls I didn't know. I do not like the fuss about me and clothes and other things. Dad can't help, he does not know things about girls.

She goes over the lines. Her features relax. That's all true. Go on then.

I love Dad's house. He loves it too. We have fun when we open the roof every morning. The chauffeur is not a Sunni like us, his name is Walid. The cook goes to church, her name is Mariyam, she is a Catholic. Nobody does Ramadan in my house, Dad says. Mum, you were right to stop me from coming in September.

She stops again before tackling other niggling thoughts.

Walid drove us up the large hill above the city where refugees live. I was upset, the houses look like ruins, there were poor people staring at us inside the car. Dad says it is our duty to help them anywhere in the world. I understand – he can't forget, I won't either. I hate the chauffeur. He is a spy. Dad does not know what to do. He has so many children Dad can't sack him because he is kind.

I miss my dad when he is away but Auntie looks after me. Tomorrow Grandad will take me to the blue and gold mosque. I love him. Now I get less upset when he calls me Seema by mistake because he loves me. I enjoy him helping me with my Arabic. That's hard but he is wicked. He tells me old stories and we laugh a lot.

I told Dad I'll never, never date Ali, he is too serious. I like my cousin Lilleth much better, we laugh when we talk gibberish, but she lives in Hama. I also talk to the budgies, they are so cute.

Dad wants me to stay until New Year. I was happy about that but now I am not sure. I love you so much, I am missing you, my dearest mummy, I am lonely without you.

She reads it through, sighs and tears it apart. It won't do.

– 13 –

Self-healing

EARLY MORNING, VIRGINIA TAKES THE OPPORTUNITY OF Ian being away for the day to rummage through an old steamer trunk kept under his bed. Has Zaida left anything of hers in that trunk? Entering his room, she looks aghast at the chaos around: soiled towels sticking out of a tennis bag, Prada sneakers perched on crunched newspapers, wires trailing to phone sockets and, on top of the console, a sleek Mac portable blinking at face cream and gel pots. Brother and sister? As different as chalk and cheese! He tall and effusive, which people take for openness and compassion; she squatty and uncertain of herself. Inside he must be as self-opinionated as ever, judging from his bickering with their father. She is on her knees pulling out the chest when Marianne comes in.

'Let me help you.'

'Thanks... but before we have a look, I apologise for our quarrel last night.'

'No need!'

'Ian was interfering as usual. It isn't his business to fly in and meddle with the clinic. That makes me angry.' Virginia throws a tennis ball at the newspaper pile and misses.

Since it isn't the moment to raise the idea of sending Ian to Syria, Marianne seeks a diversion. 'Do you have money problems?'

'Temporary, I hope. Father borrowed to pay for the extension, the refurbishing and hiring more staff. The weekend courses are heavy to run and there's a lot of competition for that sort of thing. In Oxford, Southampton, Reading.'

'Andy say it is too soon to tell.'

'Yes, it is, and to rattle Father won't do any good.'

'Is Walter taking the drug for his heart?

'I don't think so. He's as stubborn as a mule.'

Marianne looks at her watch. 'Call me if you need me.'

It is Ian's junk, of no interest until Virginia comes across a pile of school reports tied up with elastic bands. Zaida's. The blue covers are laid out with a large heading, Leaford South Fields Secondary School, and underneath in bold, Zaida Gwen Al-Sayed-Franklin. Such a midget for such a long name. Virginia strokes the crinkled paper with her thumb as if to flatten out the burden of family destinies that her daughter carries. From the day Zaida received glowing comments from school, Virginia knew each report by heart.

Compensating for her own lack of ambition, she imagined Zaida a new Cherie Blair at the bar. She has a fantastic memory, hides her passions. She used to screw up her eyes at a tug-of-war over a toy, a voice too loud, and later, Abdul's tales. What budding adolescent would not be fascinated by talk of crusades, occupations and homecomings?

She can't help feeling bitter. When a young wife, she had imagined another Syria – Zaida skipping ahead of her mum and dad on a long visit to Khalid's family. A Syria full of the vestiges of history that she read about and loved: spicy dust tasted by Lawrence of Arabia; garlands of peddlers at the Ummayad Mosque; olive groves tended since the first writing tablets. How ignorant she was then! Already weary of the day, she reaches for a brown envelope which she recognises as Zaida's. It is covered with a pencil drawing of Lascha, the female shaman Zaida played online – a powerful seal of protection, so she guesses, of the treasure inside: postcards from Syria; letters and photos, mostly from Khalid; newspaper cuttings on Chechnya and Srebrenica. Why collect this stuff? Virginia gasps. The Bosnian massacre took place before she was even born! Why? Does her baby believe only magic can save Muslim lives? Is that it? Something else drops out. Snaps of a sunburnt couple laughing and kissing on the bridge where the first crusade had assembled to hunt 'us' down, he said. The expression stuck.

Her hair now tied up into a sloppy chignon, Marianne saunters back into the room. She looks bleary, having spent the night wondering what type of a child Zaida is. She can't gather any impression from Zaida's closest friends, away for the term with relatives, one in Islamabad and the other in Cairo. Bright, reliable, down-to-earth, Virginia says. Three children with English mothers and foreign fathers. Do the girls see the same ineffable condition of their birth quarried out of their parents' idiotic coupling? Do they share , however dimly, the same rondo of questions 'why my parents/why me'? Knowing herself abandoned at birth, Marianne has long suspected that plausible answers may come from unexpected scenarios. This is why Virginia is wrong to play down Zaida's search, if this is what the girl is doing. Hopefully, she is finding in Syria something meaningful about herself, even if she has no words for it as she renews her intimacy with her father.

'Still tidying up?'

The trunk is back under the Welsh bed, ready to swallow, like any heirloom, hordes of victims. Marianne raises an eyebrow at Virginia disentangling sandals and trainers from each other.

'Let's go. There's not much here. My daughter is still a mystery to me,' Virginia says, self-mocking, unable to share her shocking discovery, her eyes watering.

When Marianne helps collect things back into the envelope, she recognises the photo of the happy couple she took in Albi.

Khalid was such a good number. An attentive husband, a good father, a fine cook and so sexy too – a combination which women of her generation have come to demand openly from their men and rarely find.

'Look at you two! You sweethearts!' Since only common-sense arguments will get Virginia out of the trap she has made for herself, she continues the attack. 'He loves Zaida. And respect your family! Trust him.' She waves the iconic photo. 'Were you not in love? It is the same Khalid then and now.'

'You're so French! Talking about principles and not what's really happening. After the divorce, he had regular access, things were fine, but he left his daughter for Syria. That's what bugs me. Why did he drop her? For a life change? To be closer to God in a Muslim land like his father? No, no! What Khalid really wants is just to be back home. Serve Syrian democracy, if he can. And make money, of course.'

'What's wrong with that?'

'My point is... we don't know what they are up to; the country is dangerous. Think of their bloody history. She already worries like mad about Muslim massacres... I bet they are still saying the two girls look alike. A raped girl!'

'Calm down. I understand Zaida is vulnerable. I have a suggestion. Let one of you visit her now!'

'What? *I* should go? Come off it!'

'Ian is free... you see?'

'He'd need a visa.' She refrains from saying 'don't be silly'.

'Syria is not a fortress. Calls from the Canadian embassy and the Al-Sayeds' address get him a tourist's visa. Quickly. Ian can use the uncle story, you know? "I am missing my only niece and..."

'What good would that do?'

'Make sure Zaida is where they say she is. And get a picture of the family situation.'

Marianne reminds her of the advice given by Reunion in cases of abduction. Check the address. Ask the British Consul to visit. Send a detective. Much better, meet the father and sweeten him so he does not hide the child away at unreachable places.

Mischievous, she asks, 'How does Mum attract Dad back?'

'Sex?'

'*Naturellement*! Let me see… one British woman had two kids kidnapped to Egypt. They had mediation. She promises Dad she will never divorce. He pays for her to stay with him and the children. Got herself pregnant. Imagine that! Happy Dad sent Mum and children back to Britain to the best doctors. Months later, she got a divorce!'

'Is it true?'

'True. Parents do extraordinary things to get missing kids back. Reunion know a few bizarre cases.'

'I'd cheer that brave Muslim mum of yours. Mind you, Khalid is not keeping Zaida against her will.'

'The point was… find what was happening in the Egyptian family. Ask Ian to go. He is a journalist, isn't he? His job is to follow difficult cases. '

The suggestion hardly surprises Virginia who has been admiring her friend's cautious moves. Indeed, why not send Ian instead of him idling at home? That would be cheaper than hiring lawyers. She bites her lips, still irresolute.

'Syria's a dangerous place for gays, isn't it?' Ian is unpredictable. Impulsive. However, he is fun, enterprising, full of – qualities that both Zaida and the Al-Sayeds would trust.

'Ian can do it. He's great.'

'Is there anything he can't do in your book? Why not ask Father? That'd be much safer. He'd prevent Ian from being too sweet with anyone.'

They fall silent. Piqued by the irony, Marianne plops down on the edge of the bed. She should have known better: Virginia is always testy about Ian.

Unhappy at having crossed her friend, Virginia collects soiled clothes, recalling to herself the brief times her brother and Khalid had met. Never shy, Ian teased Khalid about his dress sense – "suits fit only for a dog's funeral". Maybe these two would get on.

'Sorry for snapping at you when you are so full of bright ideas. But don't let Ian go on his own. He should team up with Father. Him and Abdul have a lot of respect for each other and they—'

Gwen shouts from the bottom of the stairs. 'What are you girls doing up there? Walter left for the clinic ages ago.'

They run down, Marianne seeing the lovers sliding down the handrail bellowing *Aux Armes Citoyens* before they landed in a heap of giggles.

Patrick laughs at the impropriety. The acupuncturist has left open the top three buttons of her white coat, revealing her bra.

'Shush! I can't hear myself think. Tell me why you are still coming. It has been a long time since I first saw you.'

Keeping at bay the fear of being dismissed, he bows his head into his chin, shaking it side to side like a dog baffled by life. 'Are you fed up with me? I need you to stir up my energy. Oh, beg your pardon, Miss, it isn't what I meant.' He gulps at the air. 'Prick me as much as you want, I don't mind a bit.' He bursts into laughter again.

She grins. Such a softie in spite of the pandemonium. Why should she mind his innocent innuendoes? Laughing is what widowers need most.

'I don't like you telling me to bugger off.' He sits up, head into his chin, embarrassed at the confession.

She gives him a big hug. It is this sort of playful intimacy he is craving. Khalid was the same, easy to appease when disheartened. A slight touch with her fingertips, a stroke of his creased face and he would purr for more, curling up against her chest. The thought, sharp like glass, makes her clench her hands together to contain the pain.

'You don't look too good yourself. Your daughter? What's up? Had no idea things would go wrong with a Muslim, did you, love?'

'None of that, will you?'

'I wish I could help you.'

She straightens her back. 'But you're helping me no end… when you don't pry.'

'How?'

'You trust me, don't you? That's helping.'

He sniffs, wistful. 'You're saying that to be polite to a spent old man.'

Without trust on both sides, she ruminates, there won't be any patching up. As in a marriage. She unrolls his socks and grips the finest of her needles.

'Ouch! You hurt me!' He nearly kicks her face as she bends over his feet. 'Why didn't you warn me?'

Her throat is tight. She was rough, too wrapped up in her own thoughts.

'Sorry! Now, let me warm up that energy of yours.'

Smiles are back in the room. Acupuncturist and patient are one team again. Patrick lurches down from the couch, swollen fingers struggling with the buttons of a brush-cotton shirt that he managed to iron – for her benefit, he says.

The door shut, she seals the used needles into the disposal unit. The morning treatments have gone surprisingly well given the state she was in after discovering the news cuttings and her taxing conversation with Marianne.

She interrogates the wall map showing the five cycles of energy that seamlessly flow in a healthy body. Life is movement and hope. Didn't she embrace Khalid with passion! Gripped by his stories. His Sunni ancestors merged with him – seductive male figures with a bruising courage. Us with them, always, that's what the woman in love wanted – then. And now, who is she? A dominating mother? A divorcee? Petty? Cynical? She should let go of Zaida, stop the distrust. An image of the child strolling through the Great Mosque, head towering over both of her parents, captivates her; she abandons herself to the golden mirage, then sniggers at her delusion. The Orient will ambush her daughter, as it has so many in the past.

The afternoon brings the turmoil back. Mary Angel lies flat on her tummy while the needles work on her back. She has dropped the whining of the out-to-get-you patient, which she had deployed before – her sexual life is still shit, acupuncture is useless, why bother? The battle has receded into a stillness only broken by Mary's bangles. The two women wait until the needles flop onto the side. Virginia is staring at the light picking up the soft shine of the black skin between the shoulder blades. Like the little pools of perspiration on Khalid's back when the couple lingered in bed, thankful for the Languedoc heat, blessed, having as yet no inkling of the collapse of her desire in years to come.

'I'll try another treatment. I checked it yesterday night thinking you might need it. It treats imbalances of energy like wet and dry—'

'OK, OK. Don't hurt me.'

It's over. Virginia looks through Mary's notes, making certain she has recorded in full the unorthodox treatment. She is learning to take risks.

Why can't she tackle her own deficiencies as well? Her fear of Walter. Her old jealousy of the glam brother. Her meanness in love. Her inability to deal with the Al-Sayeds. Screening her sagging desire behind Zaida, like a cockroach dreading the light.

'Are we friends?' The question soothes her. They exchange a long glance, accomplices, sensing in the other a vulnerability they do not understand and have to disguise. A need for faith, maybe, Virginia says to herself.

Mary gone, she paces her room, brooding over Marianne's crack: "love is more complicated than sex". How helpful is that?

She makes up her mind. There is no need to embitter Khalid further with a visit by the British Consul. He has unlikely qualities for a lawyer: considerate, adverse to quarrels and easily swayed by those he loves. Unlike Ian, who has the knack of getting into trouble. She ought to trust Khalid again. Zaida loves her dad and his family – that's to their credit. Marianne is right, they won't turn evil simply because they live in Syria. They will continue to love her and give her the best.

'Do I serve tea in the conservatory?'

'Coffee for me, and chocolates!' The women laugh, happy to indulge Walter tonight.

'How was Mary Angel today?'

'There's still a lot of self-destruction in her, God knows why, but she left saying she might try for children – not now, but some time.'

'Well done, Virginia.'

Ian out for the night, Virginia lingers by her father's side, basking in his reassurances, ignoring Marianne who looks at her enquiringly, unwilling to break the tranquil mood of the evening. Pretending to read *The Journal of Chinese Medicine*, Virginia ponders over Marianne's advice, reasonable and shrewd. No harm could come from a visit by Ian and Walter. Only immediate clarification and, hopefully, reassurance. And, if they both go, loads of fun for Zaida with her two families at her side.

Walter sees his daughter nodding to herself. He takes in the jerky movements, the bloated eyelids, the creased temples, her gaping mouth as she turns the pages looking for absolute truths in obscure articles. He grieves; the child doesn't trust enough in her father's experience. As for Ian, there is a similar lack of faith, irrevocable and as absolute as loneliness. Be that it may, the lad is on the ball, even reassuring about the clinic since 'debts make a business tick over these days.' Ironically, Khalid is adopting a similar "wait and see" attitude. Has he reckoned that the unfortunate email came from a panic attack?

Neither Walter nor the women can take their eyes off the newcomer. It is not the trendy casuals that attract attention but the Tintin hairdo coated with gel, short on the sides and high in the middle.

'Ian! We didn't expect you so early. Grab a chair and sit by me.'

'Dad, I hope I didn't upset you at the party.'

'Not quite.'

They hug and everyone relaxes except for Virginia, who catches Walter watching Ian idly playing with a pack of needles before putting it back into his pocket. Is he less ambivalent than he says about acupuncture? And if he brings Zaida back, it'd be unbearable! He will take over the clinic! Unless they fall out in Syria.

Father and son make a show of teasing each other.

'I won't let in any crazy therapy. We'll ignore Sue Benning's claims. As you say, son, we'll have crystal reading next.'

'And white witchcraft. It thrives in Brighton. What a story for Super Frog to take home tomorrow!'

Virginia, anxious to be included again, disrupts the fun. 'I used the Eight Principles on Mary as a last resort this afternoon.'

'What happened?' Walter manages to keep his voice down.

'The pulses became less wiry.'

'How long for, I wonder. Soon you'll be back to square one.' Hammering each word, he threatens the naughty girl. 'I'm telling you, if we lose faith in the Five Elements, our needles will stop singing.'

'Meaning?'

'Our needles empower people to talk. Together we make sense of the illness. Progressively. With thorough feedback. From pulses and, well, you know what I mean. Not from faceless experts and their expensive machines. Too busy to touch you, too busy to get to know you, too—'

'Stop it, Walter! Or I'll send you to Coventry.' Gwen's threat makes them laugh.

'Why Coventry?' Marianne wants an explanation. Then, a phone stirs the family.

'Quick, Ian, under those cushions. Oh! It's my girl texting.'

I love you so much, I miss you in the morning in the evening in the day always. And Gwen and Walter to the end of my life. Why don't you come and see us now?

'You were so positive the other night about Zaida – you're a blessing, darling!' Gwen helps Marianne pack more children's books into an overloaded suitcase. 'As I keep saying, we're sorry to see you go.'

On the edge of laughing or crying, Marianne hugs her friends for a last time as the taxi pulls in at the bottom of the steps.

'Phone me soon. Please! When they will be with Zaida.'

'Mind the future! Can't explain now. Never mind! Get a lover, will you, *mon amie*?'

The next two days will be busy for the two women left in charge of the clinic while Walter and Ian are in London applying for tourist visas. Waving through the open window, taking a last look at the house, Marianne swears to herself she will phone every day until her friends are back with the child. The late light picks out the borders, throwing into relief the patchwork of trim and wild across the garden. A perfect balance between bushes, flowers and lawn, emanating a serenity that masks the family troubles.

– 14 –

Meeting the Al-Sayeds

IN NO TIME FROM DAMASCUS AIRPORT, IAN AND WALTER have found themselves in a stunning house in the core of the legendary city. Already disoriented by the rashness of their move, both men are further unsettled by the master's absence.

Hiding his own puzzlement at their presence behind a florid complexion, the unflappable Dr Abdul Al-Sayed speaks in well-crafted Queen's English, repeating his message carefully so as to be understood by these foolish people. He has just arrived from Hama, the family home; regrettably, his son could not cancel a business commitment but he will be back shortly. Walter apologises yet again for the untimely visit, bearing in mind a tactical agreement with Ian: at first they will take things as they come.

The doctor seems a reassuring man, modest and cheerful, Ian observes to himself. Someone they hope to trust, unlike that sinister-looking man, with burning eyes above an ugly scar, who was rushing out of the house with a retinue of people, one in military uniform, just when they came in through an entrance door so low that everyone had to duck. 'My brother Omar is an important man.' No need to say. Ian wonders at the timing – did they wait for the taxi, intending to intimidate the foreigners with a show of strength? Why would they? Khalid had betrayed no hostility when they called from Leaford announcing their imminent Syrian tour, Walter wishing to grasp a once-in-a-life chance to travel with his son and, God willing, to renew his friendship with the Al-Sayeds and possibly take Zaida out for a few treats. The explanation appeared candid enough then, but now it is as implausible as a pope protesting interest in gay rights.

Ian smiles at the older men outdoing each other's politeness and good wishes like two palace courtiers. Sitting at a low copper table, they relax, absorbed by the display of courtesy and elaborate sweetmeats. A lean grey-haired woman, dressed in a white blouse tucked into a long brownish skirt, shuffles in, bringing fruit juice, minted water and dried fruit.

'Mariyam Ajemian. Our fine cook.'

In recognition of her name, she bends her head towards the guests, unsmiling, varicose hand over the crucifix hanging from her neck, then she disappears behind a plain black curtain.

They chat amicably for a couple of hours, making the most of the interlude created by Khalid's absence, about the Damascus sites and potential trips to Palmyra and Aleppo. And pious Hama, of course. Walter and Abdul enjoy sharing their jaded views of the world. The clinic isn't doing too well. It's impossible to get money out of the banks these days. Who will pay for the crisis? Not the Americans!

Abdul has taken to retirement like a duck to water, writing poetry as a new member of the Syrian Union of Arab Writers and studying the lost cities of Mesopotamia, although only Allah knows the past.

'The modern world is nothing but trouble.'

'There's no fair play in business.'

'No honour anywhere. Not even among intellectuals.'

One of his nephews could be in trouble at the Higher Institute of Translation and Interpretation of Damascus University. Khalid will have to pull strings on his behalf. Family is family. Sharply aware of the irony, Abdul stops talking, unwilling to say more.

Left to his own thoughts, the house retains Ian's attention. Authentic Damascene houses were built like forts around open courtyards for coolness and security reasons, Abdul explained. The square is shaded by awnings of white cloth flapping high above an octagonal marble fountain adorned with taps shaped like birds. The floor is covered with a mosaic of intricate blue, white and red geometric patterns. Four arched recesses act, Ian supposes, as sitting areas for the winter, with equally splendid floral patterns in gold and all shades of green. He glimpses musical instruments in the main *iwan*. Possibly an electric *oud*. That must be a bird cage hanging high up the stairs. Canaries? A fabulous place for a Leaford girl.

'Oh, here's Khalid.' The fountain gurgles on with insouciance as the men stare at the entrance from the stairs leading to the street. In rushes a clean-shaven man, his sharp features softened by a wide smile. They laugh, shout and bear-hug.

Taking a step back, Walter asks, surprised, 'Zaida is not with you?'

'She's at home in Hama. She's been over there for a few days. I thought you knew?' Khalid looks puzzled.

Walter gestures frantically, knocking a tray onto the floor. 'Sorry, let me pick it up. Khalid, I'm pleased to see you looking so well.' He stretches both hands out to his ex-son-in-law. There follow more greetings, lukewarm this time.

'My father is very tired. With the journey. And disappointed with Zaida being away. He's missed her so much.'

'We came to meet my granddaughter,' Walter explodes.

Despite the tinkle of the water spouts, the silence thickens until, stone-faced, Abdul pats his son on the shoulder; and Ian, in a similarly appeasing mood, grasps his father by the elbow.

'My sister is worried about Zaida.' He keeps his voice low and non-threatening.

'How come? Since when?'

'Since the return flight was delayed.'

'We let you know about it. On time. I believe we are honourable people.' Hardly containing his anger, Khalid pronounces these last words one by one, as if dictating to an idiot.

Inwardly fuming, Ian ignores the offensive tone while diverting the conversation onto safer grounds: the house, the trips to the Krack du Chevalier or to Aleppo's citadel. Woeful, Walter does not say anything until Khalid brings the diversion to a halt.

'Aren't you a reasonable man, Walter? But why do you behave as if we have committed a crime? Because I didn't oblige you in exchange for—'

Ian splutters an apology before Walter has time to put his foot in it again.

'I'm sorry we've offended you. The journey was tiring and my father's under a lot of pressure at home. Listen, it's a misunderstanding – quite simply, we hoped to see Zaida tonight, that's all there is to it.'

Ian gives a placating smile, wishing he had come on his own. He takes a paper hanky out of his hand bag to wipe his face and hands, not knowing whether it is the lack of fresh air or the tension that unnerves him most.

'We've arranged for you to be driven to Hama tomorrow after a good night's rest.'

Walter stomps around the fountain in a rage, making dismissive gestures, mumbling, 'Wild goose chase. Gosh! I'm whacked.' He drops into his seat, slouching back. Ian nudges him with a sharp elbow until Walter sits up straight.

Looking like thunder, unable to quarrel out of consideration for a distressed man, Khalid refrains from pointing out that

Zaida pleaded to stay on, waking up sobbing, angry. 'Mummy only cares for her patients,' she wailed. The girl never tires of drawing an aggressive-looking witch who will help fly her mother to Syria. How sad that tale makes him feel! In no way is he letting the intruders near his own pain! He hastens out after exchanging a few words in Arabic with his father.

A manservant carries in the invaders' luggage. Abdul signs to him to drop the two suitcases by the iron-wrought steps leading to the top floors.

'Abdul, I apologise to you and your son for any hurt I might have caused. I don't know what came over me. I'm jet-lagged, I guess. Please forgive me. I'm spoiling our reunion. Sorry, my friend!'

'It's OK. I also apologise for Khalid. But consider his position. You burst into his home as if we have kidnapped Zaida. However regrettable, he had to leave the room.'

'I understand. Let's retire. I'll speak to Khalid tomorrow morning and hopefully make amends.'

Abdul assures them that they will be treated well, with the attentive consideration that Syrian families like to offer their guests. It is getting late. The servant will take them to their rooms and a cold meal will be served on the upper terrace in one hour. Breakfast will be at eight by the fountain. At 10, they will be driven to Hama where Zaida, very excited, is helping to prepare festive dishes; she's spent the last two days rehearsing dances of welcome. Praise Allah to have given him an English granddaughter keen to learn Syrian ways. With rueful smiles, the grandfathers congratulate each other.

It is seven in the morning in Hama. Ian is getting ready for a jog with Khalid on a path winding through the main city park alongside the river. An intriguing invitation. A male bonding exercise? To escape relatives? Whatever. He must protect his fair skin from the November sun. While applying coats of Gucci creams on arms, face and neck he reflects on the last two days, which have not gone badly. What tickled him was observing Zaida. At ease. Affectionate. With fire in her belly. She thanked him for bringing her grandfather in a well-rehearsed speech; she was not shy of him – that pleased him. She asked if he liked *her* family. He said yes, as much as playing chess. She laughed, saying it was more fun in Damascus, then she blushed – 'I don't want to criticise', falling silent, arms crossed against a timid chest.

'Your father told me you are learning the *oud*. What do you like best, the instrument or the music?

'Both.'

'Is that why you want to stay longer? I bet you've got other reasons.'

Did she look up straight at him? Intense perusing eyes above plump little cheeks. His heart went out to the alarmed adolescent peeping from the body of the child, pleading and torn, as he had been for long agitated years when his mind and body were at war with each other.

'Is Lascha helping?

'Mummy told you?'

'I can do anything for you since I'm... Bob's your uncle.'

She hung on his arm, chatting. She had two new dolls from Aleppo. Blonde and dark. 'Lascha is a wizard and Xenobia, an Arab princess.'

'Quite a family,' he said cautiously.

'I love them to bits.'

'I bet you tell them stories?'

She did not answer, staring beyond him, drifting into her own loneliness.

'Let me see.' As though taming an unknown species, he slowly moved one step closer, raising her left hand and turning the palm over, feeling the softness of her skin and trust.

'You've nervous fingers with long tapering nails like a spider. Absolutely right for a dancer!' Her eyes twinkled.

'The life line here and the heart line tell me things about you. You're self-assured. And success and happiness will follow you whatever you do.'

'You're making it up! What else?'

'Those short lines on the side, they're unusual for a girl – they are called travel lines! See, they don't fade out.'

He was not fibbing, not quite – she was understanding that too. How he wishes Clint could have seen him, avuncular, making contact with the child.

Hama has turned up trumps. Particularly at night. A full moon sketched the silhouettes of olive and fruit trees out of the invisible terraces lining the river. Sitting in the open, the party admired the scented view. The Al-Sayeds repeated with good reasons that the fertile land below had been theirs for generations until stolen by the Ba'athist town council after the troubles. To forget their loss, the men drank an Egyptian beer once Halima and the women had left with the younger children. As Abdul played an Arabian fiddle and Khalid a small drum, Lilleth danced with the natural grace and application of a tutored adolescent who is soon to become a woman. Zaida joined her cousin after throwing off her voluminous headscarf. She did her best, trying to wobble imaginary boobs, until the two girls collapsed into fits of laughter. They were clapped. Walter, delighted, pointed out she had gone totally blonde like Grandma Gwen. According to Abdul and Khalid, the day after she arrived, she had wanted her hair – too wavy and too blonde – straightened out and dyed black, something they had to refuse. The Franklins joined the banter. When asked to go to bed, she took little steps backwards, joining her hands against her chest, mimicking a geisha's bow while keeping the immobility of her stare, a kind of constant questioning. Is she far too mature for her age? Is that what Virginia said?

Jogging along the slow-moving Orontes, Ian and Khalid are catching up with a gaggle of trendy-looking runners with sunglasses, smartphones and Kickers. The songs of the norias grow faint as they leave the bank. Playgrounds are still closed but breakfast and ice-cream bars begin to fill with a few men. Ian jaunts along, quite a picture in his electric blue tracksuit, sleeves rolled up; punching his fists in the air like an American paratrooper, indifferent to hostile looks from onlookers sitting on the peeling benches. He has to hasten his pace to keep up with Khalid before squeezing through an exiguous gate at the far end of the park. They run down a street lined with prosperous residences sighted through locked gates; they pass by colourless institutions of power – a town hall, a police station and a state-run bank – until they duck their way into a narrow passage between walls overflowing with bougainvilleas that takes them back to the chattering river.

'As I said, last night was quite magical. Jazz and Syrian music together. Good stuff.'

Khalid holds back his own question – are you that interested in our Roman ruins? Instead, he says softly, '*You* are taking quite a risk by coming here.'

'Why? Me being gay? I had to for my father. It's the first time we've ever travelled together, just us two.'

'You are safe with me. Mind you, don't watch us men clapping and hugging each other. Hama is a puritan town. People are oversensitive towards Westerners. And everywhere there are people paid to patrol the streets and report anything they come across, however trivial. Or they make things up.' He takes on a more confessional tone. 'For me, you know, homosexuality is no problem, I'm a liberal – Greeks used to do it too.' After an uneasy pause, he says, 'At times they bring girls to my house, you see the type, but it doesn't take the heaviness from my heart.'

'You're missing my sister?'

'What if I do?' He grasps Ian by the shoulder. 'Don't trust anyone. I don't want you arrested.'

'Jesus, no! I have no need for thrills like that!'

'Remember, British and Canadian embassies can't help you here.'

Ian recalls Virginia telling him to heed her solicitor's advice – don't trust either the father or the son. If they have something up their sleeve, they will smother you with words and hospitality. For all that, how can he distrust the sadness of Khalid's eyes, the proud tilt of the chin? The man has invited him for a morning run to warn him. Fair enough.

Khalid stops in his track, belligerent but also hesitating to let the skeleton out of the cupboard. 'Your father! On the game like everyone else! I couldn't believe it. Wire £20,000 and keep Zaida a bit longer. Blackmailing me! Discrediting both families!'

Ian's outrage is not faked. 'Selling his granddaughter? The old man's off his head!'

'I was too ashamed to respond. Better let him think his email got lost. He's got a lot on his plate with the clinic and Zaida being away.'

'You're most generous. Anything else I should know?'

'Has Zaida talked to you about our chauffeur? Not yet! She has bad vibes. He's a spy! She's got too much imagination. She'd like me to sack him.'

'Why would anyone spy on you?'

'That's not the point. I offered him 500 dollars to tell me who he is working for. He refused.'

'Does that prove anything? You trust him then?'

'Come off it! In a dictatorship? Full of people ready to sell you! But Uncle Omar assures me the man is one of us. One of his protégés.'

'What will you do?'

'Nothing. I've long suspected he's a pretty normal fellow. Honest one day, corrupt the next. Like your city bankers.'

'Touché!'

As they walk and talk, the river sinks deeper into a channel dug out of the limestone plateau which surrounds Hama; pools swirl around the red and white stones that litter the bed and in shallow places there are patches of green water where young men can take a dip. Khalid runs just a few steps ahead. Should he overtake him? No, Khalid is too jumpy. He catches up though, shoulder to shoulder.

'Zaida is a real treasure. I can see why you'd keep her a while longer.'

'Don't!' Khalid stands still, looking daggers. 'You're my guest. You shouldn't take advantage of it. I'll repeat until my last breath – my daughter is as free as the wind. And I always respect your family. God bless you and Virginia.'

'No offence, officer, no!' Ian pleads innocence, hands up. Amused, Khalid jostles with him for a few seconds and, after checking there is nobody around, he clutches his arms around Ian's waist, squeezing the breath out of him. 'I've got you, man!'

'You're not that strong! But let me tell you something, even if you won't believe me.' They fool around for a while, releasing the tension of the previous days.

'I thought my girl was sending daily emails to her mother when she went to the internet cafés with her cousins, so it seemed OK to say let's delay her trip back. But all they did was play games.' They laugh at the cheek of the girl. 'She has no trouble leading us by the nose! Sincerely, I thought Virginia would understand.'

'I'll stick up for my niece. Quite a bundle of fun. And the stories she notes down are amazing. They come from Abdul, she says.'

'They do. Let's walk back. There's no rush.'

'How come your father is a member of the Writers' Union? Isn't he a doctor?'

'Retired. He has a collection of poems in print. In classical Arabic. The safest way to publish since nobody reads poetry anymore! Bless him! He likes nothing better than to recite love poems on the top terrace within earshot of our Alawite neighbours.'

'A form of protest? Is that being pushy?

'Could be, but Uncle Omar has no time for it. He's up to his neck with the regime.'

'They don't get on?'

'They're family. Virginia, you know, couldn't bear Omar. She took the measure of him the only time he came to Leaford. I was a dope, she said!'

'He supports the Al-Assads?'

'That has protected me. He's not a bad man. Under torture, you, anyone, changes side. You've read, of course, about people in Hama being slaughtered. Even today many people from this city aren't allowed to travel. Sunnis. Shias. That is what I've come back to; much worse than I expected. Two or three generations condemned to fear, voiceless. House arrests or disappearances never reported. All done in the name of countering Fundamentalists.'

Khalid looks around, apprehensive about having revealed too much. There is a dusty-looking man walking fast towards them carrying a string bag over his shoulder. 'A Coptic Christian from what's left of our Golan,' he whispers. The poorest of the poor, deep dark skin, prayer beads, threadbare pants, black front teeth ruined from chewing tobacco. Khalid buys a handful of wizened dates and sends the peddler off.

'Under Bashar Al-Assad, according to the West, you've had fewer conflicts with Iran, Iraq and Lebanon. Syria is opening up to tourism. We got our visas quickly. And nobody has arrested me yet.'

They stride past a large garden restaurant. Waiters set up white plastic chairs under Bedouin tents; thirsty-looking flowers hang in baskets; there is a scorched mini-golf course – the grass looks like cement, dry with neglect. A tourist trap.

'I'd like you to come to Vancouver and meet Clint.' Khalid is still his brother-in-law. Sensitive, volatile, querulous, full of ambivalences. Like me.

'Alright. When I am allowed to travel. Be sure I won't court any favours from the Ministry, but nobody survives here long without kowtowing sooner or later.'

'Are you thinking of leaving?'

'I have loads to do – people to contact, international contracts to sign.'

On a restored stone bridge linking the centre to the park, they contemplate the city.

'*Maktoub*. I'll stay until my father's dying day.'

'You were born here. Tell me more about the place.'

Hama glorified in its religious orthodoxy until February 1982 when a radical branch of Muslim Brotherhood forced a bitter fight with the militantly secular Ba'athist rulers. In the last-ditch battle much of the old city was destroyed. To the west, a forest of new minarets is cloaked in a soothing light. Prayers and memories point to the blank sky like shards of pain between shabby blocks of flats stacked up against the hills. Khalid turns round to gaze at a more pleasurable view over the other parapet: a string of norias working on both embankments. They watch, mesmerised by the water grinding its way up each wheel in a cacophony that has fascinated people for centuries.

'Listen!'

They hear a soft singing, then the wood moans and the patched-up beams crack under the effort of lifting full buckets, each wheel exhaling whimpers painful to the ear, full of despair. Then, on the way down, the water gurgles joyfully from the buckets.

'On good days, when the water is low, our poets hear a melody tinkling through the damned town. I can't. For them, the norias are resilient, like Syria. Joyful and despairing in turn, their voices convey the twinned emotions forming the essence of our humanity.'

'You like living here then?'

'I love it, I hate it. I am in exile in my own country, but also in your country. I love Britain, I hate it too. I was a good husband. She kicked me out. Liking, you said? We live on the edge of a sword. My chauffeur may be bribed, but by whom? I invited you for a jog to warn you both. I'm attending Friday prayers. Don't make trouble for me. There are people I'm helping. Anything in their favour can go against me. You came at the wrong moment. Hama and Aleppo are tenser than Damascus. I want no trouble. I am a business man. I need a passport.'

'To get back to Britain? What about your father?'

'I don't know.'

'And Zaida in all of this?'

A smile curls on Khalid's lips. 'She has dreams too! And under our laws she is old enough to live with her father. Anywhere. She's always known how much I love her.'

'Sorry, man.' Dry mouth, pretending indifference to the threat, Ian rakes his throat to spit onto a paper tissue.

'She's already pretty clued up. Able to explain her mind to a court.'

'A child!' Hiding his dismay, he looks away from the city to watch Khalid restlessly kicking a few pebbles into the parapet wall. Ian reaches out to give him a gentle punch in the chest. 'Come on! What's up?'

'"Is the tree in the courtyard for me or my neighbour?" A proverb of ours. We all know the answer, don't we?'

'That's silly. She isn't a tree!'

Dismissive of Ian's raised eyebrows, Khalid, distracted by his own thoughts, continues, 'We're really close, her and me. You've seen how well we care for her. And to her, Syria will always be more exciting than Leaford! Sure, there is a whole culture for her to pick at and fit around her. It is what we did, you in Vancouver and me in Britain. In the end, it's no big deal.'

'What? You've just told me you don't really belong anywhere. Of course it's a big deal. Cut her off from her roots? Look at you two! You live in fear. Abdul as well. Always watching who you talk to. Zaida won't fancy that for long. That's clear already. She can't stand your chauffeur!'

'Yes, you're right. But I keep dreaming because... I fear losing her for good.'

'I wish I could help... Even journalists can't read the future.'

'Ah! Let me tell you! In my country, everyone has dreams – big dreams. Shias, Sunnis, Copts, Kurds, Armenians, Iraqi refugees, Palestinian refugees, businessmen, arms dealers, poets, daughters wanting the moon and sons demanding Kalashnikovs at puberty. If God wills it, our dreams will tear Syria apart.' He stops, then, urgent: 'Turn round slowly. Show no fear.'

Security guards with machine guns block the road. There are two police vans parked on either side of the bridge, lights flashing. There are shouts. A man they cannot really see is being pushed and kicked into the vehicle. More shouts. A senior-looking man detaches himself from the fray and marches towards them, gesticulating orders. Khalid signs to Ian to come forward.

'No photos. Put that camera away. He wants to see our papers and mobiles.'

Ian glowers at a sudden stomach pain, wishing to send a last message to Clint. He wants to pee. Radio blinking in his front pocket, the officer – fresh-shaved, stout, pockmarked – skims the visa before inspecting Ian from head to foot, cold, scornful of the vulgarity of foreign tourists.

'You no English?'

'Canada.'

'Journalist?'

'Tourist.'

'You like Syria?'

'Yes, yes, I like Syria,' he exclaims with cynical enthusiasm.

In a wink, mobile and passport are returned by hands padlocked with gold rings. The urge to piss has gone. Why travel in a country whose street culture is alien to him? He is more shaken by the motherfuckers than he'd like to admit. Will they be his death?

'Don't say a word! Smile. Let's move on! Don't run!'

Families are drifting back. An ice-cream van shuffles past. Impatient to get away, Khalid grabs him by the arm when a tall guy with a fancy camera and a woman in tow waves to them.

'Do you speak English?'

An Arab. Handsome and well-off. Ian makes a quick assessment of the man dressed in a linen double-fronted suit, probably an outfit for a wedding. At ease with himself. The young woman says nothing, all smiles, a stunner in a white outfit. Heels, lacy stockings, a knee-high dress. Bright red lips under an elaborate scarf.

'Me speak English. Read book on your king with many many wife. A good man. You know him?'

'Henry VIII was... not a good man.'

'Oh? I see. My wife in French school. You like Syria?'

'Yes, very much.'

'*Pour quoi?*' She detaches the first syllable, high, from the second lower note.

'People are nice, very nice. Syria is a beautiful country. We have Syrian friends. Very good friends.'

The couple laugh.

'*Je prends photo de vous avec nous.*'

'Oh, *non, Madame!* Look at my clothes, I'm not good enough. *Désolé!*'

They gabble away looking half-offended, half-amused by his reluctance. Khalid snarls, 'They don't mind what you look like. They just want you on their photo for good luck. It's their honeymoon. Get on with it.'

Resigned, Ian takes off his sweatband and brushes dust from the flamboyant tracksuit, aware of damp patches spoiling the top. The guards have melted away. Free of fear, people arrive for their morning walks. There is no agitation left from the arrest by the benign bridge. Innocent photos are taken, posed in front of the chattering water wheels. The norias bewail, sing or mock in turn the newly married couple who cannot keep their eyes off each other – the foreigner snapped accidentally in their midst and immediately forgotten.

'Don't tell anyone you're a journalist, or there'll be trouble.'

They walk back across the park where an unruly football game is taking place among frantic skinny-looking adolescents. 'Listen, they all speak Farsi. Iranians. Trouble, trouble!' Khalid's face mists over because Syria is a puzzle without solution. Not a good place for a princess, English or Arabic. He stops walking, rubbing his hands together in torment, eyes riveted to Ian's, blurting out, 'I'm afraid, you hear me? They can destroy me, the whole of me, not just physically. They won't kill me but I'm scared they'll destroy my self-respect, the humanist core of me. Is that meant to happen?' He takes a step back, dismissive. 'How can you understand? Virginia didn't in the end! But reassure her, since that's why you've come. I won't let Zaida see me give up my dreams. That's a fact.'

There are crippling currents of fears and resignation in Khalid that he begins to understand, together with wallops of generosity and no bluster. How can he really help? That's what has become crucial to him.

– 15 –

Touring Syria

THOUGH ZAIDA WOULD HAVE LOVED A TRIP TO PALMYRA to meet the legendary Queen Zenobia, the Al-Sayeds refuse to take their guests there. The same Ba'athist gang who slaughtered 500 Muslim Brothers in the town prison are still in control, they say. Instead, Walid will drive the two families to Qala'at Al-Hosn, to the west of Hama.

Never looking at the passengers directly, head inclined forward, the chauffeur fusses over them, gesturing to make sure they settle comfortably. The man communicates well, they say, though he has no English to speak of.

The car looks like a Peugeot, but with a horse as a logo. This is puzzling. Abdul points out the irony.

'It's indeed based on a 405, but it's put together in our factory with parts made in Iran. Of course, it is a Syrian car! President Assad drives only Shams.'

'*Sham*? Meaning "horse"?'

'Not quite. It means "sun" in Arabic. And it's the name given to prestigious Arabian thoroughbreds.'

They leave behind prosperous olive groves and irrigated crops for a desert dominated by the rugged Ansariyya Mountain dividing the mainland from the coastal strip. Having agreed not to discuss Zaida's return until back from their sightseeing, they enjoy the landscape with the innocence of people believing mankind is in charge of nature. The adults admire complex irrigation systems of lakes and canals that protect fertile land from encroaching wind and sand. Zaida, accepting that Palmyra is too far for a day trip, forgets her sulks, and points, amused, at desultory flocks of goats.

A good hour later, the girl runs from one adult to the other, tugging at their hands up and down the steps of Qala'at al-Hosn, the cavernous fortress built by twelfth-century Knights of St John. Inspired by the panoramic view over the Jebel, Zaida orders her party to sit at a round table made of gigantic stones. The four knights are happy to listen to their lady's demand. The party decides not to go back to Hama as planned but to stay together for a couple of nights since they are getting on so well. A hotel in Aleppo will be booked. The truce is so solid that they all sign the postcard to Gwen. Virginia's simply reads: "I wish you were here, Mum."

Abdul suggests a detour to a Greek orthodox monastery at the bottom of the hill where he would like to give some money to charity, a monastery dedicated to St George. To his delight, the Franklins look astonished. Throughout the Middle East, Muslims have venerated St George under the name of Mar Girgis, a Palestinian Christian conscripted and later executed by the Roman army; and they have prayed in his churches to warn off the evil of both plague and madness.

'Surely Muslims don't believe in superstitions?' Ian asks with a tinge of provocation.

'Tut tut! Is that a good enough reason to ignore a legend? What do you think, my *Shaden?*'

'Let's go and see the dragon now,' says the skittish gazelle, jumping into the back seat.

'Do tell us why *you* want to go to this place, Abdul?'

'Grandfather trusts the old monks to give the poor his money,' Zaida is sitting smug as a bug between her grandfathers – they argue too much, that's the truth – as Walid drives round steep bends to the stone-walled compound of the monastery.

Why is the car slowing down suddenly on the deserted road to Aleppo? They have just passed a limestone hill and, scattered at the bottom, a few round huts, the shape of domed beehives, made of burgundy-coloured clay. Walid is letting through another herd of fractious goats – about 20, mostly white and darkish grey; indignant, bleating at the intruders blocking their way to the village.

'You funny! Look at that beard!' The passengers applaud the silky and long-necked animals hurtling along the Sham. Ian too waves back frantically before settling into the seat, making sure Zaida has enough room to squeeze between her grandfathers. She dreams of a world, he reflects, where East and West merge – unlike her dad, who appears to dread a darker future. What did he let slip? 'If things blow up here, you and us, will we still be family?' What was that about?

Zaida is calling them to come back to the car. Oddly enough, she doesn't trust the adults talking together out of earshot. She interrupts, asks for their attention. She bursts into song and dance and then runs out in floods of tears. She eavesdrops, pulls the strings, fools everyone – why didn't she send Virginia more emails from that internet café? Quite a darling, though she may be playing up? Why not? He himself was good at playing his parents against each other!

They are driving through a barren eerie landscape of sand dunes dotted with austere crags mimicking the ruined watchtowers of vast stone citadels. Now and then ghost dwellings hang onto the roadside, wild dogs stumbling out of stone barns. There are also signs of more sophisticated buildings. Villas? Churches? Abdul tells Zaida the occupants of the dead villages have gone to settle along new trade routes.

'Were they all Muslims?'

Abdul smiles. 'Mostly Sunnis, I expect, and Byzantine Christians.'

'They really lived together?' Zaida sounds unabashed. The child feeds on hope. Abdul and Walter exchange a knowing glance above her head, tacitly agreeing that there is no need to highlight the divisions that keep communities apart even when living on each other's doorstep.

'Christians, you know, are told to care for the wretched of the Earth, but many of us never do. We can't even love our neighbours! And what about your people?'

'Good men serve peace whatever their community.' The preacher detaches each word. 'By practising our *da'wa*. I mean... we must find ways of enticing good and repelling evil. That's an everyday duty for Sunnis. Not only on Fridays! It is what I want our new *madrassas* to teach.'

Walter catches in the middle mirror the reflection of Khalid in the front seat, wincing at his father's sermon. 'What's wrong with that?'

'Bashar Al-Assad. He used religious schools to end the Damascus spring—'

'Pardon?'

'When he took over from his father, people were organising clubs, cafés were filled with talk of reform. It only lasted a few months. Since then, the regime has encouraged Muslims to spend their energy on their daily practice, religious schools and charity institutions. To draw them away from open political debate. It worked. But I'm not criticising you, Father.'

'Don't you forget I've never taken orders from anyone! I'm too old for politics. I much prefer prayers and poetry to talk, talk, talk.'

Khalid turns round at Abdul's bitter tone. 'I'm sorry if I've offended you! God bless you, Father. Do you remember what you used to tell us kids in that Iraqi camp?'

'Tell us, Dad,' pleads Zaida.

'"Orange trees can grow out of tears." That image has worked for me.'

'Like magic?'

'In your country, no. In Syria, true enough!'

'No, it's the other way round.'

The following day, back in Hama, while Zaida is taken out by her relatives, Walter and Ian are chauffeured to the anthropological museum where they are keen to see exhibits found locally, so they read, dating as far back as the Neolithic period. The air-conditioning system is in overdrive and the clinical building is freezing but in a few well-lit rooms there are echoes of an older grandiose edifice.

'The museum was blown up in 1982. We won't talk about it here.' Khalid walks to a side window with a view onto the old city. 'Can you see the gap? The size of a football ground?'

'The bomb site. You were there?'

'Trapped in a water duct for hours!'

Taxing and conflicting feelings of horror and admiration make Ian gasp. Standing straight, eyes fixed on the trauma, Khalid murmurs words Ian cannot comprehend.

Though empty of visitors, the museum is bursting with interesting things from huge black basalt lions that once guarded a Bronze Age palace to Byzantine gold-leaf figurines with lapis eyes.

'The French didn't rob us; the occupation left the exhibits undisturbed. Had your people been here,' Abdul needles, 'wouldn't these things have become the jewels of the British Museum?'

In Room 24, where high walls are decorated with a pageant of dark green and red mosaics, Walter is engrossed by Sumerian stone tablets the size of a man's hand, covered with the world's earliest alphabets.

Whispering in his ear, Abdul grasps Walter by the elbow. 'Zaida could stay until Eid-al-Adha, on 23rd December. You need money, don't you, for the clinic? We borrow from the Russians and you from us, no problem.'

Good God! Is he being asked to sell Zaida in exchange for the loan? Walter pulls himself away, clutching his hands tight behind his back, heart thumping hard, the offer blowing him apart. Tempted? Afraid to refuse? Pacing the corridor outside, he reminds himself that what seemed sensible at home is shameful to him now.

By the entrance, he asks armed soldiers patrolling the hall where the toilets are. With tense smiles, they keep saying "rwelkem, rwelkem" until, desperate, he scratches his flies. One of them, with the shorn and sheepish look of a young recruit amenable to orders, guides him to the right door. An aseptic squat-in-the-hole cubicle like those that corner you on French motorways confronts him with its gaping horror. He looks around. This is the new part of the museum, concrete and ugly, which replaced toilets once used as seats of torture, Khalid said, when the whole area down to the Orontes was crushed to the ground. A model for the handling of any future opposition, armed or peaceful.

Back to Room 26, grateful that the others have pressed ahead, Walter moves between displays without paying them much attention. Should he let the Al-Sayeds keep his precious girl? He finds himself drumming his fingers on a glass pane protecting rows of seals and bilingual tablets of cuneiform writing, full of resentment against Virginia for not facing the music herself. Lacking consideration for him and Khalid.

What is best for Zaida in the long run? The history of mankind is in the girl's blood. Hama's tragedy will not be repeated. The regime needs the West. Visiting the Al-Sayeds has been an eye-opener. They love the girl dearly; she is blooming. They would protect her with all their power as noble Sunnis with ancestors dating back to Muhammad – that's Abdul's words. Raised in Britain, she will turn at best into an ironic woman detached from her Christian heritage.

Why torture himself like this? Normally, Abdul is a level-headed man like himself. The issue is not about Zaida settling permanently but staying for another five weeks at most. This wouldn't be the end of the world. The girl will be back around Christmas. And after that, what can happen? Will the Syrian authorities let Khalid travel every year to see his daughter and then return to Damascus? How can one be sure of that? It is a quagmire of uncertainties.

A few days in Syria have stripped him of the vital layers of authority and confidence that cushioned him in Leaford. How he wishes he was home now, explaining a subtle treatment! The image – wise man, admiring colleagues, overwhelmed patient, subdued daughter – dampens his spirit further. Yet, that is what he is: the uncontested head of a declining practice, authoritarian and a know-all. Ian couldn't take it and had to leave. Tyrannical, that's what he was, putting pressure on Virginia to stick to his own style of acupuncture. Syria has dispossessed him of his certainties. He is done in and has no idea what his granddaughter needs from him. And he knows nothing of Syria's long history. The glass cases are filled with incomprehensible labels that make him squint. Damn it. He knows nothing whatsoever. And worse, he feels sick.

What can he tell Zaida? She too has been playing games by not answering all her mother's emails. 'Couldn't be bothered,' she said. She wants the impossible – both families together. Realistically, is one family more deserving than the other? Stirred by the question, Walter stops in front of a well-preserved clay pot the size of a watermelon. It is a funereal urn, that of a small child, buried in the floor of a Bronze Age kitchen. Ordinary folks kept their dead close to them. The beauty of it affects him deeply in ways he cannot quite fathom, and to regain his composure he twiddles with the pack of needles he always carries in his trouser pocket.

'Are you alright?'

Smiling, a middle-aged woman in a brown gown, heavy gold earrings peeking from beneath a brightly coloured scarf, has joined him in front of the burial items. They exchange the statutory questions – where are you from and how many children do you have? – in a matter of seconds. She speaks English, French and Italian, having lived four years in Florence.

'Syria is getting safer, better with President Assad. I have four children, you want them to go to university, it's difficult, our president is clever. Tell your people at home.'

Would an English woman bat for her country unprompted like that? Or is this woman paid to accost foreigners?

Time to join the others. Ian is already waiting outside the museum gate. A few tents have been set up on the large space, left empty once its houses were demolished one by one, as a memorial against any future rebellion. Flags with a crescent and a red cross tell them what is going on at present. Animated boys and girls of about 10, dressed in red and white uniforms, surround dummies laid on the floor to practise what seem to be first aid exercises. With a microphone and shoulder-high camera, a Muslim woman, beautifully made-up, presents herself in French. She would like to interview the foreigners for the main radio channel: Where are you from? Do you like Syria? The Syrian Red Crescent? Our president?

Ian quips in French, 'President Assad is a good man. His First Lady was born and educated in Britain. My brother Khalid married my sister. She is English too.'

The journalist hoots with delight at a perfect censor-friendly response.

A hefty-looking man in his fifties, tanned prematurely into old age by the desert sun, addresses the foreigners in ebullient

English with an offer of beads and bracelets, chains and necklaces, which he conjures out of invisible bags sewn into a swirling grey gown. They like the trick. He is a Badawi, a Bedouin normally herding goats and camels south of Palmyra. His wife and eight children make the jewellery. Times are hard. Wells have dried up, there is salt in the water and leaks from the drilling. Impressed by the man's patter and the size of his *kuffiya*, Walter and Khalid bargain for a delicate necklace inlaid with turquoise beads. 3000 Syrian pounds are not too much for Zaida. Will the chain lose its shine? Base metal, not sterling silver? The idea of being cheated enrages Walter, who is usually capable of bargaining effectively.

What about the real negotiation over his granddaughter? He starts panting and rushes back to the museum, past the bemused attendants to the loo where bitter greenish liquid slithers out of his stomach with lunchtime salads. Liver and kidney are at war with each other. Drained of energy, he shuffles back to his people waiting anxiously under the entrance arch.

'Too much travelling, it's getting me down,' he apologises.
'I'll give you a treatment back at the hotel if you guide me.'
'Great, son, I'm game,' he croaks, patting his pocket.

Late in the evening, Ian and Clint share their anxieties in a long call.
'Is Walter OK?'
'The heat, the worry, it's taking its toll. Looked really ill this afternoon but he's pulling through after that treatment.'
'How come?'
'He is water-deficient, he said, and we went from that. I loved it but he won't consult a proper doctor about his heart.'
'Why not?'
'Allopathic medicine is against his principles. Statins? Mere poison! He wants to treat himself with his own system.

Show us the way, I suppose. Out of an integrity, not just the inflexibility I used to detest.'

'Good work, guys. Fancy having his son back! As in your birthday book.'

'What about the end – the nasty eagle, the tomb?'

'Whoops-a-daisy!'

– 16 –

By Themselves

STIRRED BY THE DECISION TO LET WALTER AND IAN VISIT Syria, Virginia paces her bedroom reading for the hundredth time the email she received the day they left.

Sorry, Mum, for not being in touch. In Hama they won't let me go out with my cousins. We go to the mosque and I don't understand the prayers. It's boring. I am missing you, Mummy. Lascha will zoom over and drop you here if you don't come on your own.

That's fighting talk! Virginia beams at the thought of Zaida claiming that Lascha has been on overdrive, flying two relatives across, and not just one.

I had a bit of blood in my knickers. Don't fuss, my cousins – who are nice girls – look after me. They have given me a bra. I don't like it, I don't wear it. Daddy is in Damascus and I am missing both of you.

She is proud of her girl. Despite that bad timing, Zaida doesn't seem too daunted and, fingers crossed, she'll be spared further bleeding. She doesn't mention any cramp. Is she trying to spare her mum? It is a real shame mother and daughter have been robbed of that first time together, sharing confidence openly: 'Did your tummy hurt, Mummy, first time? What did you do?' How crucial! Being at strangers' can't have been that comforting, although Khalid roped in his sister. He is sensitive to women's matters; at heart, a deeply romantic man. And so devoted.

She searches for the postcards she found in the trunk. The most recent shows the popular waterwheels of Bechriyyat with water cascading down five meters. "When I was a kid I loved riding the highest noria. One day, I'll show you how to dive at the weir. Love from Dad, who misses you so much."

She too has kept a few of his letters from a long time ago when he promised the English bride that he would ride the norias for her. She gropes for her breasts, flabby and redundant, yearning for the tart smells of sex. Did her grandparents turn in their graves when she screwed a Muslim? Puritans, they were! But not Gwen and Walter.

She should have gone instead of Ian. At the airport, Zaida, gobsmacked, rushing, dissolving with laughter, throwing her arms around her and pushing Khalid forward for the blissful reception, the two families together at last. She should have gone, let waves of hope wash over her. Could she care for Khalid again? Would she want to?

She hurries across the garden, shocked to feel a slight pressure between her legs, a tingling urge – rather indecent. Is she overripe fruit? The thought tickles her pink. Relieved to see that the waiting room is empty, she has time to shoo away ill-timed delights.

Patrick the rogue is unusually late.

To people like him and Mary, she chants the benefits of self-healing, but what about herself? She too has been stuck in stagnant emotions, re-enacting the scripts of raw infantile resentment.

Better start now by looking up a well-known site her father would belittle. Biting her lips, she scribbles points down in a rush as though hiding a dirty secret. Rueful. Of course, she is her own woman: confident, trusting, receptive, flowing, in charge of herself. She loves the image, but the next minute she mocks her presumption, longing for Zaida embracing her. Pray Walter help her put a call through tonight. Emails are too clinical.

Patrick Brookside watches Virginia in a pristine lab coat spraying surfaces with antiseptic as his wife would have done, light on her feet, bursting with good news. The lady is short and is no dark beauty but she has a startling vivacity that is compelling for an intelligent man like him. She won't remain single now the daughter is old enough to not be in the way. Personally he has never been for people mixing their blood. English and French, only trouble; to get better jobs, Irish lads marry our girls, just like the Poles. He still remembers the GI mongrel posted at Greenham Common who married the first wench he proposed to. Those two were divorced within two years as the English lass didn't want to live in a New Orleans backwater. Blacks marrying white girls, that's foul. But his marriage to Edna was a true union – that's the truth, without being romantic about it.

Since she can see through him just like his wife could, he doesn't say much as she needles his wrists and his legs. Because he has some dough on the side, they pester him with promotions for rejuvenating baths, testosterone tests he can't be bothered with or counselling for the over-sixties. They stink! So what if he's losing his marbles a bit? He doesn't need to be told his whatsit isn't as good as it used to be! He loves a good massage though. When the lass spreads cream on his legs, he, eyes tight shut, heals at the touch of Edna's hands.

As he searches for the car keys in his trousers, his mind drifts back to their honeymoon in Majorca, where Edna first anointed him with sun cream, from a blue and yellow Piz Buin tin box, messing around on the dunes where they had their privacy. She was a waif in those days, her waist so teeny he could make a ring of it with his hands. She had a big heart. He spoilt her, making sure she never saw the dirty bits in his mags. Never. He taught her everything. In the forces, they look after you; they let you take your nookie where you can. There's nothing wrong with old British values. And now he has Virginia Franklin to thank. She raises his spirit, as she says. Don't make me laugh. Nowt to do with bloody needles and Chinese grass! How daft can you be? The old fella will make it this time – to Scarisbrick Road. It isn't that far. It can't be bad for you to clock out when giving it a shot.

All day Gwen coaxes staff, takes bookings and rearranges appointments to cover for Walter's absence, her outward calm belying her worries. Her gratification shines through when she shows people how the practice has been refurbished but will the new look carry the clinic through the next decade?

The cars have gone. She is glad to have refused the invitation to dine with Sue, one of those well-meaning people who in time of crisis keep stifling you with a concern against which there should be a remedy. No more speculating with her about the Al-Sayeds' welcome, or the two families' whereabouts. They will be back soon enough with plenty of tales for them all to enjoy. With Virginia out at a concert in Birmingham, she does a few jobs before leaving the clinic in time for the late news programme.

The work will help rein in thoughts of the empty house across the yard. In an M&S linen frock where quality wins over design, glasses perched on a prominent nose, hair permed, radiating fortitude, she flips through the evaluation sheets collected at the end of the Acupuncture For Children course, run by Sue and Andy. As usual there is a high degree of satisfaction and yet, regrettably, she may have to cancel the winter session since only a couple of people have registered so far. The pool of acupuncturists who can afford further training is shrinking fast.

What about the accounts? Walter is unwilling to discuss the situation with her. 'Leave it to us,' he says. She resents the assumption that she is uninterested in the business side of the clinic, particularly when fewer punters take up the in-house courses that are so expensive to run. Why keep her out of the discussions with Andy and that second-rate accountant who would have messed up their tax returns a few years ago, had she not pointed out his mistakes? When the cat's away the mice will play. She flicks open the latest Excel sheets. A shortfall of £30,000 is predicted by the end of the next financial year. How bad is it? She will tackle her husband when he is back next week. Would the bank lend them the missing sum?

Gwen closes the file, her thick-skinned confidence ruffled. Khalid has not mentioned a loan, nor the preposterous email, Walter conceded on the phone when she probed.

Marianne's daily call interrupts Gwen's train of thought. They share the good news. The two families plan sightseeing together. It was a short call – the Hama line was cut off – but it was thrilling to catch a "hello Granny"!

The following day, Gwen looks at the rose beds critically. Too many suckers, too much powdery mildew. This autumn, severe pruning is required to counteract the neglect. She unscrews the cap of a concoction devised by her mother and, ready to spray, waves to Virginia, who is tending to Zaida's patch with the gardener.

'I was thinking of that Patrick of yours. He has a crush on you!'

They smile, knowing there is no harm in the man, only a corroding loneliness; and as he says, one treatment does him more good than a dozen lagers.

They are doing well holding the fort in the absence of husband and brother. They hug briefly.

'Mum, I'd give anything to be a fly on the wall! Right now they are touring Zaida's dream castle! Or was that yesterday? I don't know!'

'I'm thrilled they're getting on so well. Your father has forgotten the clinic. That has never happened before!'

'What if they're being fooled into thinking all is well?'

'They've three passports and three flight tickets, they'll be back soon. Trust them!'

'The calls are so short!' She picks the secateurs from her mother's basket and angrily deadheads a few withered roses, which she lets drop onto the ground. She works fast while her mother watches the arched back, the knitted brows, the refusal to let go.

'Mind my Abbaye de Cluny!'

Virginia pretends not to hear as she drags the plastic basket to the vegetable patch, lurching over young shoots poking through the gravel. Jesus Christ! How stupid to have bamboo! As saplings they trip you up, and fully grown they make you look short and fat. Ouch! She presses her lips onto the pearl of blood running down her right forefinger, sucks hard and spits the thorn out while shaking her hand, annoyed with herself for being so careless, so sloppy with Mum, so cross at Ian earning yet more brownie points. Mind you, to give her parents their due, they also made a fuss over Khalid from day one, treating him like another son, spoiling them both rotten because they have balls! Of course, she was the dumb daughter, the predictable and dependable one who would return home! And she did!

Heck! It still hurts, there's another bit of thorn left. It serves her right. Outside the acupuncture room she is altogether too slapdash. As her mother goes in, she follows, sucking her finger, a miasma of longing taking over. Whenever Khalid has visited Leaford he has been appreciative not only of her work but also of her appearance – her innate modesty and grace. Fancy him still saying these sweet things! A rare talent, according to patients complaining of husbands cold at the table and frozen in bed until death do them part! The woman under treatment is not really the sick one, but what can you do?

She rummages for a Boots first-aid pack Gwen keeps in the reception desk. Sticking a white plaster on, she remembers that, bizarrely, Marianne had advised against letting Khalid leave. Somewhat pompously, her friend declared, 'Parenting, more so than marriage, can be shaped and cut for different fits. Act positive!' And even on the phone, shameless Marianne recommends seduction! Echoing Angela Wright, who had singled out cases where the offer of sex was used to trick the ex into bringing back the child.

Have an affair with the father of her missing child? A good man, certainly, but constrained by traumatic times! Oh! The joy of Zaida flying home soon! No need to think the unthinkable. She bursts into smiles as she pushes the first-aid kit back into the drawer. Would she have screwed Khalid to get the girl back? Too late. Tearful, she wipes her face with the silk handkerchief Zaida gave her.

What will her baby look like? In need of rest. Brimming with stories, she'll sound quite grown-up at first. Or shy away from questions. Virginia skips out of the office, hearing her voice: 'Mum, Mum, I'm dying to go back to school!'

The indoor plants do not need watering and feeding. What annoys Gwen is the ficus, a dingy plastic addition by the interior designer that gives the annex the air of a cheap *hôtel de charme 2 étoiles tout confort*. She will drag the ghastly thing out with Zaida's help. Well, not really. They'll have to give her their full attention, without making her feel bad about having to be fetched.

She turns to a glass cabinet, where dozens of pie birds have found prime place in front of a mirror placed at the back so that the objects and their reflections give the uncanny effect of a multitude. Patrick Brookside whistles "four and twenty blackbirds" whenever he comes in. What a hoot! Time to do some dusting. At the risk of being obsessive, she keeps cotton buds, paper tissues and white vinegar in the desk for that purpose. As she wipes beaks and contorted necks the size of sunflower seeds, she wonders how Walter is coping with the trip; it can't be good for his heart. With rapid strokes, she brushes the glazed folds of the feathers, unable to forgive her husband for refusing any drug to relieve arterial pressure. He's as stubborn as Ian. She'd love to know how those two are getting on. In the long run, Ian will manage to make a good living anywhere. He has bags full of curiosity, talent and warmth; and the knack of getting his way with all sorts, as Marianne said. He should settle well to journalism. Virginia, if the clinic went to the wall, would never learn another trade. And how will they keep the clinic running when Walter goes? Gwen rubs hard her favourite creature lying in her palm as if forcing it back to life before placing the amulet on the shelf, safe, shiny black and yellow under the mirror light, throbbing with reflections.

Back in Chateau Mourel, Marianne cocks her head to listen to house martins bickering under the eaves while making the bed, satisfied that it shows no more sign of her shenanigans. The flight back is booked for the three of them! Last night, uplifted by the tremendous news, she pleased herself, as happens when there is no partner on the menu. She celebrated by herself, waves of joy pouring into her.

Waking up, she continues to rejoice. Getting Ian and Walter out there was the right strategy in spite of Virginia's misgivings. Her pride blends with the astonishment at things working out so well.

To calm herself, she resumes the routine that never fails to steady her by transporting her to the girls' dormitory where a well-made bed was seen as the apex of obedience, personal hygiene and a pure mind. Literature had been French since *Tristan et Iseut*; Art resided solely in Le Louvre; History and

Religion had the knack of betraying *le Peuple*. Unlike internet generations, she was taught by acerbic females in awe of the subjunctive, harsh on mediocrity, patois and spelling, who believed in the power of books to combat womb-shaped destinies; praised for thinking for herself. Will Zaida be equally fortunate when wired up to social networks? How can she grow through the rupture from the Al-Sayeds? Which talismans will she hang on to? Prayers and books in Arabic, and what else?

Virginia won't change, paralysed by distrust and pessimism. She was still doubting that dramatic call from Aleppo, saying she can't be in seventh heaven until she sees them. Never mind! There will be no drawn-out lawyers' war.

With orderly gestures, she folds up her Thai silk pyjamas and rearranges the two pillows. No-one can accuse her of neglecting her duties! She is untied, thoroughly liberated from that 17-year-old self. Owing to Ian. Friendly enough, he helped her shred what little was left of the romance, an imprint for the paper basket. Jolly good! Good riddance to her befuddled yearnings for the Franklins. Virginia sees in her a needy orphan, always on the lookout for substitute parents. Certainly, she has taken to the Franklins instinctively; and not just because father and son are irresistible. She saw in them that sense of the common good and discipline, generosity and respect for civic values that her godmother was also nurturing in her. Let Zaida carry the baton!

– 17 –

Aleppo's Citadel

HOTEL AL-RAIS, WITH OODLES OF CHARACTER INSIDE AND a sprawling rooftop terrace, could not be better situated. The 18th-century hotel is close to Bab Antakya, a medieval gate leading to the thriving heart of Aleppo and the Christian warren of Al-Jeida. On Friday, as night falls, throngs of Muslims join Christian and Jewish crowds who jostle past each other, as they have done for centuries, in the narrow stone-flagged lanes to patronise shops, bars and restaurants sprouting in the courtyards. Abdul shines with good will when his friends congratulate him on the booking. A World Heritage site, Aleppo has much to offer to all faiths. They had better not lose any time. After choosing rooms facing a leafy inner courtyard, the group splits up.

Ian switches off the television, where what seems like a burlesque opera has replaced the generally unintelligible news. At least he could make some sense of the political importance of an international weightlifting event, fascinated by the shivering Syrian flags tattooed on chests and biceps. Then more suicide bombers in Iraq. It struck him that he had not missed the news all that much... McCain and Obama bickering over the right number of troops to withdraw in 2013, as if politicians could predict that far ahead! Journalists, too, collude in the pretence that somebody, somewhere, has things under control. Assholes! Well, he shouldn't remain at *The Vancouver Sun*. Clint is dead right – he lacks the cynicism, the hardened heart, the objective eye. It'd be good to talk. He'll try and ring after exploring the city. Changing his tired jeans and naff trainers for something less American-tourist-on-the-prowl, he wonders why he should bother about his looks here. He buckles the red leather belt carrying his wallet and mobile and slips in his passport, just in case. Grabbing a map of the old city from the reception desk, he puts on the smart white basketball cap that Zaida likes him to wear.

Abdul proposes to take Zaida to the Great Mosque for the evening prayer. Super. She likes to watch the children playing in the side alleys of the prayer hall. Afterwards, she will look for an internet café where she can email her mother: "I am living a dream, signed Princess Lascha." She has enough sense not to mention Grandpa being sick. She won't say either how brilliant Uncle Ian is with his needles – *that* would annoy her mum no end!

Walter rushes to the reception asking for a new phone card. It is not too late to make a call and find out how Gwen and Virginia are getting on with the clinic. He will babble on, but keep to himself his fear that Zaida may be staying behind for several weeks. International numbers are so expensive that his calls never last more than two or three minutes. Back in his room, he cannot take his eyes from the decor, imagining his wife exclaiming at each opulent detail: mother-of-pearl inlaid furniture; handmade fabrics swirling from floor to ceiling; latticed windows with carved shutters; a ceiling patterned like a rug. Here's an idea! Give Gwen one of the heavy-textured tablecloths Damascus is famous for. She is prodding him about the accounts. He helps himself to icy water, thinking that in less than a week the business side of the clinic has become such small beer to him. There is a pleasant feeling obliterating the early disorientation and that weird sickness in Hama, a lightness of heart that pushes the question of Zaida's return to the back of his mind. Perhaps he ought to consider letting go of the clinic altogether; think of retirement, travelling, leisure. And return to Syria with Gwen and Virginia for a less pressured visit. Tomorrow morning, he will feel light on his feet, free of fatigue, the faint pains having gone after a few treatments; bog standard, of course, but Ian does them with good grace. He will get postcards and then pop into one of the coffee bars by the gateway to the citadel, thankful not to have the overprotective Al-Sayeds at his side. With the city map at hand, he will enjoy finding his way around the maze of alleyways; and he will cope nicely with touts pestering tourists by scoffing them off – "Allah will show me the way!"

Khalid checks Abdul is happy to unpack by himself before the evening prayer. Afterwards, should they take their guests to the rooftop restaurant in the new city where Italian and French dishes are on the menu? His father prefers an old favourite by Souk Ibn Al-Khashab where the finest cherry kebabs are served with spicy aubergines. Not the bland tins of tuna fish and baked beans they had lived on as refugees.

Careful not to draw Zaida's attention, Khalid tiptoes past her bedroom intending to have a quiet time, however brief. His luggage has been left by Walid on top of a low wooden cupboard hiding an ugly metallic safe. He flips through his attaché case where he keeps his papers and a work file he has not yet opened. That can wait. Nobody has been through his things but what's the point of checking, or even changing his passwords? He is small fry! And Omar is bound to play fair with family. He won't unpack apart from the clean white T-shirt emblazoned with a large CND sign that Ian gave him. Disregarding cotton shirts – too formal, he slips it on, pleased to look like a tourist.

Khalid's mobile rings. Ian. Surrounded by police.

'I beg you, talk to them. I'm in deep shit.'

'Where are you?'

'The citadel. At the gate of Khan Al-Sabun, something like that. Help me, please!'

To let a minivan squeeze through Souk Al-Zerb, Khalid flattens himself against a stall, spilling nuts and sweets before falling flat on his face on the rough cobblestones under a torrent of well-practised insults from a shrivelled face peeping from the shade. 'Who wants to kill this dog for me?'

Before anyone moves, Khalid apologises and throws a handful of Syrian pounds into an empty basket. As he shuffles off, there is a shooting pain in his left knee. He stops walking, swearing for wasting so much time. Luck returns at the sight of Walid moving out of the vine-hung trellis hiding the regulars' side door to Hammam Bakri. There is no time to explain anything as, waving in the direction of the citadel, he urges Walid on.

'Forget about me! Get my guest out of the police's hands! Take this purse and go!'

One hour later Khalid leads the way up the stairs, limping to the empty top terrace of Hotel Al-Rais where one may not be overheard. He tugs at a glass of pomegranate juice while glaring at Ian who, crestfallen and apologetic, is recounting the bundles of Syrian notes he has just stacked on the squat coffee table separating them.

'How is your knee?'

'No fuss, please. I should be fine tomorrow.'

At first they talk in whispers, blind to the view sweeping over minarets, domes and arcaded gates leading to the natural mound whose fortress walls and fortified bridge dominate the old city.

'Is that bribe enough to get my passport back? How much will Walid keep for himself?'

Khalid grunts with impatience, his good manners pushed aside. 'Forget the money for the moment! Tell me what happened before Walid found you. Before you rang me. Everything. Not so fast this time.'

Flushed, Ian leans back, screwing up his eyes to revisit the scene. 'It's bloody stupid! I was strolling along the esplanade taking photos, stopping to check the map, enjoying the crowd at the café tables, and…' He draws his breath in. 'It wasn't planned, I swear… I found myself following this kid.' He gives Khalid a sly look.

'You're bonkers, man, following a pimp in the full glare of the police! I can't believe it!'

'The guy came out from nowhere, or an alley on the right, just a few steps ahead of me, balancing his hips, mincing steps, slowing down. I was just behind—'

'Spare me the details! What was he wearing?'

'A black shirt, loose over tight jeans. Nike football boots, black and red. Quite posh. A light blue canvas handbag over his left shoulder. He knew someone was following him – he turned round and gave me a kind of twisted smile. The next thing, I was surrounded by security. With guns. Three guards in camouflage gear shouting at me, doing my pockets, my bag. The smart kid ran off. That scared me. I managed to call you, before I was punched in the stomach. A security van arrived, they got handcuffs out. Everything went so fast. Then, thank God, I heard Walid shouting.'

Khalid looks more thoughtful as the story unfolds in fragments.

'They let me go. I couldn't believe it was over. They turned their backs on me, ignoring me, smiling and chatting with Walid as if nothing had happened. Jesus, it was close!'

'You goat, you fell for it. No bum dresses like that unless he's a pimp cruising the tourists. Or, much worse, these shitheads could be on the game too – I mean, a bit of extortion on the quiet since no victim complains officially.'

'I'm so sorry. I wasn't thinking. Not that I saw that guy properly.' Maybe he did… a shape at his side in the shop selling old prints... a flick of painted fingers holding a book... a whiff of perfume, a yellow streak of hair, a glitter of an earring. How resilient and swift these impressions are! He can't tell Khalid about them. And why did he ignore the obvious? The tawdry pinch on his buttock, the narrow alley... the dope vendors scampering away at the sound of heavy stamping. Did his mind register all of these warnings to no effect?

'Forgive me, please! What can I say?'

'Forget him! Whether he was working on his own or not, in the end they are sure to get him or another guy to swear the bloody American was soliciting. Pure and simple. Looks like they can charge you for indecent assault – quite a crime.'

'I'm not an American! And being gay is not stamped yet on passports.'

'Makes no difference.'

'I can't tell you how sorry I am.' Ian jumps to his feet, searches frantically in his bag and looking contrite drops back into his seat. 'The bastards! My mobile, gone for good!'

Khalid can hardly control his voice, mocking Ian. 'What do you expect, you bloody journalists? The red carpet treatment? Amnesty International on tap at your hotel? Plenty of people here would cheer at the prospect of a disgusting American queer ending up in jail.'

'I am a Canadian journalist and I have done nothing wrong,' Ian mutters in a desperate effort not to quarrel. This annoys Khalid even more.

'Wake up, man! Canadian, American... it's the same if they decide to go for us. They set you up with a suitable crime – indecent assault, illegal documents found on that mobile. They'll get onto your blog.' He pauses. 'They'll make us dance!'

Groaning, biting his lips, Ian shakes his head in disbelief. 'I get what you are saying, but why? They have bigger game to catch!'

Khalid sighs. 'Me, probably.'

Ian bends forward, studying him, speaking slowly. 'Because… you're a lawyer?'

'Could be right.'

'Doing Human Rights work? Underground?'

'The less you know, the better for you.'

'And that's why you left the family you loved – Virginia, Zaida?'

Khalid scowls back, but does not answer. Rigid. Determined not to let go.

'Come on, tell me… you've taken a few risks?'

'Not recently. With Zaida here.' His lips hardly let the words through. Face screwed up. Back straight. Frozen. Waiting for the blows. Yet again.

'We are all in it together?' Ian bangs the table with a clenched fist before flopping into the seat, blurting out, 'My fault, my fault!'

His agitation pulls Khalid out of his trance. Back to the present, on his feet, reeling across the room, storming. 'If only Virginia hadn't been such a fool! We had no plot to keep Zaida. And you dare accuse us of kidnapping! Try to understand us for once!'

Ian prefers not to retaliate. 'Tell me how much Walid paid the police?'

'Forget it.'

'Please. I must pay you back. A question of honour.'

'800 dollars.'

Ian whistles. 'A good business for Aleppo. I'll wire you the money when… we are back in Britain.'

'I'll drink a pint to that,' Khalid sniggers. 'And tell me, are you sure Walid had met the security police before?'

'I was too churned up but yes, they didn't seem to ask him who he was. What else can I say? Forgive me, I was in no state to understand what was going on. Could he be on it too?'

Khalid shrugs. 'Walid in cahoots with the pimp and the security police? Possibly. Syrians gamble on who is going to win any given race. Why let your family be trampled for the sake of obsolete principles? That's how things work everywhere, just to make a point – in Britain too.'

'Meaning?'

'Nowadays, everyone ignores collateral damage in the name of democracy, national interest, a war to be won, money to make on the side.'

'Look, Khalid, it was *you* who bumped into Walid, not me.'

'So what?'

'Forget it!'

True, Walid turned up at that crucial moment, Khalid thinks to himself. Hammam Bakri is the only hamman his people patronise when they are in Aleppo. Was it a happy coincidence, or was Walid stalking his master as well as Ian?

Someone is calling for Khalid outside the door. Left on his own, Ian throws the bloody American cap onto the floor and stamps on it, raging at himself until Khalid's prompt return.

Shaking with fear and anger, he screams, 'Talk of the devil! Walid's been in touch with Omar to tell him we are delayed in Aleppo. Damn it! I could swear on my father's head that Mustapha Al-Dari, that Alawite rat from the Ministry of Petroleum, is behind all this. He's sure to demand his pound of flesh in exchange for visas and passports.' He eyes Ian venomously, hissing, 'God the Merciful, the sooner you leave the better. Your peace mission is a stink! Don't mistake us. Uncle Omar is a patriot who has committed our family, the Al-Sayeds, to Bashar Assad's side. Like many people, he believes only Ba'athist regimes can squash the Islamists. Bear in mind, in Syria, not all Muslim Brothers are rebels these days – some have reached a comfortable accommodation with Assad.'

Ian wants Khalid to confide more, to trust even. 'If you're neither a patriot nor a Muslim Brother, whose side are you on?'

Khalid offers a tired smile. 'In Britain, Muslims ought to be liberal. Follow your traditions. I believed that. If nothing very deep was good enough for the Brits, it was good enough for me. In Syria, I don't have that choice. I'm an ordinary Sunni businessman who knows that any change will be fraught with violence and injustice. Never trust anyone. Let alone a bloody pimp!'

Like any Englander wrong-footed away from his native land, Ian claims flawless decency, but is brutally interrupted.

'Shut up, will you? Syrians are in jail for lesser crimes than hosting a foreign journalist taking illegal pictures!'

'I never did! I came as a tourist. I have no such photos.'

'They won't believe you. They'll make me sing for it precisely when it suits them – tomorrow, much later. Liberal Sunni families like ours become their scapegoats. You understand nothing about the violence shaping our lives! Damn you and your family!'

Khalid is called out again to talk with Omar on the phone.

An hour later, he is back, collapsing into an armchair, drained of life, refusing to look at Ian directly, muttering to himself in Arabic, searching for English words.

'Ian, it's not your fault – both of us have been… hooked. Like I said, what I dread… is being… set in place.'

'Already? What are you talking about?'

'Your flights are cancelled. We are to wait… inside the hotel. My uncle takes charge, tonight. He's coming… to offer us a deal. How to get back your passports and exit visas.'

Muezzin calls drift uselessly over the forest of minarets and satellite dishes, leaving behind a mournful quietness.

'Walter – can he leave with Zaida?'

They burrow their eyes into each other.

'Walter, yes. Zaida, no, not yet.'

Ian's fingers tighten around the armrest in an effort to prevent himself from lashing at Khalid's throat.

'Christ! Why not?'

Long pause.

'I can't cross Uncle Omar. I wish I could.'

'What sort of a deal is it?'

'They won't return any exit documents unless I guarantee to be a good boy in the future.'

'To do what?'

'Pass on information on underground groups they'll name when it suits them. As long as Zaida remains in Syria, they can blackmail me. Accuse me of withholding vital information. Or else… something might happen to her.'

'And if you accept?'

'You and Walter are free to leave. You'll get the flight tickets and passports at the airport.'

Behind the words Ian sees the cruel smiles which make Aleppo a death trap for Khalid and for himself, the nauseating Brit.

– 18 –

Opening Gambits

BEFORE SETTLING FOR THE NIGHT, ZAIDA IS TOLD THAT Uncle Ian's passport has been lost and unless it is found in a couple of days there will be a delay in their departure. That's OK then! That's why she was sent off to the souk with Walid earlier on; why her father was short with her.

She is on her own, back in her room, which is huge with horrible twin beds. Alien. Like a tomb. Cluttered with black furniture, heavy tapestries and curtains covering the doors. It is dark, night and day. And there is no computer, only the air-con command to play with. Hot or cold air blows into her hair.

She disliked being fobbed off with the chauffeur who treated her like a stupid girl not understanding Syrian pounds – but she does now. He sniggered at shop windows showing models wearing naughty bras and knickers but she had covered her hair and shoulders with a shawl without being told to, out of respect. She can tell he isn't a nice man; he gives dirty looks and shouts at you in Arabic. He has bad breath, a bad aura.

She hated him pulling her out of the shop, shaking her like a puppy! Hadn't she the right to take time buying jewellery for her mother? Later she watched him telling fibs on his mobile, smirking and checking no-one was listening over his shoulder. His eyebrows stick to each other in the middle. And the left little finger is missing. He got shot! Does her father know? He wears big gold rings on seven fingers. She can tell the police if he disappears. That can happen to chauffeurs in Syria. Maybe that's what happened to Aunt Seema. "You've got her beautiful face" – it's awful! She's dead!

She knows how to behave in Syria. Like the other girls of her age, she has to put up with a bra. It's no fun. Conscious of it sticking out, she took care to walk behind the chauffeur, feeling cross with her father for sending her out alone with this man.

There was another upsetting incident. After showing the few dance steps she was learning, a male relative exclaimed in English to her dad, 'Let's engage her to my son! She's old enough!' They laughed, her father nodding. Of course, a nod doesn't always mean yes, but she isn't sure anymore. There is so much she doesn't understand and there is nobody she can talk to. In Hama it got worse when her other relatives, young and chatty, played with her, patting her cheeks or dressing her up for hours as an Arab doll, forcing cotton pads onto her. She had no clue as to what they were giggling about. Sure they called her names. But she didn't text her mother about it.

She allows herself a moment's longing for home. They let her down by not taking her to Tadmor, that's what Palmyra is called – it has two meanings in Syrian Arabic, 'the bride of the desert' or 'dates'. She'd love to see the temples. And tonight they have been rude, entertaining themselves upstairs, too busy to talk to her down in the courtyard. Her mum would never cut her out for the whole evening! And without being told anything, she would see her daughter's tummy is hurting. And after the treatment, the two of them would give each other cuddles and talk about women's things.

She ignores the television. At Grandad's, she had her fill of endless soaps; and in the end, very few new words to show for it.

She switches on a standard lamp by the mirror crowning the bulky dressing table, but no, she'd rather not examine her breasts tonight, she isn't in the mood. In fitful movements, she undresses fast to slip into the cream pyjama top and shorts that her granny had packed for her, and at the thought she stifles a few tears.

In the middle of the night, she is woken up by fierce shouting coming from the yard and, a few minutes later, by heavy footsteps marching along the corridor to her father's room next door. Uncle Omar's face is terrifying. Cut by scars as big as a hand! She was warned of his late coming to discuss some confidential business.

There are quite a few people in the room. Someone is getting angry and she can pick out her father calming the man down. She could get up, open the door and shout like Max in that children's book roaring to the wild beasts – 'Shut up!' But she's too old, that'd bring shame on her. She shivers; something terrible is happening, she doesn't want to know Uncle Omar's secret, she's only a little girl. Grandad Abdul took them to the... *mausoleum*, a new word meaning a grave for important Muslims. She saw what he did not see: the place, tucked away from the main streets, was shabby – no flowers, no grass, no photos, paving stones cracked or missing. He bent down at eye level, squeezing her hands too hard, speaking slowly. 'When you're old enough, we'll tell you our secrets, our family history, our wars. Will you like that?' 'Yes,' she said, but she won't want to grow up that much, if it means carrying secrets that make you angry and memories that are sad and scary. She doesn't want to be told anything about Aunt Seema. She hates it.

And there is the BIG question. Adults can tell Allah from God but she can't, not yet. It is a worry that makes her itch all over. Inside the mosque, she believes in Allah but once she is out she is far less sure.

Her tummy is rumbling and aching. What to do? Mouth closed, she takes a few deep breaths, as her mother had shown her, to calm stomach pains; she fills her chest again and holds the air in, then with caution she releases a thin flow. She is making a sacred promise. If her mum and dad are back together, that'd be cool – believing in Allah or God, she doesn't mind which.

If the cramps get worse it is a punishment for telling lies. To her father, she pretended she was sending long emails home from that internet café. And to her mother, on the phone, a few times she overdid it, going on about how much she'd like to stay and why-won't-you-listen, that sort of crap. In truth, she isn't that sure herself anymore. Let another girl with proper periods get engaged to that man's son – not me!

There is more shouting from next door! Rattled again, she buries her head under two pillows to block it out. Slowly her favourite vision fills her mind: she is sixteen in a bridesmaid's dress, with make-up and lipstick, stepping down the front steps of Saint Stephen's church. Her two families are cheering for the cameras. Her mum and dad are kissing.

The images sink into her every cell, reconciling her with her future. The ache gone, she curls up on her side, falling into a foetal sleep undisturbed by the occasional searchlight sweeping across the windows. Security is being reinforced at Hotel Al-Rais.

When Ian wakes up, the Western-dressed guard, a slim stinking ferret with a Saddam Hussein moustache, has retreated outside the door of his room. Fearful that a device might have been planted while he was asleep, he remains silent when the hotel attendant collecting the copious breakfast he hardly touched engages in Pidgin English.

Walter has not been in this morning. Nor Khalid. His pulses are wild. He is left to stew on his own. He throws himself on the bed, raving and howling his impotence into the brocaded cushions. How he hates the sordid deals, shoddy compromises, maimed bodies discovered in dumps in the early morning.

Biting his lower lip, he turns onto his back, resentful of the extravagant ceiling, aching to get away from the mocking décor. He will be interrogated while being well-fed between sessions. There will be repeated questions about the Al-Sayeds' involvement with Amnesty International and Human Rights Watch when they lived in Britain – material that Military Intelligence is likely to know about already. And their supposed connections to radical Syrian intellectuals, paid by the West. Or, even more insane, their affiliation with Muslim Brotherhood Jihadists in Hama, financed by Saudi Arabia.

He will say nothing, explain nothing, just wipe off spit and sarcasm with the aloofness of a beggar. That won't do. With glee they will deride him, stamp on the gay man, a traitor by nature, a repulsive detritus. They will take him where no man wants to go.

Only the Al-Sayeds interest them.

How long will they burn his flesh and blow his mind, hour after hour mocking him for having stepped outside the brotherhood of men, unhurried, confident he too will come to loathe himself? How long the crucifixion before he turns their allegations into truths? The birthday book ended with an eagle sweeping over a grave! Whose grave? The question writhes in his stomach. Bloated with terror, he searches for the few needles left from the pack he last used for his father. He braces himself at the gleam of the steel. Stripped to the waist, he props himself up on the bed, forefinger following the meridian from the perineum up the belly, right in the middle, underneath the rib cage. Leave that needle in for ten minutes. Fumble for a point about one inch either side of the median line that should also calm the nausea if he finds the right spot. Lying still, he wills the needles to work.

There must be ways of not betraying a family he respects and loves.

Father. Everything rests on him.

Walter must find a way to contact Gwen and Clint; ask them to alert Human Rights Watch, the Western media, the embassies, *The Vancouver Sun*. Marianne. Everyone. Get petitions off the ground, all energies focused on Syria.

They have to make up plans, however shaky. Cultivate hope. Let it grow, or the thugs will bury him as well as Khalid under layers of deception and despair.

The same day, a gang of people in civil dress have taken over the reception rooms, top terraces and inner courtyard of the Al-Rais Hotel without giving any sign to the punters that something sinister is unfolding on the third floor.

Passports and other papers left at the reception by the Franklins and the Al-Sayeds have been confiscated, together with flight tickets. The service is faultless. Anyone wishing to complain has been advised to deposit their request at the General Information Commission housed in the Military Academy, close to the Republican palace.

Day and night, the bedroom door is being guarded by security people, who Khalid addresses with courtesy even when Omar Al-Sayed is let in at midnight to kick off a fateful row. Putting his hands on Khalid's shoulders to keep him seated on the bed, he towers over him.

'Only you, Khalid, can release that fool of yours.'

'How?'

'By helping us trace and arrest the people you've been conspiring with, people who want to destroy our country.'

'Nonsense! I deny that – this is an outrageous lie!'

'Why did you return to Hama? To develop contacts with dangerous people, didn't you, to avenge yourself for those terrible nights?' Scorn swelling the veins of his neck, he glares at Khalid, ready to grasp him by the collar at the merest sign of defiance. Seeing the kid paralysed, the bully smiles. 'Don't be a damned fool! I'm your uncle and you'd better listen.' During his frequent visits to Hama, Khalid was seen meeting children of the disappeared. Officer Walid Hadidi filmed them together two months ago beside the family tombs. 'The Minister, the merciful, has protected our families and now demands names. Mustapha Al-Dari orders you to fight the enemy within.'

'Who? Every Syrian who isn't a Ba'athist member? You will dishonour Syria again with more blood.'

'Ian will be allowed to leave immediately. Not Zaida. Keeping her here will make you talk. In three months, you both leave – if the traitors are under lock and key. Syria's a modern secular country like any other. But with Islamist madmen to deal with.'

Omar sits down on the bed. Too close. Khalid disguises his deep disgust at the pro-Assad rant that follows. Once an army officer who fought in the Lebanese war, Uncle Omar had not yet been polluted by cynicism and self-interest. The family loved the captain for his bravery and the way he had confronted ruthless savagery with dignity in a Lebanese prison. And today there are millions of honest people like his uncle who support the emergency laws, so long as the regime modernises the country and protects the constitution from the most radical Islamists. He understands the logic, even while, as a pro-democracy lawyer, he has defended those unfortunates caught up in the mechanisms of the system. Like their trump card... Zaida!

Pinned down by Omar's rapacious grin he remains as still as a gecko working out an escape while gripping a branch. Abdul has to find a way out for her. How? His lawyer's brain starts to tick again. Understand where Omar is coming from. A life deserving of respect. Transferred to intelligence missions in the Golan Heights and Palestine. Snubbed by the Alawite cadres, he resigned on health grounds. A principled man, open to reason.

'What's your evidence against me? From tortured people? Absurd! I've never condoned armed violence. Why would I risk my life helping Jihadists? I loathe them as much as you do.'

'What did you do in Britain? You came across scoundrels in Leaford and that's why the Military Intelligence put Walid Hadidi on your tail. You'd better be straight with me.'

Now lumbering around the room, Omar argues and shouts until Khalid admits that when working at Leaford Refugee Centre he took on two cases – their bodies mutilated from lashings and cigarette butts on the genitals.

'Asylum seekers? Had I known it, I'd never have sent for you. Damn the day I did! Who were they?'

'A Muslim Brother. A sheikh in charge of a *madrassa*. And a Kurdish Communist Party leader. Both tortured on orders from the Supreme State Security Court.'

'Curse impartiality! That'll be the downfall of our country!'

'Curse you and the day I listened to Father! I should have stayed in Britain and carried on with Human Rights.'

'They want names. And the Syrian Bar Association will disbar you once and for all!'

Omar examines the tip of a cigarette, his scar quivering, restive as he studies Khalid, who has sunk further into himself, head in hands, trapped and crushed. Omar feels a tinge of sympathy – he himself had been terrorised in a similar ambush in Lebanon. He falls silent, which helps Khalid clarify his mind.

'Names from me? These bastards already have them! Tell them! There's nothing new to spill even under torture. And Zaida won't be part of a deal. I'd rather die. And if you kill us, you'll see my father destroyed too. You'll be a pariah. You'll live in hell for shedding the blood of your own family. And there are no grateful sods in Syria! The villains will turn against all the Al-Sayeds… sabotage your business. Think hard. No more profit from those pipelines to Jebel Al-Akrud.'

Puffing at another Marlboro, Omar takes in the sharp-edged shadows of resilience ageing his nephew's face. The boy is of his blood, although the split is irrevocable. And he lacks cunning. He takes his hand with affection.

'Time to decide. Make sure you know which side you are on when I report back. I'm going.'

'Wait. Give me two days. I beseech you, just two days. Let Walter and Abdul look after Ian and me in our rooms. We won't run away without Zaida! Get someone to take her out to the souk, please. I don't want her alarmed more than necessary. Remove the security from the corridor. Post them outside at a distance. Walid is enough of a guard dog.'

'Walid saved my life. Allah is the merciful.'

They have no more to say, both knowing that there is nothing unusual about families being caught in deranged machines fed by generations of deception and brutality.

'Nephew, let's drink to happier times!'

On waking up a few hours later, Khalid has a splitting headache and his knee hurts more than ever. Blurry-eyed, he watches, in the glass of water on his side table, the tablet dissolving in small sputters like a dying soul. His mouth is parched. No wonder, given the amount of beer and whisky that Omar forced on him! He wills himself to get out of bed, his left leg buckling underneath his weight, invisible ants in the inflamed joint. He scratches the skin. He'd better have a long shower but he can't be bothered to shave. An ashen figure wrapped in a long white towel looks back at him: pasty face, skin flaking on the temples, stubble sticking out of the dark mop, a few deep creases outlining the scimitar nose. He drinks another glass of water and belches at the family trait, Uncle Omar's revolting nose.

He paces the room, leg and head throbbing with pain. He shouldn't have brought Zaida to this fratricidal country. Virginia's fear is being realised. He was too cocksure of the patronage of the Al-Sayeds, naïve about his own ability to resist the rot. He abhors the fortune that forces pigeons to fly with hawks.

He should pull himself together – Zaida would expect no less from her dad.

His princess must vanish. There is one way left. Get the Franklins out of Syria. All three of them. Let them take their chance up north, God willing.

He lies down. Fucking beer! His head's burning!

Were the winds of a cruel destiny at work when he met Virginia?

He was deeply in love. And she was keen then to probe him about Syria, unlike later. Gratitude and joy welded him to her when Zaida was born, his life hooked onto theirs. Now more than ever.

He hears again the perverse taunting: 'your daughter is a mongrel, unreliable, with no loyalty to either family.' Mollified by alcohol, he did not take in Omar's insult, but now he goes berserk, swearing out loud in Arabic and English as he hurls his canvas shoes at the bottles infesting the parquet floor. As these roll and crash into each other, the sound brings him back to his senses. Quiet! Zaida is asleep! On all fours he gathers the bits and pieces into a paper tissue until an invisible needle pierces the skin of his knee, making him yell and hop like a mad man again. A few minutes later, he finds himself on top of the bed, crumpled into a ball, broken.

He did not shed a single tear in front of Omar, who stayed until early morning cajoling, accusing, falling silent, wild. He didn't do too badly, having gained time to take counsel with Abdul. And all the wheeling and dealing that goes on in his uncle's world might open a way out in the next two days. The old fox will hesitate to nail his brother's skin.

Abdul must sort out false passports for the Franklins. That isn't such a crazy idea! For years, dissidents have organised a flow of people out of the country. With Allah and dollars on his side, Abdul can tap into the Kurdish networks and have papers made overnight.

Walid Hadidi is a dark horse. What rank has he? Can Abdul buy him? Yesterday night he came in greasy with dishonesty, head lowered to the ground, gloating and blackmailing with excessive politeness: 'I saved that dirty foreigner from prison. What can you do for us in exchange?'

There is a scuffle outside. Zaida. Screaming, she scratches at the double handles of the door, unable to turn them. There is a youth in uniform on her heels. Furious, the guard pulls her away, shouting insults as she kicks at him. Orders are orders. She must stay in her room like everyone on this floor. Khalid murmurs a few apologies while handing over five thousand Syrian pounds. The door slams closed. Still dressed in her pyjamas, his baby breaks down onto the carpet, crushing her ragged dolly into her mouth, whining, 'Daddy, when am I going back home?'

– 19 –

The Deal

THE NEXT DAY, WALTER CREEPS OUT OF HIS BEDROOM TO appraise the guard standing at Ian's door, who glances back at him with more interest than hostility. Short. In his fifties. Pot-bellied. Scruffy in spite of the uniform. Bored with the job. All good signs. Walter makes his move, quick as a thief. A finger on his lips, he drops a few banknotes into the man's hand before slipping into Ian's room.

They puzzle over an early morning note from Abdul. It is strictly forbidden to use hotel phones, outside phones and the internet since they are under "official security surveillance". Ian and Khalid remain confined to their rooms. Walter and Zaida can walk in and out as long as they stay inside the hotel and speak with nobody. Zaida will be taken out sightseeing by reliable people. "Don't make a wrong move now. Have trust in Allah. I hope to get your papers by tonight."

'Maybe I'd no need to tip the guard, son. They've relaxed. That's progress!'

'Poppycock! That note was dictated to Abdul. It's a cat-and-mouse game. To sap our nerves. They're bloody good at that.'

He throws himself back onto the bed where he lies prostrate until Walter insists on giving him an emergency treatment to sedate his nerves. It's futile, but it will please the old man.

Zaida is led out of Hotel Al-Rais by three females wrapped in flowing *abayas* and escorted by a bearded security guard wearing a tight T-shirt and jeans – all muscle. They have come to take her out for another round of sites and shops, a nice gesture from Uncle Omar. The charming cousins are overjoyed, so they claim, by the opportunity to practise their English on their young relative, who follows them, grudgingly aware that she has no other option but to play their game. She's the bait! That's the ploy! Why the gun? She won't talk to them. The tallest says she will get her favourite ice-cream at the Bab Antakya stall. 'Lemon, isn't it?' How does that woman know? She coughs it up with her breakfast and the whole thing splashes onto the orange and green gown, who stops smiling. 'You dirty girl!' It serves her right. Seeing the vile women shuddering in revulsion while cleaning up, Zaida bursts into a hopeless run, a rabbit blinded by terror. She is caught by the guard, who slaps the sobbing girl round the ears before dragging her back to the hotel. The Aleppian cousins have slipped away.

After the evening prayer, Walid enters Hotel Al-Rais's courtyard through a low panelled door reserved for staff which opens directly into the souk. With apprehension, Walter watches him slipping past French, German and Russian tourists packing the reception hall after fairy tale trips to the past – Xenobia's Palmyra and Roman Apamea serving as antidotes to the reality of Gaza, Bagdad, Hama, Kabul – so Walter tells himself. Being a forced recluse has taken the gloss off the tourist trail.

'Allah is the merciful! Look! What have we here, Sir?' Walid Hadidi, in a khaki uniform, taps the older man's shoulder.

'Christ! You speak English! What's up?'

The scruffy servile look has gone. The officer does not deign to answer as he waves one British passport. Not Zaida's. Not Ian's. Walter feels faint while flipping through his to check the exit visa has not been cancelled. It has been extended by a fortnight. He can stay or go. Do as he wishes. How very kind.

'What about Zaida's papers? Ian's? And our phones?' He hisses, unwilling to attract the attention of a group admiring the mosaics around the central fountain – tourists oblivious of the prisons behind the décor. Bitter.

Walid beams back at him. 'You are free to leave or stay longer with your son. The girl's papers are being looked after by her grandfather. Tell your country Syria is a good country.'

Walter secures the passport in a breast pocket, making sure it cannot fall out while giving Walid a long icy look, refusing to thank the man. People at home are never that corrupt, except for MPs. How much has the tosser put into his own pockets when getting this thing back?

6am the next day.

'Allow me to come in.'

'Checking on me already?'

Fully dressed, Walter is sitting on a low couch, trying to fathom the next few hours from the view etched by half-closed curtains: an enigma of buzzing lanes, covered streets and rooftop terraces sprawling to the towering defences of the Mameluk citadel; a baffling array of churches and mosques impervious to the agonies below.

Abdul has come to take his pulse, which he has done two or three times since Walter's malaise, but never so early. In the faint light seeping through, Walter appraises the sombre-looking visitor. Overcast. The aristocratic features have taken on an unhealthy bluish hue, the eyes are bloodshot, his breath foul. God, don't let Abdul collapse too.

'Let me check your pulses and pay back your kindness.'

They buy time playing at doctors until Abdul squeezes Walter's hands with obvious affection. 'There's no need to tell you what you need for your heart … Rest, and more rest.'

'How, when our children are under house arrest? And what about our princess? Why, oh why did Ian come back? Virginia and Khalid should never, never have got together.'

'*La la*, my brother, you're wrong. It's not the children but our countries that have let us down. Didn't I tell you Khalid can't get an entry visa from Britain anymore? Even if he could leave Syria legally. Since the War on Terror. Blacklisted as a lawyer defending Muslims!'

'I can't get my head round it all. Our little girl is a pawn! That's indecent!'

'With trials like this, my friend, I also feel guilty. I put pressure on Khalid to work for us in Syria. I tell myself *Allahu akbar*, Allah is the greatest. I pray he is showing us a way.'

They lock onto each other's eyes – old men's eyes; reddish, watery and puffy with impotence, but also proud of their boys. A long stare until Walter shuffles along the couch to make room for Abdul. Each sees the other as self-blaming; neither is ready to engage openly with the unspoken.

They have become brothers scheming in the hope that orange trees grow out of tears. Secretly comforted by the other's affliction, they sit in agony while pretending to be absorbed by the ramparts sketched out against the steely sky. Both urged their sons to return home while imposing the same historic burden – that imperative demand of kin that crushes individual destinies; Mafioso fathers taking blood from ill-fated generations.

'Zaida should leave with you and Ian tomorrow. You will have plenty of rest – I mean, soon, in Britain.'

At sixes and sevens, Walter makes a huge effort not to scream at this man, his only friend who is making no sense.

'What? So soon? Do you have her passport back?'

'Not yet. I've got a solid contact. He's getting the papers ready. For everyone.'

In the midst of crisis, however dangerous, Abdul never departs from his patrician bedside manners. 'Listen. Because of our political convictions, we've prepared ourselves, knowing we might have to leave quickly with false papers. We see no other way. If we can get you three out of the country, they can't blackmail Khalid with the same force.'

'I see. I see! With Zaida here, they've got him by the balls!' Walter exults for a split second.

'With her safe, Khalid has a better chance to leave the country.'

'Why doesn't he try to escape with us?'

'We'll create a diversion. They'll look for four people. That ought to fool them for a while. And give Khalid the night to be driven to Lebanon or Jordan. A short journey. With professional smugglers.'

'Trustworthy?'

Abdul lowers his head, as ever eloquent with his silence. Walter is unable to find the right words. How can he ever apologise enough for the trivial suspicions that have led to this tragic trip?

'We'll travel by coach up north. Not by car and not to the nearest frontier, Lebanon. That's what they'll expect us to do. We'll go to the Turkish frontier, beyond Qamishli, a Kurdish town. We'll travel in the same coach but separately, my ailing deaf and mute granddaughter wrapped in a cloak. You and Ian will be sitting alone as ordinary tourists in the front. Strike up a conversation with me, a complete stranger, when the coach comes to a stop. You're on the way to Ras Al-Ain because you are interested in the excavation of the tells, you know, the artificial mounts dotting the Jezira.'

'The Mesopotamian settlements? How ironic! I fancied visiting the area since I saw the giant statues in the Aleppo museum. We'll be alright. How long is the trip, do you reckon?'

'Six hours. Seven. It's the longest route to Turkey. With tolls and roadblocks. There are tensions in the North-East region at the moment.'

'That's bad!'

'Not really. The militia has enough on their hands searching coaches for Jabhat Al-Nusra fighters, Iraqi refugees and armed Kurds. Not an old man with a sick child. Or an elderly tourist feeling nauseous because of the bumpy drive. Your son is concerned about you. Play up the father-son bit, any Syrian likes that – even the police.'

'But why this way out of the country?'

'It's a region where the regime's control over transport is not that tight. With a bit of luck, once we are safe in Qamishli, Allah be praised, we'll rest with a family working for us. The frontier is just one kilometre away.'

'What people? How come you trust them?'

'The old man is my brother; his mother was my wet nurse. You see how far back we've been together! Their sons work for the Democratic Union Party and Khalid has helped them more than once. There's one danger – armed men setting up roadblocks, that happens now and then – but… money goes a long way. That's better than choosing more obvious routes.'

Abdul's look of absolute calm unbalances Walter. How can anyone who has never pulled any strings understand even 10 percent of what is going on? At the end of the road, how many thousands of Syrian pounds will he owe the Al-Sayeds? Someday, he'll try and repay them in dollars.

'We've talked to the son. They've decided to smuggle the three of you across the border late in the night.'

'You don't mean… smuggle! Why won't we be showing our papers and going through when we arrive? Why waste time?'

'The frontier is open from nine to three, when they close the barriers. We'll arrive at nightfall. You all wait for the following day and try one of the two guards with your papers. Or much better, they go off for a piss or a cigarette – that can be arranged. Long enough for the 500m walk to Nursaybin.

If that doesn't happen, my people will give you a donkey ride over the mountain pass.'

'I feel less daunted knowing there are alternatives to bribing the guards.'

'That's a way of life for frontier people. Dealing with refugees. Militia. Intelligence officers. Smugglers. And in Nursaybin there are five or six hotels to choose from, all with telephones. I am told there is a minibus to Adana – a town with an international airport.'

'We will never be able to thank you and Khalid enough. To have worked this out for us when I was spending the night despairing! I trust you won't return to Aleppo straightaway, will you? We need you to negotiate things with your Kurdish friends.'

'What else you want to know?'

'How can we leave the hotel without raising suspicions? What about Walid Hadidi?'

Abdul's face relaxes into a warm chuckle. 'No fear. Walid turns out to be quite a decent man by today's standards. He will help Khalid escape tomorrow by one of the service doors to Souk Al-Attarine.'

Walter nearly chokes over the turn of events. 'Isn't that suicidal? How can you be sure of the man?'

'How long can you trust any man? Two days? I've made Walid understand that by letting us go he is helping Omar and the Minister in the long-term.'

'How so?'

'Walid is one of the security men working directly for the Minister to spy on Khalid. That's why we can trust him. He already knows everything that may be of interest to them. And he's unhappy at the idea of Khalid being... knocked about for nothing.'

Shrunk inside a grey *jalabiyya*, unusually disorderly, Abdul stands up, ostensibly to examine the view, slowly regaining his composure. 'We haven't told my brother anything. Omar should not be compromised. He must be free to fight our corner. Normally he is quick at picking up the way the wind blows at the Ministry of Petroleum. Much depends on what goes on between that Ministry and the Ministry of Information. Khalid being under house arrest, that's a plus already for them but they'll fight as to who takes the credit for it. There are bullies, as you say in English, barking instructions without always wanting to be obeyed. Mao, Hitler, Nixon were like that. Blunt men of power, unstable, ruthless with rivals. With no honour. And they must know that once Zaida is safe, Khalid will never make the accusations they want.'

Abdul sinks back into the seat. 'Pray Allah they realise the game is not worth the... candle? That's what you say? Khalid is a marked man inside Syria, where nobody will contact him for legal advice. Once he is outside they'll keep on his trail from country to country. That's the sort of reasoning we hope they'll work out. With the help of Walid and my brother. There is no-one else to turn to.'

He has his faith, Walter thinks with some envy – I have none. He feels empty, beached like a salmon at the end of its course.

'Don't despair, Walter. We need you. I've ordered breakfast on the top terrace with Zaida. Ian already knows about our plans. You two talk and make her understand the situation. She can't cry on the coach! Help her pack but not until tonight. Well, that's all for now. I have to go and book the seats at Al-Baron station.'

'Understood.'

'Later I'll take her to the mosque. We'll be back within an hour, as I promised Walid. For tomorrow we'll buy *toshkas* at the stalls, her favourite sandwiches.'

It will be their last visit to the mosque together. For a time Abdul loses his nerve, pacing around the room, tossing his head violently as if to wake up. He stops short, shaking Walter by the shoulder. 'You understand, don't you? We'll split up if anything goes wrong. You understand? You'll have her papers. Hide them. And I'll have other papers for her, just in case I have to return to Aleppo with her. She is to be kept safe at all costs. We'll have all the papers tomorrow morning. And a lot of cash. Money is our best ally, as ever.'

'How do we pay you back?'

Abdul gives him a rueful smile. '*Shukran*, my brother. Be a grandad and father to our princess. Give her my poems. Tell her... I've loved her as much as our blessed Seema.'

'I promise. And I swear she will study Arabic... Do you really think Khalid will be alright?' Walter's voice, hoarse and hardly audible, suppresses all the impossible questions he could ask while watching the blood drain from Abdul's already ashen face.

An ear-splitting silence.

Abdul's hands have pale nails, neat and trimmed, and long and graceful fingers: doctors' hands. Like his. He bends over and clasps them both into his, making a silent wish of eternal friendship, dogged, 'Back in Leaford, our place will be under surveillance by a whole range of intelligence people – yours, ours, Americans – depending on which groups claim your son. Tell him to contact our very good friend Marianne Castagou. He will remember her. Virginia took him to her place in the south of France. We'll send her dollars so she can wire them to him wherever he is. Her place is so remote, tell him it is safe. For him to stay there, I mean.'

'With Allah's will, my brother.'

Waiting for the impeding storm, eyes clouded with dark tears smudging the grey sheen of the morning, unshaved, the elderly fathers look at each other beseechingly, wishing that at least the other would believe in salvation. At that instant, bereft of gifts for the next generation, trumped by fate, bereft of hope, Abdul Al-Sayed and Walter Franklin can no longer comfort each other: their souls are laden with stones. What will be will be. A cacophony of deaths and no redemption.

They embrace tightly. Farewell. *Allah ma'ak*. They let go with a gentle rush like the wave parting from the sand at the turn of the tide.

– 20 –

On The Road

IT IS THE LAST AFTERNOON COACH TO QAMISHLI WHERE Abdul's relatives would see to their crossing. Sympathetic to the Kurdish Democratic Party, they know how and why Khalid has been blackmailed; they will do their utmost to get the British girl out of Assad's claws. There are passages through the porous border manned by different groups, unpredictable in their allegiances, but they can work together against the regime.

Ian and Walter pour over a tourist map of north-eastern Syria. Back into their third coach from Aleppo. Things have been uneventful. Long-distance coaches are comfortable and equipped with Bollywood films on receding screens that pop out at the press of a button. They sit near the front, acting out the frail gentleman enjoying his trip with his devoted son. They do not acknowledge Abdul and Zaida when these two, dressed in hooded grey and white *djellabas*, walk past to reach their rear seats.

Walter seems engrossed in the Lonely Planet guide but, to Ian's amusement, his head soon rolls to the side, mouth open, snoring slightly. His authority has melted away during the journey, relegated to the role of *flâneur*, not a boss any more. All the decisions have been taken by Khalid and Abdul. Necessarily. And there are plenty of reasons to accept the fatigue enveloping them both.

Ian snaps closed his iPad with *The Girl With The Dragon Tattoo*, the Swedish thriller everyone else has read. He is too whacked to take anything in. Pushing the seat into a sleeping position, memories float back of mindfulness workshops he shared with Clint. Eyes closed, he attempts to relax every part of his body while paying attention to each breath. Don't rush. Filter out negative thoughts. Give your full attention to positive emotions. His mind drifts off to a Vancouver Island beach. With Clint on towel mats watching a boy playing by the ramshackle reservation for the Nuu-chah-nulth. Don't lose the detail. Scrawny and naked, the kid pats the sand into conic tepees with seagull feathers for flags, shingle for paths, shells for pots and seaweed for fires. With an odd smile, the boy walks away from the ancestral camp. A ritual only Clint understands: 'Hold on, man, let go of the guilt. You stole no land. Breathe in and out. From your tummy. Not too fast. Anchor yourself onto me. You betrayed no friend. Listen to the incoming surf. Good. Let it wash away the tepees and the self-blaming.'

The Franklins appear to be resting from worrying, so Abdul guesses. Whatever front of confidence he puts up for them, he is well aware that Zaida's life is being moulded by too many hands. It's imperative to keep an eye on each move in and out of the coach and make sure they are not being followed. The number of travellers has gone down since Hasakak. In this semi-arid steppe, families carrying the paraphernalia of the urban – leather bags, sneakers, comics etc – have been dropped off in austere villages to call on impoverished relatives. There are too many signs of the encroaching desert. Dried-up wells. Abandoned settlements. Abdul feels in his arthritic bones the fragility of the country he has returned to. The Khabur river, once sung by Mesopotamian poets, stopped flowing months ago – a shocking sight from that bridge. Since the Euphrates, he has seen new villages exploiting scarce water resources for seasonal crops instead of herding goats and camels. There will be wars over water, like over oil. Abdul is engulfed by a surge of nostalgia for vibrant diverse communities; when people respected the land and each other's way of life. But why be so gloomy when the trip is going so well? He should just care for his 'sick' grandchild. He smiles. At the last stop, he brushed off an inquisitive mother who asked why his child was left inside the coach. The matron backed off. Pray Allah it will be as easy with the next nosy parker.

Just on the other side of the alley there is a young female he observes with tact – as in his clinic when he could practise discreet admiration of femininity as an occupational perk. A ravishing profile. A student travelling on her own? With a guitar and a backpack covered with red, white and red stickers – the Kurdish flag. Not a spy! Head crushed by a woolly bonnet. Wearing a black military jacket. Lost in her thoughts.

Why is the coach pulling to the side? There are murmurs of annoyance and surprise at being parked beside some rudimentary garage-looking sheds. Piles of tyres spill outside breeze block walls; rundown cars rust between a trailer and two Toyota vans. Why stop so close to Qamishli? The driver shouts some explanation before disappearing inside the workshop.

'Everyone is to leave the coach. To wait outside. Child, they're just checking the water tank.' Abdul helps Zaida gather her clothes before leaving the safety of the coach. Bemused, Walter and Ian find themselves in a café of some sort. The other travellers settle at the wicker tables, buying Turkish coffee, chatting with the mechanics carrying buckets of water and preparing for a long wait. When her grandfather takes the girl to pee in a tuft of weeds behind the shed, people drop their glance out of respect as these two sneak past.

At the zinc counter, the foreigners buy tins of Pepsi and offer bottled water to the elderly man waiting to be served. Fancy him addressing them in English!

'Are you British? Let me explain what's happening. The water gauge is red. The driver is checking how serious the leak is.' He introduces his granddaughter, now happily munching through a bag of Walkers at an isolated table. Black hair curling out of the hood, she contributes with brio to the agreed pantomime when thanking them for the soda – tight-lipped, she bows and joins in front of her chest her beautiful hands, manicured and henna-tattooed. Abdul misses the blonde child but Aunt Halima insisted on the disguise to facilitate the escape of an obviously local pubescent girl.

With Zaida settled in the coach, Abdul is free to engage with the driver. An usually coarse face with eyes Abdul can't read anything into – a studied blankness acquired over generations of service.

'Only 50 kilometres left.' He shares his suspicions with Walter and Ian. 'I can't figure the driver out. He won't talk, I mean, to a bossy Sunni. But he isn't that upset by the delay. Does he get a bit on the side from the café?'

Tyres screaming to a halt deafen them. A Ford pickup pulls in. Hoods, goggles, shouts. Defiant Al-Nusra black flags sway from the open rear. There is a rush to the coach door. The truck roars, storming out in the opposite direction. Lost youth playing at war. Abdul's heart praises Allah. A futile panic.

Zaida likes sitting by the window, on the right side. They have the back of the coach to themselves now that most people have left. Sinister clouds of sand are creeping up above the horizon, bleak and threatening. She snugs herself by her grandfather, holding his hand tight under her cloak – no-one is watching – listening to him humming a prayer until they are disturbed by the coach coming to a brutal stop. Again! A police car is parking on the verge. There is a persistent banging on the door. A security patrol! There is some furious barking. The student, with guitar and pack, hobbles into the seat next to them. 'Please, help.'

Groaning at their bad luck, Abdul figures out that she has no papers. She leans an imperceptible weight on his shoulder, bonnet over her eyes, frozen. He spreads a blanket over the two figures immobilising him, reassuring, 'Look sick and moan if someone comes close to you. We'll stay inside the coach. We're family.' He takes out his beads, deep in prayer, ignoring the passengers spilling out onto the macadam. Jumping up the steps, a policeman, rubber baton in hand, urges Walter and Ian to get out. They pull out their travel documents but the officer waves them off as the group left inside attracts his attention. But he is pushed out of the way to make room for another olive-green uniform handling, with some difficulty, a sniffer dog. A German Labrador. Excited, yelping, growling, lips turned up at the mouth corners. A beautiful beast. Abdul recognises the race trained by the Nazis to sniff out hiding Jews. The same dogs are now trained to find dealers and terrorists. As dog and man search up and down the alley, Zaida, terrified, squeezes her body further into Abdul's lap.

'Shush. The dog won't hurt you, he is looking for drugs! See! They're leaving.' Tail down, impatient. No drugs. No guns.

On the road again, passengers sigh with relief. The raid has failed. No-one was arrested. They applaud the return to an apparent normality. Free. People move seats and chat for the first time across the rows with strangers. Zaida listens to their new companion talking to Abdul. As a mechanic engineer, she works for Kurdish women resistant fighters. Why the guitar? A singer, she rewrites ancient melodies to sing protest songs – 'All about Azadi,' she explains, 'our freedom. In Arabic, you say, Houriya.'

'In English, freedom. In French, liberty,' Zaida whispers, raising her head to show that, having recovered from her fright, she has had enough of acting dumb. Do these words all mean the same? Abdul wonders. Is there anything gained as well as lost in translation? Abdul hugs his clever girl, dreading their parting.

Qamishli: eight hours from Aleppo. Dragging their bags out of the coach storage, travellers exchange their last farewells. The student embraces Zaida and Abdul, all smiles. 'You good to me. *Shukran.*' She vanishes like a firefly into the night. Will she become a martyr, like his fallen daughter? A blasphemous question!

'What was her name?'

'Whose name?'

'Your girl friend, silly.'

'Promise you won't get upset? Her name is... Seema.'

She stifles her cries. Is he senile? She glances at the deep wrinkles, the warts masking the upper lip, the receding chin, the overgrown eyebrows. Pity fills her heart. Sensing her dismay, to restrain her trembling, he holds her up against his chest, struggling to express an intolerable cocktail of sadness, anger and hope that any young person would find inconceivable.

'It's a good sign, dear. Her name is Seema Mouslem! She's asked for our protection. It's not a coincidence. It's Allah's way to show us we are not abandoned.'

No, she won't faint. She has to trust Him or Grandad.

She runs to Walter and Ian, waiting at the entrance gate to the parking lot where deserted coaches spend the night on the outskirts of the small town. There is no-one else around. It is pitch dark except for the occasional lights sweeping from the road leading to the centre. Zaida tells them about Seema Mouslem. They comfort her. Her brave friend knows the region; she is bound to reach a refuge among like-minded people.

'Here is my brother Shervan.'

Nervous exhaustion is being replaced by feelings of pride and hope at the sight of a red and white kerchief jumping out of a battered Red Army 4x4 – short and scruffy, so unlike Abdul, but with a scintillating laughter. They cheer frantically, praising their hosts. 'Hurrah! We've done it. Owing to you, Abdul.'

Walking up and down the yard, the brothers have a long conversation in half Kurdish, half Arabic, keeping the Franklins waiting, now glum and crotchety, inside the jeep.

'What's going on? I'm done in.'

'Sorry, Walter! I needed to check every step of what's left of your journey. Zaida, listen. My heart sings. Your dad is nearing the Lebanese border.'

'How do you know?'

'He phoned Walid, who contacted Shervan today.'

'How far from the frontier?'

'5 kilometres. Chin up, child. Allah is bountiful.'

Exhilarated, high on the news, the Franklins congratulate the brothers for their cunning. Chanting 'Khalid, Khalid', Ian runs around the car, punching the air like a footballer celebrating a goal. Zaida joins the rampage as Walter turns to Abdul.

'What about you? Back in Hama? Do take care of yourself! Don't phone anyone. Be as quiet as a mouse.' Walter grasps his friend's hands, holding both for a while, eyes fixed on Abdul's, mouth shivering with fatigue and apprehension.

'Wait, you two!' She sprints to her grandfathers and hangs onto each neck in turn, perusing the floppy flesh and uncouth hair covering their tired faces. She kisses their cheeks to blow their frailty away. In this blessed instant, they register the strength of her affection – she loves us equally! Over her head, they grin at their own vulnerability.

The British Consulate has confirmed that her family will be on the plane to Heathrow tomorrow, but Virginia craves for more news. Cleaning the practice room every morning is quite a bore usually but today she rubs the taps with febrile energy. She has already transferred her three afternoon patients to younger colleagues keen to help, and Andy will see to the reception so that she can take her mother to the airport.

Her joy is dampened by the bewildering information filtering through since that first invigorating call three days ago from Nusaybin. She doesn't yet fully understand what happened in Aleppo: why were the three of them on the run to Turkey? She suspects this is to do with Ian being a journalist, but would that endanger Khalid as well as the Franklins? Khalid has gone underground and fled to Lebanon, so Walter claimed, adding that he "sacrificed himself", at which she heard Zaida burst into sobs. Why? Initially she resented Khalid spoiling the thrill of Zaida's return since the girl, distraught by the separation, would exaggerate any threat to her father. Is he still crazy enough to dabble in dissident politics? Never mind. Knowing the child will be safe in her arms tomorrow triggers an immense surge of respect and affection for Khalid – sacrificing himself… for their daughter? What has he done?

Forget him! The exhausting wait nearly over, she skips a few dance steps around the couch. Elated, her whole body is shuddering with the thought of hugging and kissing her girl. She'll have to watch out and not spoil the fun with too many questions and reproaches. Zaida will be physically depleted, emotionally drained and her spirit in turmoil. Just sit close in the car; say little for a day or two. Once settled, she will unwind. She has probably acquired a veneer of sophistication after handling another family for a month or so, and this in a tough country. How else would she have changed?

Throughout the morning, her silver needles once more help her take her mind off her own concerns. Mary Angel is doing quite well, much steadier, although troublesome symptoms will persist for a while. The treatment over, Virginia realises that Walter, back at the helm, will be told soon of her use of the Eight Principles. If the boss doesn't like it, tough! The two approaches can be complementary; there's no need to drop the golden rules that the practice has taught over the years. God forbid!

Lunch time. Andy and Sue put their heads through the door to propose a party with Zaida's school friends in the next few days. Virginia jumps at the offer. The place will remain a solid family clinic whatever its financial problems. Walter will accept her experimentation as a continuation of his life work. White coat off, ready to join her mother at the reception, she opens the curtains which she earlier drew close to protect patients from today's blinding light. She looks out at the street, at the young women with pushchairs, the trio smoking on the doorsteps of the library opposite, a Sikh youth scampering along talking to a phone, bright sky above the horse chestnut at the corner. She takes a deep breath, thinking that, like her acupuncture room, the world out there has rules and codes ready to be deciphered. Zaida is flourishing in this mysterious world and doesn't want her mum to stay a mere spectator. Why not join Khalid in Syria with her one day? When she turns back, the light pours in, illuminating among other things the watercolour he gave her for their first anniversary. The frozen lake glistens. A good omen? She focuses on the picture, sensing his face emerging from the frost, as it was then on the bridge, shimmering for a few seconds. Long enough.

– 21 –

Flights

FOUR DAYS AFTER REACHING QAMISHLI, THE FRANKLINS are flying to Heathrow from Atatûrk airport, where a miraculous call to the Hama house had put them through to Abdul. They were elated to know he was safe and well but he had no news of Khalid yet.

They sink into their seats too exhausted physically and mentally to talk. Zaida's jumbled emotions trigger more weeping followed by hysterical joy. She is on cloud nine when thinking about her mum but sick at the absence of recent news from her father. And she is already missing her Grandad. Is he at the souk, being saluted at every stall *kayf il'ayli – "how is the family?"*, or at the norias with her cousins? That hurts. For all that, she hasn't seen her mum and gran for ages and ages! She can't believe it! On her lap, there is a bag filled with a wool cushion cover exploding with bright red and blue flowers. For her mother. That's what her dad would have bought, she said before embarking, her jaw clenched, rigid, resolute – I won't weep anymore!

Amenable, Walter lets Ian check his pulses once more. He shuts his eyes, ready for a rest. Ian needlessly worries about the effect of the four-hour flight on his arteries. The rascal! He has just felt the tinkling feeling of needles being inserted into the source points. He half opens his eyes. They smile at each other with a blend of relief, recognition and mutual respect.

'Welcome to our trade, son.' With no hint of irony.

'Don't raise your hopes, Dad.'

For a while, Ian fiddles with the earphones, zapping from one crappy film to another, exasperated by the Turkish Airlines catalogue. Too overwrought to sink into a police drama, he unplugs the set. Zaida has already fallen asleep, head back, plump mouth half-open, vulnerable. He has enjoyed looking after her. Maybe he could make a good dad. He wraps the flight blanket around her after moving her head gently into a less awkward position, hoping she does not wake up bawling as she did the night after leaving her dad. Other images flood in: the undistinguished silhouettes of their Kurdish hosts enveloped in dusty gowns and headscarves against wind and recognition; the donkey shed where they slept on straw beds and washed from tin buckets; divine dishes of stuffed peppers and eggplant salads brought in by a decrepit sun-baked manservant with the silent courage needed to serve folk on the run. The hideout was only an hour's walk from the Turkish shacks marking the promised land. Didn't they cheer at the sight of the first star and crescent, flying by a petrol station with minivans for hire. Too expensive for the Iraqi refugees queuing at the coach stop nearby, but the shell-shocked trio paid without blinking – whatever it cost to resume their privileged lives.

Other scenes, imagined this time, also flash by. Abdul being shouted at by Omar at Hotel Al-Rais, spreading his hands out to calm the captain down, persuasive – they won't be answerable for the gay journalist anymore. Nor for Khalid. And for Mustapha Al-Dari, business can be business again. He also sees Abdul back in Hama spending hours in the Grand Mosque negotiating with Allah: 'Take my own life, not my son's.'

Ian wails. He is the criminal who should be punished. He can still see the brash balancing hips, the flaunting hand, the practised elegance designed to ruin families. Is this the destruction Clint foresaw in the birthday book? He pulls out a Kleenex to wipe his blotched face. Keep real! Khalid has to get to Beirut unharmed. Where is he now? Probably half a day south of the border after being driven through the dry side of that mountain marking off Lebanon, overjoyed by the green undulating hills. Parched of news about Zaida's flight, he is bound to contact Virginia and perhaps Marianne Castagou. Ian blows his nose, swearing to himself that he will do whatever it takes to help his friend rebuild his life yet again. Clint won't mind in the least. The hotel in Nusaybin was the first place where the two of them talked at length. Zaida, he was emphatic, had never been in any danger until the Franklins, the fools, came to her rescue with an unaccredited journalist in tow. Searched by security officers in Aleppo. Accused of entering the country without a press visa. The whole truth would be better told face to face. What truth? Would he have screwed that rent-boy? Was he flirting with prison and death as well as sex? Impelled to wreck the omnipotent father behind the trip? He has stumbled into the scene so often he doesn't perceive any compelling truth any more – only volatile impressions. Why bother about what really happened if any credible story is a kind of do-it-yourself job suiting particular moments? Damn it!

Sensing Ian's agitation, Walter heaves himself up in the seat, scratches his neck, bitten yet again by the Franklins' debt to Abdul. Khalid is made of flesh and blood, not mere money. How will his children live with such a burden? They have different debts: Ian owes his freedom, and Virginia, her child's release. What about the damage done to Khalid himself? Their visit, Ian says, was ill conceived and badly timed but that's not the whole story; ironically, the regime did Virginia an immense service by chasing her relatives out. Zaida will never be brought up in Syria. But at what cost?

The trip has wrecked something in him too. He is disoriented. Anxious. At the end of his tether. He hasn't cared for the clinic for days. Has his sense of self-respect been drained as well as his Qi? Why not retire? He could go within a year. It'd be a gift for the old girl. Will Virginia be capable of raising money for the clinic? She could borrow, Ian argued, to restructure, modernise, get new therapies – even electronic machines! Enough! It's all mumbo-jumbo, but if it gets the clinic out of the red for the time being, let it be. He is dog-tired, corrupted, blown apart. There are tremors running down his left side. He should take the statin.

The talks with Ian have also been too emotional; and seeing him handling the needles, listening to advice but also making it clear he'd never come back – and that decision wasn't anyone's fault. Children are golden eagles, Ian concurred: they mate for life away from the parents, fighting the wind to build their nest in their own ways. Ian left Britain feeling alien, he said, full of resentment – but why put an entire ocean in between? The children were close to each other, whatever they both say now; and the house was full of kids running in and out, sleeping over. Gwen went to no end of trouble. Where was that lonely kid? Rubbish! Too wiped out to contest stories of neglect, he attempts to console himself. With youngsters, as with patients, one has to accept their fickle truths at face value, however partial their accounts.

His thoughts drift back to the idea of retiring. Virginia. He will have to trust her wholeheartedly. And stop being a meddling old fart!

He shakes his head, muttering. Jesus! It's too early! In a conscious fantasy he marries his daughter to Khalid and the Leaford throne; the couple will visit the Al-Sayeds' mausoleum with Zaida and her younger siblings. Hooked together through travel and Skype, the two branches of the family will fuse into one; and the patriarchs will become birds of a feather, both sustained by faith and conciliation. The rosy-tinted story makes his eyes water. He's becoming such a fool! Will Gwen realise it? How much has he changed? He can even enjoy idle thoughts.

'Tell me,' he nudges his son, 'do you think our ladies will understand what we've been through?'

'Sure, Dad, but not this evening! There's no rush to unsettle them, is there?' Especially his sister! Ian recoils at the scene when she grasps the full blazing tale. Virginia, cock-a-hoop and vindictive. Being laughed at when she'd been right from the start. Overruled by idiots and that treacherous Marianne etc, etc. She'll blow her top! So smug. Though to her credit, she took no time to size up the situation when he phoned her from Turkey. She had prepared herself, she said, since the decision to let Zaida visit Syria. Her solicitor acted fast and organised a Turkish bilingual solicitor registered with Reunion to take the Franklins to the Canadian and British Consulates in Ankara – a chatty man who first thought Ian was the girl's father! As he expected, the Brits, less on the ball than the Canadians, took another day to produce a passport for Zaida – eager to hide from the media yet another British daughter held against her will by an uncaring Muslim father. As a journalist, Ian understood that such cases test the best of condescending diplomats by destabilising negotiations skilfully woven over sugary mint teas. Yet, he was not prepared for the outburst when some official congratulated them for getting the girl out swiftly, since abductions to Muslim countries are all long, drawn-out cases. Pricked, Zaida blurted out she wasn't abducted! 'That's stupid!' She wanted to stay with her father and... she got muddled up, lost for words; blushing as her tale, he thought, was incomplete, too hurtful to tell. The know-it-all spat out memorable British nonsense. 'The child's brainwashed! No need to apologise. We understand.'

Ian bends over to Zaida, who is rubbing her eyes with her fists. 'Sand in your eyes? Remember the snob at the Consulate? Talking rubbish?' Ian takes on a posh voice. '"I'm proud to say we run excellent workshops on British values and respect for cultural diversity."' The clowning over, he says with fondness, 'You really did us proud.'

'Thanks, Ian!' She clicks her tongue, staring hard at him for a few seconds, before confiding, 'There is a Koranic verse Muslims recite to protect people.'

'Your father?'

She bows her head to hide her face. 'I prayed with Grandad. But in England it won't be that easy.'

'You are a child! Enjoy coming back home, sweetheart.' She sniffs her tears back, looking so much older. What else will her mother notice? Tightening his arm around her shoulder, he chews over the idea of an article about Syria for *The Vancouver Sun* with his niece as the heroine.

'We are landing in one hour. I can't wait!'

Zaida's eyes are sunk but they shine like polished ebony above rings of fatigue and a tight expression round the mouth. She is fiddling with the lucky charms hanging from the leather bracelet given to her by one of the Kurdish boys who took to her when guiding them to Nusaybin. There was a short climb over a few boulders to a rail track. He held out his hand to pull her up two or three times – 'Miss, Miss, good here.' She had fun. Can she tell her mum that?

Nearly there.

Walter tells Zaida that when Gwen and Virginia drive down the M1 they will glimpse Lyn Hall, an imposing square building. He grew up on the farm, behind clusters of oaks and elms. 'You knew my father bred cows? Deep red, almost black. With soft white underbellies and vicious curly horns.'

'Look! We're flying so low! Are these things your cows?'

'Are you teasing? They're ponies! Our English longhorns have gone. So has our farm!'

They were beauties! How can he not be pessimistic when age-old skills disappear? In Syria too. Jute replacing silk; plastic, wood; indoor farms, outdoor grazing; computerised probes, his silver needles!

He ought to cut out the sour grapes! Like any adolescent, Zaida venerates the Unstoppable March of Progress, however deceptive this is. Hectoring his own children did no good. How can he do better with her? And not be defeated by the brutal business optimism of the age? He can hear Abdul. 'Time is short. Yet, brother, tell her of your longhorns. Of our mosaics. Of cruel graves. Of healing. Of reconciliation.'

Old people, Walter realises, gnaw at the same questions like dogs over a bone. Have their lives been expressions of unreliable judgments and erratic actions – at best, haphazardly useful? Will their descendants do better? The reflection triggers yet another fit of loud coughing that disturbs Ian, who squeezes the hand resting on the armrest to prevent it from shaking.

'Please see a doctor! Listen to Abdul!'

'There's not much wrong with me apart from exhaustion. Andy Gibson will see to it. Don't fret now. I'm sorry I scoffed at your own projects years ago. Can't we let go of... whatever... made things difficult? What do you say?'

Good Lord! The grey withered face, the pleading and the fact that he is leaving for Canada make Ian sputter with a passion that surprises both of them. 'Our bruises? Our battles? OK, Dad, let's grow up. It's a deal. But you see a doctor. And... you put less pressure on Virginia?'

'And Gwen?'

'You old bugger!'

'What's the joke, you two? They won't be late, will they? Will they like Grandad's poem? It came to him on that horrid coach. I never want to act dumb again!'

220

'No fear, Zaidouna.'

Clint was wrong. There is no death lurking on the trip. Ian gives his niece a steady look. He sees something of himself in her. She makes up her own stories… about emails, not snails. She is fun with her fierce loyalties and a dogged refusal to compromise. The first thing she told the staff at the Consulate was that she was Syrian and British. Fair enough, but when they asked what she was first of all she disconcerted them – 3/4 British and 3/4 Syrian. A witty formula he could borrow one day – 3/4 English and 3/4 Canadian. She is a real hoot, with the generosity that made some goys wear a yellow star; and now, straights wear pink ribbons. He can see her aged 16 demonstrating with a placard saying, "A Palestinian British Syrian Jew. For Human Rights. Not bombs". Concerns he himself may take up again with renewed conviction, alongside Clint, who is already mobilised against the destruction of pristine Alaskan glaciers. The thought of working together cheers him up.

'Listen, you two.'

Zaida wants his attention as well as Walter's. 'I have Grandad's poem. Allah is the gardener and the rose is… I've forgotten, but I love it.'

She darts a hesitant smile, scrutinising their faces for signs of derision. Reassured, she recites softly:

'I rushed into the garden and picked a rose,
Afraid to be seen by the gardener.
I heard the gardener's voice speaking to me:
'What is one rose? I shall give you the garden.'

Getting out of the car with his large bags, Khalid feels an electrifying relief. Since crossing the *djebel* with the help of another well-paid thug, nameless, hired by Walid, their plan has been flawless. Nonetheless, he is glad to see the man off after the silent drive from Homs. The less they see each other, the better.

Al-Faour seems an unassuming place in which to start yet another exile, but in this town, at least, he's safe. Unbelievable! The next step is to register at the Hotel Ahiram, a bland overpriced place, which is, as he has expected, close to the coach station. It takes no time to check in. Key 156. He takes in the tired room at a glance. Peeling white paintwork, stale cigarette smoke. So what! For now it is his chateau. He rubs his chin as if to quash the corrosive bitterness spilling into these first hours of freedom. Why is life so treacherous? Why him? He dries his eyes on his sleeve. Locked out a second time. Why? He curses the broken handle on the bathroom door, manages to get in and, as he feared, there is no hot water. He will miss again the small things – the Zabadani sweet apples, the Halawani grapes, the oranges without skin that Zaida so loved. The street peddlers' calls. The muezzin's. All these treasures that nursed a congenial childhood that left him unprepared for this nomadic life. The cold shower helps him recover his spirits. He won't stay in Lebanon for long. As Omar says, a man's life on the run is made up of 50% planning and 50% chance. Is that why the precious papers worked at the border? His luck will hold through Rafic Hariri and Heathrow, where, in two days' time, he will take Zaida in his arms and bear-hug Walter.

7.30 am. Refreshed after an excellent night. Too early to ring his father. Abdul will be at his old friends' in Hama, the Minas, who are not yet bugged. So first he'll have an espresso downstairs and, to celebrate his exile, a *pain au chocolat* which the Lebanese do so well. Then find a public phone. Then off to enquire about today's schedule for coaches to Beirut. He makes his way to the reception hall. The shutters are still closed. Wilting furniture, a couple of kids playing table football in the dim light.

Piercing screeches startle him. Not the kids. Cats. Probably scavenging in uncollected rubbish – not like Syria, where the firm hand of dictatorship keeps the streets clean. The irony makes him cough. From the gloom behind the reception desk two men emerge, moving onto him, in military uniforms – whose he can't tell, though they look familiar. There is not enough light. He holds his breath. An accented voice shouts at him in English.

'You British passport. You no look British.'

'My parents were Turkish but I was born in Cambridge, England. I am a British businessman.'

'Where you live?' asks the arrogant mouth.

'Leaford, Britain.'

'What business?'

'Textiles, carpets. I've come back from Syria where I have my business partners. I can show you my cards and… theirs as well.'

The man consults the acolyte. Khalid, displaying a feigned ignorance of Arabic, retreats slowly towards the door. A roar drags him back.

'What you name? Erdal Neyzi? No! You real name? We check you at border.' He grabs Khalid by the arm. 'What you business?'

An immense sadness overwhelms him. No divine intervention in Al-Faour. Were they tipped off? Walid? Damn them all!

The officer slices up the passport, his lifeline, with a pen-knife, while the sidekick searches him, down and up. His body stiffens into a corpse. Finding nothing on him, and nothing in the luggage he left in his room, their suspicions are confirmed.

'Why you no phone? Why you no address book? Why wrong business cards? Why 10,000 dollars? You do bloody arms? Who you work for? Hezbollah?'

They change tack, in Arabic and French now, voices suave with threats.

'Well, well, brother, *qui es-tu*? What prayers do you say? *On va t'aider*. We prefer business with Christians.'

Silence.

'Your name? Brother, your name.'

The bully, his face too close, bears his teeth, growling insults: "pig, pig". That black uniform! The badge on the beret! Seema's tormentors. The flashback sparks off seconds of pure madness as he jumps for the throat, squeezes it, victorious, yelling, 'Got you, bastard!' Trained in self-defense, the officer tears the lunatic off, pins him down. The colleague takes over with two clean hand chops that send him crashing onto the floor tiles, head first. Khalid's howling in agony triggers a flow of ardent abuse and another vengeful kick to the groin to suppress the "pimp". The team turns the half-conscious bundle over and ties the arms at the back with professional knots before getting back inside to celebrate the arrest, well-orchestrated and justified, with a Beirut beer handed out free by the appreciative barman.

Long since inured to violence, the little boys abandon their football and skip over the body into the sunlit street.

Returning from the mosque, Dr Abdul Al-Sayed turns the corner from the grand Al-Hassad Square, buzzing with traffic and edged by swish cafés wedged between sinister municipal buildings, to enter a tangle of quiet pedestrian lanes lined with semi-derelict shops and graffiti. There is Abu Reen, as always at this hour, sucking a tacky-looking *nargile* in front of the only inhabited block of flats, a sad confused man he has no wish to cultivate tonight. An Alawite who rabbits on. They exchange their evening salutations.

'*Masa Al-Khayr.*'

'*Masa An-Noor.*'

And Abdul hurries past, shamed by stories dishonouring the Sunni community. Years ago in a neighbourhood, Sunni or Shiite, depending on his spleen, the caretaker saw a banner barring the street saying "Access forbidden to Alawites and dogs". That was before Hafez Al-Assad shifted power in favour of the Alawites.

Putting down the white plastic bag full of mangos he had carefully prodded one by one at his favourite stall, Abdul fumbles in his baggy trousers for the heavy key that opens the wrought-iron enclosure surrounding the Al-Sayed mausoleum, built in 1786. He reads the date every week, praying, talking to himself, stroking the slabs; feeling close to the generations of imams, scholars and doctors who made Hama's reputation as a place of Sunni learning. He steps in and freezes, glimpsing an image from way back when living in Leaford: his wife's grave desecrated with human excrement. He weeps. The tears bring back his grandfather sent by the Turks, Arab cannon fodder for Gallipoli, he never recovered; his other martyr, Seema, her body mixed with Lebanese soil in September 1982. His wife, unable to bear the tragedy, buried in the land of unbelievers in 1994.

He talks to his dead aloud. 'My dearest, I will leave for Mecca as soon as our son returns.'

He also prays silently for his three daughters and their families, so that the living will enjoy peace and honour, in Hama and in Britain. He thanks Allah for protecting his enduring friends, the Franklins.

He prays aloud for his beloved granddaughter, the well-named Zaida, the Fortunate One. 'The All-Living, give her the grace to bloom as a Damascene rose in an English garden, and the strength to be guarded from evil. Allah the merciful, take my life and spare my precious Khalid. A compassionate son and father. A courageous man with the heart of a falcon, whose body deserves to be buried in this grave under your protection. Alongside his father's.'

To protect his son, a traveller in this world, he chants A*yat Al-Kursi,* his favourite Koranic prayer. 'Allah – there is no deity except Him, the Ever-Living, the Sustainer of all existence.

Neither drowsiness overtakes Him nor sleep. To Him belongs whatever is in the heavens and whatever is on the earth. Who is it that can intercede with Him except by His permission?'

His throat is dry. He has the mangos and, of course, his pocket knife. With assured slashes, he slices the fruit into two halves, ready to cross-hatch the pulp swiftly so as not to waste the sweet juice.

There are fatal shots. Blood spills from the neck onto the yellow fruit. He falls forward, kneeling towards Mecca, furious, demented with the burning pain thumping through his lungs, hallucinating a rose garden for a final reunion.

There will be no investigation concerning the disappearance of the scholarly Dr Abdul Al-Sayed. Abu Reen rolls his eyes, flicks the dandruff from his cloak, swears to Omar Al-Sayed that he saw nothing in the darkest night, heard nothing after the two gun shots. 'Nothing at all. How could I, a meek man like me, half-blind?' He spits at Omar's well-shod feet. 'Death is liberation.'

Epilogue

For Those Who Like Tidy Ends

THE FRANKLINS LEARNED OF THE AL-SAYEDS' TRAGEDY IN long letters from Aunt Halima. Her saintly father was among the heroes who would never return home. After discrete enquiries, her relatives concluded that he had been murdered – by whose cursed hands they would never know. 'Allah, forgive us for not burying our dearest father!' There followed more devastating blows: to insult their dead, the family mausoleum was bulldozed and Uncle Omar was jailed for three months for facilitating his nephew's escape.

Then, a second letter. "Rejoice, Zaida, your father is alive. Alhamdulillah…" Snatching the letter from her mother, Zaida runs around the William Morris room, laughing. 'All praise is due to Allah alone. You see, I'm not forgetting!' She reads on. "The bad news"… Oh?… "my friends, is that he has been tracked down to Roumieh, a Lebanese prison"… No! No!… where living conditions are poor."' She collapses into Virginia's arms, in tears, whispering, 'Mum, can't we be a normal family?'

'We'll look after him, darling! We know where he is, we won't let him starve. Aunt Halima, look here, has already brought fresh food and clothes. We'll send him lots of money to—'

'How, Mum? How? God doesn't help much, does he?'

Her mother strokes her hair down. 'Look, Halima is right. There's good news. Uncle Omar has been released already! He'll be invaluable; he has enough connections to get Khalid out! With Halima he'll find out how to deal with the guards, how to get him the things he needs, and sheets of paper so he can write to us.'

'Maybe they've seen him already!'

'We can help from our end by getting legal advice relevant to Lebanon. And, treasure, I'm going to alert Marianne and Ian. Let's see what they say.'

Advised by Amnesty, Marianne hires an experienced Syrian lawyer who confirms Khalid's true identity to a Lebanese court. The judge, convinced by the prisoner's testimony that the Assad regime murdered his father and forced him to flee, acknowledges Khalid's status as a political prisoner. A generous move.

For Walter, Syria is proving fatal. While his family feeds on every grain of hope, Walter has no illusion about Khalid's wretched life. Is it his fault? And Abdul's murder? If they had all been more trusting, the friend he vowed to cherish would still be alive. Sinking into depression, his interest in the clinic wanes. There are other inexorable shifts. Patients, short of funds, fall away. Fewer practitioners register for Walter's long courses, preferring to train quickly in more profitable therapies which only deal with tangible bodies, not the person as a whole. A sure sign of mediocrity.

Undeterred by her husband's dismal decline, combative as ever, Gwen does her utmost to resist bankruptcy. She is forced to borrow at high rates until finally the business has to be sold. Robbed of his craft, plagued by guilt, Walter's heart gives way and he dies of desolation.

Soon after the clinic's closure, Virginia is hired as an NHS consultant to practise the Eight Principles; but to appease her father, wherever he might be, she resorts on the quiet to the Five Elements for her more difficult cases.

Supporting Zaida through tidal swings of grief and rage, Virginia and Gwen work smoothly together to wrap up the business. Gwen, free of her husband's bemused glances, indulges her passion. The unused space in the clinic is repopulated by her growing bird collections. Should she open it up to the public as a local attraction?

'Go ahead, Mother, you're the boss.'

On the order of the court, Khalid is released from "the indignities of Roumieh prison", as he writes, and is moved to a better-equipped camp where political prisoners are allowed to buy their own food from outside. Eager to help the friend whose downfall he provoked, Ian moves mountains to set up a solidarity fund to top up Khalid's miserable allowance from the International Organisation for Migration.

The camp swarms with spies, happy to gain credit by alerting the Syrian authorities to Khalid's accusations. Damascus retaliates, identifying him as an Islamist Jihadist, an indelible tag certain to block his application for permanent residence in Britain. Another request to enter Fortress Britain on a temporary visa as the father of a British child is also rejected after months of waiting.

Among fellow prisoners there is whispered talk of fanciful escape to Turkey or Egypt by buying the conscript jailers. Khalid ignores these pipedreams. "My spirit is not yet full of dust. Every hour of the day I wonder why my life has been preserved. My dearest friends, my time here is not wasted. Together we share our stories of injustice, courage and fury. I want to come home a stronger man, free from either the hope or the hatred that, for some, are more destructive than prison itself. Please send me history books of the Middle East. I mean recent history. And more poetry from all around the world."

In March 2011, pro-democracy protesters take to the streets of Darea, Aleppo and Damascus demanding the fall of the regime. Massive crackdowns by the security forces draw more people into the conflict. This very month, Khalid is allowed his first visitors from abroad. The news sets off a bitter phone conversation between Marianne and Virginia. They should both go over Easter, urges Marianne. Virginia refuses.

'You're frightened?'

'No, it's not that. How can I see him? He's bound to act... I mean... the hero...the victim!'

'Well, he is a victim of history!'

'Big words, Marianne! But face it – in his letters he takes no responsibility for what happened. Unlike Ian.'

'You forget... *censeurs* read the letters.'

'He was a fool and still is! Why believe in Bashar Al-Assad's promises about reforms? Why go back? The Al-Sayeds were naive. Their connections melted away one by one! He was arrogant, crazy! How could he bring human rights to that place?

'Really?'

'It's tragic. Ian beats his chest, but not Khalid... He kept Zaida when he was in danger. No, I can't go, I want some explanation – why didn't he get out of all that shit when he still could? Was that a way of punishing me? So selfish!'

'Don't be *ridicule*!'

'Marianne, don't mock, it's the truth.'

After the phone call, Marianne shudders at the tormented story of Virginia and Khalid. There will be no reconciliation, that is ghastly enough, but more appalling is the prospect of Khalid remaining interned for years in Lebanon. Equally deplorable is a future where Zaida's yearning for the fusion between her two worlds will never be fulfilled. *Mission impossible.* Deeply distressed, she paces the terrace, trying to beat off the nightmare. Indifferent to her turmoil, the chateau's peacocks strut about with the arrogance of a Ritz butler. She can travel without Virginia. Why such venom? She kicks a bird out of her way. She has not seen Khalid for years. How will they get on? Will he be disagreeable, bitter, vindictive? Halima suggests otherwise, but is she sugaring the pill?

A month later, Marianne is glad to report back. How much she admired Khalid's resilience and integrity whenever he argued against those prisoners drawn to more violence and revenge.

In years to come, after her retirement from Médecins Sans Frontières, Zaida Franklin-Al-Sayed will publish in Arabic and English the collected works of Abdul and Khalid Al-Sayed. Words as soft as snowflakes, hard as courage.

About
Yvette Rocheron

I grew up in France, married (twice) in Britain, and have one son. Graduated in English (Poitiers, France). PhD in Sociology (Warwick, Britain). I worked at first in sociological research and latterly taught French Studies. Now retired in the Languedoc, I have enjoyed moving away from academic writings to return to literature.

My first novel *Double Crossings* (2009) focuses on a troubled Anglo-French couple living in France. *Homecomings* also dramatises international family bonds but this time across Britain, Syria and Canada. The current civil war prevented me from writing for about two years, after which Bashar Al-Assad's survival in power, contrary to Western predictions, encouraged me to strengthen key characters and let them heal beyond the blockages of fear, distrust and blackmail.

Acknowledgements

I owe a great deal of thanks to the few people who have read earlier manuscripts for their support in the course of the writing: Joseph Périgot, Frédérique Beaufumé, Faith O'Reilly, Sandra Freeman, Michel Aubeneau, Françoise Aubeneau. And crucially, Ben Evans, literary agent for Cornerstones, whose sensitive advice gave me the confidence to launch into some substantial re-writing.

I would also like to give my husband a big hug, James Hinton, who helped me bring to fruition the novel. Once a poet and now a historian. Watchful, he read the text tirelessly, underlining for the umpteenth time Gallicisms and many other blunders. Doing the job of an old-fashioned copy editor, he generously claimed. He did far more: he respected my voice.

My thanks to all those figures who peopled my imagination when writing. Tutors at the College of Chinese Acupuncture, UK. Also, Martine Gallie with whom I enjoy spending time discussing the craft of the acupuncturist and other mysteries of life.

I also acknowledge my debts regarding legal advice about the movement of children across borders to my friends at Reunite International Child Abduction Centre, for whom I worked as a volunteer for too short a time.

The poem *I rushed into the garden* is adapted from Rûmi, thirteenth-century Afghan poet, quoted in French by Malek Chebel in *Dictionnaire amoureux de l'islam*, Plon, 2004, p. 531.

As half the novel takes place in Syria and I do not understand Arabic, I relied on translated works to evoke scene and atmosphere. A seminal book for detail about female family life in Damascus under French occupation was Siham Tergeman's *Daughter of Damascus. A memoir*, 1994. And about current Damascus, Nathalie Bontemps's *Gens de Damas*, 2016, was particularly helpful.

Finally, I wish to express my gratitude to an engaging member of the Syrian Writers Union, a poet dissident, and his son, a maths teacher barred from travelling abroad, for their open-mindedness and generosity one day in Hama in April 2010, when they engaged in French with me, an unbeliever, about their threatened Sunni heritage and their dispossession. I felt their presence throughout the writing.